THE PIANO TEACHER

Karl Viklund

The Piano Teacher

A Magnus Markusson crime novel

By Karl Viklund

1

I had just put the noose around his neck when the wind howled. It was a relief to have some wind blowing through as the summer was hotter than ever. It was a strange time to be thinking about the wind. When I am about to kill a man. He was pleading at first, but then he had stopped and hoped that maybe I would reconsider. I would not. All that had to be done now was to take away the base from under him. Then it wouldn't take long. I did so. I watched him struggle, trying to find that air to breathe, which was disappearing as if you were drowning. The choking and the struggling. It was a tad bit uncomfortable at first, but I steadied myself and watched the man start to lose the battle with the rope. The body went limp, and the battle ceased. He was dead. I am not a lunatic, some deranged killer. I am merely righting wrongs. Wrongs that could only have one punishment. I had to remove all the traces I could from the area, and once I had done that, I was ready to leave. I looked once more at the man in the tree. The swaying had stopped, and he was still. No more hanging like meat would in a butchery. I had regained a bit of something inside of me. Would my wounds ever be repaired? No, certainly not. But at least the man in the tree had paid. He wasn't the only one who was going to have to pay. I drove off. It would now be on to the next one who had to pay. I was looking forward to collecting the payment.

2

The phone rang at the Varberg police station. The lady on the switchboard answered the call. Inge Björkman was on switchboard duty, and at this time phone calls were quite rare.

"Varberg police, Inge Björkman speaking, how may I help you?"

"I've seen a dead body. I want to report it." The voice was a man's. The line was crackling a great deal.

"Just hold on a second sir," Inge Björkman said to the man, grabbing a small notepad as fast as possible and tearing off the page which had her scribbles all over it. She got a black pen that was stationed next to her and was ready to write on a fresh page.

"You say you saw a dead body?" she went on and continued.

"Whereabouts was this?"

"There are some woods next to the Läjet camping site. You know the one?"

"Yes. Where—."

"As you come into the woods, you won't have to go far until you see the body. He's hanging from a tree."

Inge Björkman's hands quivered slightly.

"OK sir, and —," Inge Björkman couldn't finish her sentence. She heard the drone of the dial tone in her ear. The man had hung up abruptly.

Inge Björkman at least had a location. The man who had called seemed in a hurry to get off the phone. Inge Björkman assumed that having just seen a dead body would have been quite a shock for most people. Inge dialled a number as fast as she could. Inge was calling Chief Superintendent of the Varberg police department, Magnus Markusson, to explain the odd and slightly chilling phone call she had just received. The clock read 11.17 pm. Magnus answered.

"Magnus speaking," Magnus Markusson said. It sounded as if a TV was blaring in the background.

"Hi, Magnus. It's Inge here from the switchboard. I have just had a rather odd phone call from a man who said he saw a dead body just off the Läjet campsite in the woods nearby. He had said the man was hanging from a tree."

"OK, let me go and check it out," Magnus Markusson said.

Magnus Markusson hung up and called Eva Lindqvist and told her to get ready. Eva needs to come with, Magnus thought. If this turns into a case, she's the one who will be doing the donkey work.

Magnus Markusson hung up and headed towards Eva Lindqvist's apartment, which was nearby his house. He found Eva waiting outside when he arrived. Eva Lindqvist was a superintendent at the Varberg police department and worked closely alongside Magnus. Magnus, who was now forty-nine, thought that Eva Lindqvist, thirty-six, was the perfect person to take over from himself in the future. Eva liked to really dig into the cases which suited Magnus because he did not like to. Eva got into Magnus's new car, and they continued onto the campsite. Magnus had his window open. He had recently bought a Volvo V40 cross country T3 model, second hand. He was reasonably well off, but he didn't have money for a brand new one. Magnus had needed a decent car, something that he could also zip about in. He had found this car on the blocket.se website. Two hundred and ten thousand kronor had been the asking price. Two hundred was Magnus's final offer. Deal. Magnus had been thrilled with this purchase. Everyone that had driven with him since this new purchase had become infuriated with his constant explanations about what his vehicle could do. Magnus had even raved about the air conditioner, amongst other things.

Sweden was about two weeks past mid-summer, and on this day in July, the weather was still hot, even at this hour. However, there was a slight breeze now. During the day, it had been a scorcher. 31 degrees Celsius. Varberg, as well as many other cities in the south of Sweden, had been experiencing a heatwave. There was even talk of a chance of the record temperature in Varberg, which had been set in 1901, being broken. That had been 33.6 which wasn't far off. Magnus looked out at the sky and heard a rumbling, which sounded menacing, and it seemed a distinct possibility that a storm was on its way. The sun had set an hour and a half or so ago, so it was dark. Magnus knew where the Läjet camping site was and turned off Västkustvägen onto Strandbackavägen and down the road that leads towards the campsite. A sign pointed out that if you were looking for the campground, you were on the right track. The sign had seen better days. There was a road, more like a trampled thinned out patch of grass that leads to the woods. The woods were of moderate size and probably attracted some foot traffic during the day or evenings, but at this time it was presumed devoid of any people. Magnus followed the path quickly, steadily and got to the entrance to the woods, and switched off the Volvo. He rubbed his beard for a second and felt the bristles on his hand as he moved it up and down against them. The beard had two colours. Predominantly light brown with sweeps of elephant grey in places. Magnus had hardly dressed up for the occasion. A pair of training pants, some cross trainers and a t-shirt. However, on a normal day's work, he hardly dressed much better. Magnus and Eva Lindqvist got out of the car at around about the same time, with Eva moving a bit of her blond hair from the front of her face that had escaped the bun she had in her hair. She usually had a resolute look to her face, but now she had that deer-caught-in-the-headlights type of look. Eva was very attractive, and a few had thought she had no clue how to be a cop, but they were wrong. Eva was smart and as tough as nails. Three years ago, Eva, along with a few others, had chased a gangster into a car park and then split up. Eva went the right way, and with the criminal having no way out, he decided to try and take Eva out. After taking a few shots at them earlier, he was out of ammo and thought Eva would be easy to walk all over. He cracked Eva in the ribs with two heavy punches as well as a stiff one to the jaw, and then left as Eva lay on the ground, dust in her face. Somehow she had gotten up and called for backup and run after the gangster at full pace. She caught up to him, and with other members of her team having gotten word of the criminal's whereabouts, he was outnumbered and had nowhere to go. Afterwards, Eva had been looked at and had found two of her ribs were cracked. No one had believed she had somehow run with those ribs, let alone catch up. Lately, Eva had been battling mentally. A month prior, Eva was involved in a serious domestic dispute and had her weapon drawn due to the nature of the husband involved. His wife had been nearby, and it seemed as things had calmed down. Suddenly he had drawn a big knife and ran at the wife with one intention. That's when Eva had fired. She had shot him in the chest, and he had gone down the second the bullet struck. The man had been taken to the hospital; however, he died shortly after. Eva had never used her weapon before, and now she had killed someone. Of course, Eva had done the right thing. But that hadn't mattered. A week after that, the incident had really started to hit her and still was in her head, upsetting her a lot.

The path through the woods lay in front of Magnus and Eva, and they entered, keeping their eyes open. The camping site next door had a festive atmosphere to it. Magnus and Eva both took out a flashlight. It didn't take long to find what they had come to look for. They spotted the body. The man was hanging in a tree, the body limp.

"Fucking hell," was Magnus's response to seeing the body.

Eva said nothing. She looked at the body for a few seconds and turned away and took a deep breath.

Magnus took out his grey mobile and looked at Eva. 11.35 pm. He hit a number that was in his contact list, and the phone rang. He heard Inge Björkman's voice next.

"Inge. Hi, Magnus here. I need to get everyone down here immediately. We found him."

3

The crime scene had been cordoned off with blue and white checkered tape. The rain had started coming down, hardly ideal conditions for going through a crime scene in the woods. Portable heavy-duty lighting equipment shone brightly from the perimeter of the scene all around the body. Forensics technicians were combing the immediate area for anything of interest. The heavy-duty lights also highlighted Magnus Markusson's eyes - they were as red as a fire engine. Eva Lindqvist was standing frozen like a statue, presumably thinking. She had a troubled look on her face. Magnus prodded Eva on her shoulder. Eva gave a start when she felt the tap.

"What are you doing?" Magnus queried.

"I, I was, just umm, just—."

"Concentrate for fuck's sakes. Get it together."

Eva tried to knuckle down to the task at hand but was still having a hard time focusing. Rolf Jonsson and Alexander Holström, part of Magnus's homicide and violent crimes squad, were hard at work, with Rolf Jonsson taking photographs and Alexander Holström taking notes on a small note pad. Stina Wahlgren was the newest member of this squad. She was still wet behind the ears. However, Stina was incredibly bright. Some people thought she was odd. She was thirty-four, had a sweet smile, and was naturally pretty. Stina was busy making her own notes, as she made her way around the crime scene. Magnus stood looking at the body. It was just hanging there, an unsavoury viewing experience. Everything seemed darker after viewing the sight in the tree. Magnus scratched his beard again, then wiped some of the rain off his face. The storm had threatened to devastate the scene, but luckily it had started to calm quite quickly. The rains still came out, but it was manageable. The pathologist, Kerstin Beckman arrived, donning a raincoat and began to get to work. She asked two of the uniformed officers guarding the entrance to the crime scene to please get the body down after she had taken a few pictures for her own records. The officers had to be careful, with one holding the body, which wasn't something he found pleasant — especially now that the body was damp and getting wetter — while the other cut the cord while atop a small utility ladder. Another officer then joined in to help get the body down slowly. The body was set down gently on a white, thick plastic sheet. Kerstin Beckman could now proceed. She checked the body temperature of the corpse, hoping to get a good idea of the time of death. She peered behind herself to Magnus when she arrived at her conclusion.

"33.2. So he's been dead around three hours," Kerstin Beckman said. The time was now just after midnight.

"What else?" Magnus said.

"Hang on. I'm getting there."

Magnus waited impatiently and tapped his trainers which now were muddy on the ground while Kerstin Beckman studied the body. Kerstin was not going to be rushed. Magnus thought about the findings and the possible crime in the interim. It looked as if someone had hung this man out here in the woods. Sure, it could be a suicide, but if Magnus's first assumption was correct, then it was a murder. And murders didn't' come along much in Varberg. And they definitely didn't come along as meticulous as this. This was nasty. Someone really had gone to a lot of trouble here. Whoever did this must be disturbed, Magnus thought. Just as Magnus was pondering more, Kerstin Beckman gestured to him with her index finger to come to her. He lent down on his haunches.

"Cause of death is pretty obvious. Death

due to asphyxia from strangulation. Some telltale signs. His eyes are bloodshot, kind of like yours."

"Lovely comparison," Magnus said. I just want to go back to bed, Magnus thought.

Kerstin pointed to the neck.

"Ligature marks," she said.

Before saying anything else, she took out a tape measure and measured the victim's body. 180 centimetres. She passed this information onto Magnus.

"Murder plain and simple," Magnus said.

"Let me tell you what I think. The first thing is that the branch the victim was hung from is a fair way up, so there's no doubt if our victim did this, then he would have had to have used something to stand and tie the rope around the tree. He could have placed the rope around his neck and then kicked away the device he used to get up there but —."

"But then, where's the thing he would have stood on?" Magnus chipped in before Kerstin could finish.

"Exactly. If we were to suggest that the victim climbed the tree himself, not an easy task, you would expect to find a trace of him having done so. Some bark falling off, some marks on the tree, but there's nothing. It's also a thick tree, so it's not easy to get up there. Also, if he managed this and jumped, I'm quite sure you would see the trauma to his neck being much more pronounced. The ligature marks much deeper. It doesn't add up. I think someone put him up there, made him stand on something, not a chair or stool, something a bit higher than that, and took it out from under him. So yes, Magnus, you are correct."

Magnus thought for a second, then turned to one of the forensic technicians and asked him to check for other ways in and out, and to look for any tire tracks. To set up this murder, without question, you would have needed a vehicle. Magnus dusted the top coating of rain off his hair. His hair felt frazzled. Another forensics technician was bagging items of importance found on the victim. Each piece of evidence was put into clear zip-lock plastic bags. Magnus grabbed some white latex gloves, placed his hands in them, and started to take a few of the items out of the bags to peruse them.

A wallet was first. A credit card, as well as a debit card. An ID card. Magnus took some interest in that. The victim's name was Sven Julin, fifty-two years of age. While Magnus placed the evidence back in their respective bags, a swab was taken under one of the victim's fingernails as the technician had detected some small trace elements - little bits of red under a few of the victim's nails. Red something. Magnus heard a commotion behind him and turned around.

"You must be joking. Not these people now," he said to himself and started walking briskly to the herd of reporters that had arrived and stationed themselves at the entrance to the crime scene. Magnus's steps could be heard slushing into the ground as he thundered off to speak to the barrage of journalists.

4

It hadn't taken long for the reporters from the various newspapers to find out about what had happened. It was always fascinating how the news got to them so quickly. Representatives of Hallands Nyheter, as well as a few other smaller local publications, were sniffing around, hoping to get that scoop that would earn them the plaudits of their bosses, and get those papers sold. After all, that's what it is was all about - selling newspapers. Magnus walked right into a beehive of questions. Magnus told everyone that there were no comments at this time and followed that by turning around and buzzing off. Magnus then issued for two men on duty at the scene to move the journalists back and create another barricade using the police tape. After some coaxing, the journalists moved back. Fuck, Magnus thought. How do these people find out so quickly? Magnus wondered what the dramatic headline would be this time.

Magnus, while walking back towards the

body, took a detour across to Rolf Jonsson, and informed him of what he needed him to do next.

"You know I don't like doing this," Rolf Jonsson moaned at Magnus once Magnus had told Rolf he was to get the details for the next of kin and go and notify them about the terrible thing that had transpired. This was to be done immediately.

"Well, Rolf, there are many things I don't like either. Just suck it up. I don't have time for this," Magnus snorted.

Rolf Jonsson was a quiet man who handled investigations well and was reliable. He wasn't ambitious and liked his job as it stood. Rolf was happy in the middle of the ladder. He wasn't one to show too much emotion. He was sixty years old, wore glasses, and had a moustache. His resounding feature was his fat stomach. He was always trying to lose weight but never shed any. Lately, he had actually gained weight. The recent death of Rolf Jonsson's wife, Camilla, had been an enormous blow to Rolf, and although he was getting his work done, he often looked down in the dumps. Everyone could tell he was struggling with acute grief. Rolf's sadness would surely intensify when he had to go and deliver this kind of devastating news. He knew what it felt like to hear that. He was there when Camilla had passed away. She had died from colon cancer, and it had been detected in the latter stages. It had spread by then to Camilla's lymph nodes, and her decline was rapid. Four months had passed since her death, and Rolf honestly did not know what to do with himself. The pain. The longing for Camilla just to come back, although that wasn't going to be happening. He had been having dreams too. Those unpleasant whirring images. Sickening ones where he would suddenly wake up in buckets of sweat. Ones where he would wake up shivering cold. Camilla would be across the street from their home on a sunny day. Always the same beginning. She would see him from across the street. She would be returning home. She would give a big wave and have an enormous smile on her face. Then the dream became a nightmare. Camilla would then be killed. Run over by a car, shot by a sniper, heart attack. Once Rolf Jonsson had dreamt Camilla had been run over by a car after she was shot by a sniper while having a heart attack. Sometimes he would get repeats of the dreams. Then an old man would walk past him standing in the garden, look at him and say, "Get over it." What was the old man thing all about? He had no idea. Rolf Jonsson had a cat. Sylvester. Based on the famous looney tunes cartoon, you would have expected Sylvester to be black and white; however, he was not. He was a fluffy orange cat, with white streaks in between the orange. His tail was powerful. He would whip it around when he felt like it, and if any ornament got in the way, the whippy instrument always came up trumps. Sylvester also had a powerful personality. He was always off on his own bat, busy finding new places to sit in the sun. He would be at home right on time for food however, and then would sleep in many different places in the house. Sylvester was not a big fan of winter and usually just ate and slept more. Work and his cat are what Rolf had. He had to hold onto it. Rolf couldn't give up, no matter how bad things got in terms of his grieving. He made the way to his car. His work was done here. Once he got the details of the family, which he would get shortly, he would have to contact them and then see them the following day. Rolf had no idea how he was going to speak to Sven Julin's family in person about what had happened. Even though it wasn't the same thing, it would bring back memories buried in his mind of being told that Camilla wasn't going to get better. Rolf's chest started to burn like a fire.

5

"It's over here," the technician said to Magnus Markusson as he pointed to the area of disturbance. It had been apparent that someone had manufactured their own convenient driveway into the woods, as the run over blades of grass indicated. Magnus surveyed that particular area. The rain had thankfully ceased by now, but although it had not been a massive storm, it had still muddied the waters in terms of tire tracks. Magnus ordered the tech to try and get a cast of the tire track, even though it was going to be difficult. Usually, people wouldn't go out of their way to find an alleyway into the woods unless they really didn't want to be seen. The technician was able to get a partial tread, which was undoubtedly better than nothing. So, Magnus thought. Someone drives in here and hangs this poor old chap—more than enough for me to think about. Magnus turned to leave the crime scene. Eva slid into the car with Magnus and still had a shell-shocked look on her face. The silence spoke volumes on the ride to Eva's apartment. She just wanted to go home. Get some sleep. Let the mind disengage its thoughts for just a little while. Eva was a divorcee and had been divorced for two years when her then-husband Ragnar had been having an affair with his secretary. Eva knew nothing of it until she dropped by his office unannounced at the end of office hours one day. Ragnar had been dipping his pen into the receptionist's ink on Ragnar's office table when Eva had walked in, Ragnar probably having forgotten that Eva had spare keys in case he ever lost his. She had slapped the woman, which had made an impressive sound, and called her a "slut bag," which she had always found amusing.

In the silence on the way to her apartment, Eva was fidgeting with her fingers and rubbed her forehead and eyes a few times. She used to be the epitome of cool, calm, and collected. Since the shooting in that apartment, she had been pretty close to a nervous wreck. With thoughts in Eva's head of her pulling the trigger and killing the man who had the knife, Magnus suddenly hit the brakes very hard, and the tires screeched to a halt. Magnus was looking across the way. Two young males whom Magnus estimated himself to be in the region of nineteen, twenty, were getting some cheap laughs at the expense of an animal. There was a white Labrador retriever behind a fenced gate, which appeared to be the worksite to an automobile workshop. The dog's tail was down, and the two student delinquents had found a small pipe and were taunting it as well as cracking the gate several times which upset the dog more. The dog was barking a lot. It almost appeared to Eva that smoke started to come out of Magnus's ears. Having got to know him extremely well over the years, this kind of behaviour was the kind of thing to piss him off completely. Eva rubbed her forehead again, unsure of what Magnus intended on doing and just hoped whatever it was, it wasn't something stupid. She was about to ask him what he intended to do, but before she could, he got out of the car, shut the door and went across the road.

"Can I help you two with something?" Magnus questioned.

The two gave him an unpleasant look. Magnus clenched his one fist together hard to try and calm himself down.

"I noticed you seem to think its fun to tease animals," Magnus continued, now raising his voice.

"You better fuck off; otherwise, we will beat the shit out of you."

The person who said that to Magnus slurred his words. Drunk as a lord, and unfortunately for him and his friend, unaware that Magnus was very adept in combat if needed be. Magnus's look sometimes was deceiving. He was in reasonable shape, maybe a touch over a decent weight. His attire and general facial stubble and messy hair gave the impression that he couldn't handle himself if needed. Magnus snickered, and then looked at both of them, a more primed look.

"So let me get this straight — you two. You two are going to beat me up? Yeah, right." Magnus was now very close to both of them.

The first delinquent took no time in swinging the pipe in his hands. Magnus ducked and felt some water drops hit his face that had come off the tube, which went to show how close the pipe had been to connect with him. Magnus grabbed the attacker's hand and squeezed hard. A clang of the tube hitting the concrete was heard as the pipe swinger couldn't withstand the pain any longer. It wasn't long before the young upstart followed suit and hit the ground as well. Two punches in the stomach and down he went, making a sickly wincing sound. The next upstart ran at Magnus and took an inexperienced swing. Magnus followed the same procedure, two to the stomach and down like a ton of bricks the other guy went. After a minute or so, in which Magnus tried to make friends with the dog, the youngsters started to get onto their feet — albeit very uneasily — and started to get going as far away from Magnus as possible.

"Move it. Get out of here," Magnus said.

The two drunkards didn't need a second invitation to depart and continued away from Magnus, moving very gingerly. Magnus went back to his Volvo and got out some bolt cutters that were in the boot. He snapped the whimsy lock off and ushered for the dirty white dog to come to him. The dog had a fair amount of trepidation as to whether she should listen to Magnus. Magnus managed to get the dog to follow him across the road calmly; however, the dog took a while to decide if this was a good idea. A few gentle pats helped the dog make a decision. The dog seemed to have a gentle and calm nature, even though she had been barking at the teenage imbeciles. Magnus was very good with dogs. He already had two others at home. The dog hopped on the back seat without much hassle and proceeded to get comfortable. The dog was still looking a little unsure, but a quiet dry back seat seemed miles better than being behind a muddy, wet gate. Eva didn't say a word for the rest of the trip home. Magnus pulled up outside Eva's apartment. Their places of abode were not far away from each other.

Eva opened up her front door, got inside, shut the door, and slid to the ground, leaning against the door. She was expended—what a dreadful day. Eva started weeping and continued to do so even once she got to her feet and set off for bed. I can't go on, she thought to herself. My head is going to explode from all this. Her blond hair hit her comfortable white pillows, and within seconds, she fell asleep. It wouldn't be long at all until her mind started to race again, replaying the same scene again and again. A slow-motion replay of the domestic disturbance incident. A close-up of the bullet circling towards the man's body. Eventually, Eva fell asleep until morning.

Magnus Markusson got home at 2.58 am. He took his new friend out of the backseat and started talking to her as he did with his other two dogs. He had a wire terrier named Smilla, and a Tervuren named Buster. Smilla was a small dog but was not lacking any energy, while Buster was a lot bigger and took the role of the lead dog in the house. They both got along very well and were well behaved if running into other dogs when Magnus had taken them on walks. Magnus didn't foresee the new dog being a problem for anyone. He unlocked the back door and already heard speedy steps coming to the door to see what was happening. The two dogs pushed and shoved to get their first licks in and then diverted their attention to this new dog. Cue the sniffing. All three took part in this game. What the hell is with all the sniffing, Magnus thought. Also, they always have to smell each other's bums.

"Who's this?" said Magnus's wife Lena, who had just wandered into the kitchen to greet him.

"Well, hello to you too," he replied.

"Don't you think we have enough dogs? I mean, how many more should I expect you to bring home?"

"This is the last one. I promise. The dog was behind some gate, in a shit hole of a workshop, no food, no nothing. I couldn't just leave her there." Magnus refrained from discussing the details of his little fight.

Lena nodded and grinned, her long brown hair moving gently. She was an elegant woman, a face that was comprised of class and sex appeal. Lena, who was forty-three, had been married to Magnus for sixteen years. Their relationship was the opposite of what was the given at most police stations. Divorces, angry fed-up children, and general resentment and disillusionment were frequent problems in marriages around the police station. All based on the parent who was a cop never being around. Magnus's and Lena's matrimony was different. Apart from one shattering family problem around four years prior that still lingered on from time to time, this had been and was a very happy household. Lena had some silk pyjamas on, as well as a robe. Magnus was more interested in her footwear. Lena had slippers on that were fluffy white, with a rabbit's face and long ears sticking up near the front of the slipper.

"What the hell are those?" he asked.

"Saw them today. They are so comfortable and cool at the same time."

"Bit odd if you ask me."

"Well, no one was," Lena smiled.

Lena then stated she was back off to bed, slippers and all. Magnus was left to deal with sorting out the new dogs sleeping arrangements. Before he organised new dog a comfortable spot, he found her some food, which she wolfed up. Smilla and Buster stood looking at Magnus, expectantly waiting for some food too. Both sat and looked at him, not moving. Magnus caved in and gave them a treat each, which he found in the pantry. Some twirly meat sticks, which apparently helped their teeth as well. The new dog, yet to be named, looked undernourished and had a rough, dirty coat. Bath time tomorrow, Magnus thought. Lena can do the honours.

Before Magnus went to bed, he wanted to sneak in some food, as he was a bit peckish. Lena would do her nut if she knew he was digging in the fridge at 3.30 in the morning. He dug around their expansive white fridge quietly and found some meatballs in a Tupperware container. He poured himself some water from the tap and proceeded to sit on the comfortable couch in the television room. Magnus ate a couple of the meatballs and then closed his eyes for a second to relax after a torrid and tumultuous night. A few hours later, Lena prodded him, and he woke up bewilderedly. Magnus, getting up after sleeping on the couch, had slept with his neck in a most awkward position, making it as stiff as a board when he limbered up and walked to go and shower. What a start to the day, he thought.

6

Magnus Markusson continued to mumble. Often, he would be able to sleep in for a good while and roll into work later with some excuse or another. Lena assumed that was the sort of time the chief detective would go to work, but in actual fact, Magnus made up his own time on many occasions. This particular morning, due to the previous night's murder, a sleep-in was out. Magnus was now the chief detective, a position he had gotten because of his great track record in closing cases and service to the police force. As far as his work ethic was concerned, Magnus was hardly burning the midnight oil trying to solve cases. Magnus had been given a morning hug and a kiss from Lena, who had gone back to bed after waking him up. The dogs, including the new dog, were all tucked in their respective spots. Didn't take long did it, Magnus thought in regard to the new dog making herself at home. Lena Markusson ran a pretty successful website, easycooking.com, in which she aimed at doing elaborate type dishes in a more straightforward way. Lena also had a baking and dessert section, and a calorie-conscious section for those trying to shed some weight. She ran the website very well and made a good steady income. She always made her own hours but had discipline in updating her site almost daily. One of the fruits of this was not having to wake up early. She was a one-woman show, working from home. Magnus, on the other hand, was working for someone, namely the municipality. The police department was headed up by police commissioner Erik Rosenberg, and Magnus couldn't stand him. Rosenberg, fifty-five, was the type of boss who talked a good game but had a lack of experience for police work. He had been drafted in from some or other municipal post as he was very good at running a tight operation. The problem was a police department was just a little bit different from running a business. Magnus had heard via a few people that the Varberg municipality and Hallands county, in general, liked to save money. He wasn't against that, but did they have to get a dimwit in? The two did not see eye to eye at all. There were arguments all the time, and Magnus never listened to Rosenberg, which made things worse. In Magnus's defence, nothing was ever Rosenberg's fault. So, all in all, work was a difficult proposition any time Rosenberg stuck his nose into Magnus's business. Magnus sat down and sorted out some breakfast. He was trying to behave himself and eat healthier in the mornings. So, he was supposed to take Lena's orders and go for yoghurt with some blueberries. What he actually had was a quick fry up while she was sleeping. Eggs. Bacon. Sausages. Toast. Magnus was a vast coffee consumer, and this was a part of the breakfast as well.

After this hearty meal, he looked at the big black circular clock near the breakfast table and reflected on his life in general with the few minutes he had to spare before going to work. Magnus felt secure and happy. He then felt a pang of guilt and sadness. What about his son? He and Lena would often think back to their son, Sebastian. Even though their household had been a loving, caring one, for some reason, Sebastian had ended up being an extremely tough teenager. He did poorly at school, got into fights, and after that, became involved with the wrong kind of people. Deviants who were involved with drugs amongst other things and it got worse and worse. Lena was always constantly worried. It was very serious. Sebastian finished school, and showed no ambition to study, and was hardly ever home. The breaking point came one night when two of Sebastian's so-called friends arrived unannounced, saying that Sebastian owed them 1000 kronor for "some stuff." And they wanted it right there and then. They weren't leaving until they got it. Lena had answered the door, and they had barged in looking for Sebastian, who wasn't there as usual. One of the two young men was Felix Corvin, a friend of Sebastian's from their time at school. Sebastian was nineteen at the time, and Felix was around the same age. Magnus had never liked him, as he was sure that Felix had led Sebastian badly astray. Sebastian had never mentioned to Felix that his father was a cop, maybe fearing he would not be accepted into those types of groups. Lena tried to calm Felix and the other scruffy layabout down but to no avail. Felix decided to get serious and pulled a gun out, which freaked Lena out. To go from a calm evening in a calm town to have a gun pointed at you was a big shock. Just then, Magnus had pulled into the driveway, not sure who was at home with Lena. At this time, they did not have any dogs. He came in slowly and saw the problem in front of his eyes. Lena was sitting on her legs on the floor, leaning against a kitchen cupboard, crying and trembling, trying to avoid looking at the weapon. Magnus was quite far across the room, unable to do much. He told Felix to drop the weapon in no uncertain terms.

"Drop the weapon you fucking bastard," said Magnus.

"We just want our fucking money," said Felix.

"Yeah, just hand it over," the other guy said.

Magnus knew he needed to do something quickly. With his wife having a gun pointed at her, he wasn't going to hang about assessing the situation. Magnus had a shoulder gun holster, and with that, a gun sitting cosily in the holster. He said a quick "1-2-3" in his head while remaining still and in a submissive stance, and then made a gesture as if he was dropping to his knees when he pulled out his gun and aimed straight at Felix's accomplice. Now it was who would crack first.

"You so much as move, and I shoot your friend," shouted Magnus, spit peeling off his tongue.

"But I shoot this bitch of yours," said Felix venomously.

"By the time you do that, I would have already put a bullet in your head."

Felix's shoulders dropped slightly, his eyes blinking once or twice. His buddy was petrified—advantage Magnus.

"Here's what we are going to do. You want your money. I'll give you your money. Then you will get the fuck out of here and never come back. Before that, you will drop your weapon, otherwise, believe me - you ain't leaving here alive."

The two lowlifes looked at each other before Felix replied.

"How do we know you won't shoot us if I drop my weapon?"

"You don't. However, if you keep your

weapon, then there's an excellent chance of both of you being shot. I should also add what would happen if you shoot a policeman's wife. The whole force will want to take you out. Five minutes. That's how long it would take for them to hunt you down. Also, your sentence would be like a holiday compared to the treatment you would get. And that is if I don't get you first."

Felix flinched when he realised Magnus was a cop.

Lena had now rolled up in a ball, her head between her knees. She was looking straight at the floor, hoping that this would end.

After some hesitation, Felix put his gun down on the floor. Magnus asked him to slide it along the ground to him. Felix obliged.

"Now my wife is going to get the money from another room. Lena, go and get the money." Luckily Magnus and Lena kept some money in the house for emergencies. This wasn't the type of emergency they had envisioned. In actual fact, with Sweden, a largely cashless society, cash being in the house wasn't really needed. Lena got up and was still crying and shaking. She left the room, and while she was gone, the room was silent. Everybody just looked at each other. She returned with the money.

"Give it to me," said Magnus.

Lena handed it over, shaking.

"You can forget about getting your gun

back. Also, once I give you this money, you walk out this door and never come back. I hope that's crystal clear. You *ever* come back here, and you're done," Magnus said with authority.

They both nodded. Felix Corvin looked like his friend did at this point. Afraid.

"Right, let's wrap this up now," said Magnus, who surprised Lena by putting his gun away, and motioning for the two to come and get their money.

Let them try and attack me, Magnus thought.

They came towards him, and Magnus handed Felix the money. Magnus restrained himself well. He would have much rather liked to have beaten Felix as well as the other guy to a pulp instead.

"I'll catch you later." More emphasis clung onto the word catch.

With the gun down, Felix Corvin's fear had dissipated.

"Fucking loser. I could fuck you up in second. Then I'd slap your wife around in front of you."

"Is that so? Why don't you try that? I know why. Because deep down, you are a coward. A pathetic waste of space."

"Yeah, whatever. It's too easy to take you out. Besides, I wouldn't want to touch that greasy wife of yours. Who knows where she's been?"

Magnus, all of a sudden, grabbed Felix Corvin's neck. He held it tightly for a few seconds and stared right into his eyes. Felix's friend did nothing. Magnus then pushed Felix away.

"Let's hope we don't meet again. Now get out of here."

Felix gave Magnus a hateful glare and left with his friend.

Lena ran and held Magnus so tightly and didn't want to let go. Magnus held her for a long time. After about ten minutes, he told Lena to sit down while he made her a cup of peppermint tea. He then dropped a bombshell, and even though Lena was upset at first by this, she agreed it would be best once she thought about it. It was time to put an end to this nonsense. Magnus or Lena could have been shot. One or both of them could have been killed. They made the decision even though it pained them to do so. Sebastian would have to go and find somewhere else to live. Sebastian would have to leave. End of story.

As soon as Magnus stepped into the office, he walked into a beehive of activity. Apart from their murder enquiry, there seemed to be lots of other things on the go. A blur of noise and papers appeared wherever Magnus turned. Looks like a bomb has hit this place, Magnus thought. There was a meeting scheduled at 9.00 am, which everyone had been made aware of by Rosenberg.

Magnus didn't have time to organise himself a cup of coffee, which annoyed him. Lena had kept telling Magnus that all the caffeine wasn't the best thing for him. It had travelled in one ear and out the other. He was burning it off and using it in energetic ways for crying out loud. The meeting room was in desperate need of renovation. It was a plain room, pleasant enough, but rather small and very dull. Everybody was by and large seated when Magnus strode in and sat down on one of the black swivelling chairs that were quite comfortable. The everybody consisted of Alexander Holström, Stina Wahlgren, and Rana Zia, as well as Eva. Rana Zia was the administrator slash receptionist for this division. An immigrant from Iran, Rana Zia had a bubbly personality. Magnus could never think of a time he hadn't seen her with a smile on her face. The heatwave was back in full force, making this small room stuffy and uncomfortable when Erik Rosenberg walked in and shut the door. Rosenberg went to sit at the head of the ivory coloured desk. Rolf Jonsson was the only member of the homicide and violent crimes division that was not there, presumably because he was speaking to the family of the victim when the meeting got underway.

Rosenberg kicked off, stating the grounds for the meeting, which everybody with half a brain cell was aware of. That murder had taken place the night before, that a discussion needed to take place regarding this, and everybody needed to work together to ensure the swift conclusion to this case. Rosenberg asked Magnus to please brief everyone with the findings thus far in this serious matter. Magnus wondered as he stood up and moved over to the whiteboard how many more times he would have to hear the case referred to as serious by Rosenberg. Magnus had thought when a man was found hanging in a tree in Varberg, it was a given that it was serious. Magnus started talking and jotted down some notes with the red marker on the board as he went along.

"Sven Julin, fifty-two, was found hanging in the tree in the woods just off the Läjet camping site. He was estimated at being dead for three hours before we arrived. We retrieved some evidence at the scene — his wallet, which contained nothing out of the ordinary. His fingernails had a small red trace substance. That has been sent off to be analysed so we will have to wait for that. Once the autopsy is completed, I'll know more." Alexander Holström raised his hand and began talking when Magnus nodded at him.

"I take it there's no doubt this a murder?" he asked for confirmation, even though it appeared pretty clear.

It's a bit early for thick questions like that, Magnus thought.

"If he had done this to himself, there are many questions. How did he get there? Why would he go to all the trouble of going to those woods? Also, then how did he do it? It would make sense for him to tie the rope to the tree, put it around his neck, stand on something, and kick it away. However, there was nothing there he could have stood on. The other way is to climb up the tree and jump from there, and again we come back to how he got up there. It was a thick tree, so he couldn't just grab hold and get up. He had no scratches at all, which you would expect when you are struggling up a tree. I think what happened is that someone took him there, made him stand on something, which would have had to have been taller than just a stool as he was a little more off the ground than that. The killer then pulled it away, hopped in a car and took off. So no, there is no doubt. This is a homicide investigation."

Hopefully, you get the message now, Magnus thought.

Everyone took note of the disseminated information. Magnus then continued.

"We did manage to collect partial tire print a forensics guy of ours found at the scene from a vehicle entering the woods using a back way that you wouldn't deem a natural path for entering and exiting. We can run the partial and hopefully get a hit of some sort."

"What else?" Rosenberg asked.

"Well, as I said previously, not much until the autopsy has been completed. We also need to dig into the case a bit deeper."

Rosenberg looked around the table and thought that everybody was too relaxed about proceedings. He slammed his hand on the desk and wiped his hand against his greyish moustache.

"Is everybody aware of the gravity of the situation? I need to send something out to the press, and I need to convey something to the regional commissioner. This city needs to know we are well on our way to solving this."

"Why can't you convey what we have thus far?" asked Stina Wahlgren, not understanding why facts couldn't be utilised.

"Because everybody needs to see that we are moving swiftly so they can go on with their lives as normal."

"But I don't think it's going to go as fast as you think," Stina countered.

That's it Stina, Magnus thought to himself as he grinned slightly.

"Oh, for God's sake. We have to be PC. We have to give the impression that we are dealing with this efficiently. I thought you knew how law enforcement worked."

"Whoa, hold on a second. There's no need to take it out on Stina," Magnus said and continued.

Speaking of law enforcement, you wouldn't even find the building unless it had Police written on it, Magnus thought to himself.

"The bottom line here is we have what we have. It's as simple as that," Magnus said in a way to cement the fact that there was nothing more to add. Rosenberg didn't look impressed at Magnus coming to the aid of Stina, nor having nothing else to go on and got up in a huff.

"I will get something written up for now, but I better get some news soon. I have a meeting shortly, so I won't take up any more of your valuable investigation time. Everybody better sharpen up." Rosenberg gathered his things and left quickly. Magnus addressed everyone else once Rosenberg had left.

"Right, listen up, don't pay any attention to that idiot. Let's start chipping away at this case."

Magnus started to assign parts of the case to the team. One thing was certain. This case was a problem. Murder cases were always a problem. Varberg had a calm, relaxed atmosphere. Why had this happened? The town's residents would certainly want to know what was going on. They would be nervous about something like this. And who knows if this was the last victim. With a killer being this specific, maybe more victims were lined up.

Eva Lindqvist was to go through all Sven Julin's personal effects and other items found at the scene. Was there something extra they could tell them? Alexander Holström was to start digging into Julin's affairs. Bank statements, cell phone records, things of that nature. Stina Wahlgren was to work on the tire tracks and try and narrow down what vehicle it could have been that was at the scene. Stina was very good at finding little details. Magnus kept it to himself that although Stina didn't seem leadership material, that she was maybe the best investigator of them all. And Stina was supposed to be a rookie. In the short time Stina had been with the team, Magnus had been very impressed. The meeting was adjourned. Magnus was relieved that he could finally have a cup of coffee. Before doing so, he sat in his office, and after a bit of thinking regarding the case, nothing new and ground-breaking sprung to mind. Magnus decided to go to the morgue to see if Kerstin Beckman had anything thing to tell him that would brighten up his day. Maybe she had something to turn the case on its head. Magnus was about to get up, but before that glanced around his office. It was a mess. He had a large, smooth dark brown desk, which was camouflaged by the number of files, photocopies, and reports that had found permanent homes there. Magnus liked having lots of stuff around. If anyone questioned what he was doing, he had lots of files to point to. Magnus had a computer in the middle, a Lenovo laptop. Magnus wasn't one to take many notes. The laptop was mainly used to check what was going on in the horse races every day. Magnus pulled at his collar of his blue golf shirt, trying to get some fresh air through. God, another oppressively hot day, he thought. The weather forecast had been for the heat to continue for another good few weeks or so, with not much rain predicted. Magnus needed to grab that cup of coffee. Magnus went out to the communal coffee machine, a weathered old thing, but capable of a good brew. It wouldn't operate properly. Magnus gave it a tap on the side, but there was no sign of operation.

"I wouldn't bother," said Alexander Holström as he walked past, flicking back his jet-black gelled hair.

"Things bust," he added.

As Magnus walked out, he shouted to Rana at the front desk.

"Rana, I want someone to come and fix that fucking machine. Today!"

7

Magnus stopped at a McDonald's on the way to the morgue. With the coffee machine out of commission, he needed to find another establishment for his coffee needs. McDonald's would do. In the times he had been there, and when he had ordered coffee, it had been perfectly fine. Magnus went in and ordered as there was a queue in the drive-thru. He walked back to his car, taking a sip from the plastic cup that had the standard white protective lid over it with the small slit where you could drink from. Magnus suddenly felt more invigorated as he turned his key in the Volvo's ignition. He proceeded to the morgue with a more optimistic outlook on things. Could Kerstin have found something more incriminating? Hopefully, that was the case. Let's get this done, Magnus thought. Magnus's phone then rang, and he answered. It was some salesman type pest asking him if he was happy with his banking needs because this gentleman had the "solution" just for him. Banks didn't make calls like this, so it had to be some kind of chancer making the call.

"Look, you can stop right there. I'm not interested. I'm really swamped today, so if you don't mind," Magnus said, hurriedly trying to drive and talk, with his coffee resting between his legs. The salesman was undeterred. Magnus didn't quite get what he was saying, according to the seller. He wanted to elaborate on things.

"You know what? I really couldn't give two hoots arsehole," Magnus elaborated in his usual manner and hung up.

While hanging up, he took his eyes off the road for a second and misjudged how close he was to the car in front of him, causing him to brake hard when his eyes hit the road again. The thudding of the brakes sent a cascade of coffee out of the cup. The protective lid couldn't save all the coffee. Magnus's jeans softened the coffee's landing, wetting them in the process. Magnus frowned and started swearing to himself. He was angry; he hadn't used his cup holder located right next to him but had not been thinking at the time. Off to the morgue with wet pants. Great, Magnus thought.

The sun stood in the sky, not a cloud to keep it company, and the temperature was already up to twenty-five degrees. The cold chamber in the morgue was grey and metallic as far as the eye could see. You could almost taste the metal. That and the disinfectant as well. Kerstin Beckman welcomed Magnus when she saw him. She had a bright smile on her face.

"You don't have a towel or cloth, do you, Kerstin? I managed to spill coffee in the car on my pants".

"Yes, I have some napkins over here. Help yourself," Kerstin replied.

"Thanks."

"You will be pleased to know I have completed the autopsy on Sven Julin, our man from the woods."

"Find anything special?"

Kerstin invited Magnus to come and sit in her office, which was filled with several personal pictures. On her desk, she had various portraits of her family. Her two children were quite the artists it seemed. She had a boy of six and a girl of seven, and there were various works framed on her desk and on her walls of the usual type of thing children paint. Some animals. One with Mamma and Pappa outside their house with a big snowman outside. They had used lots of different colours. Very lovely indeed, Magnus thought. Kerstin Beckman was forty years old, and had black hair, with a length going to just below her shoulders. Her eyes were sharp and brown. Kerstin's office was the opposite of Magnus's. It was spick and span, and the desk had a lavender smell.

It had been polished recently. Kerstin Beckman took off her white pathologist's coat and placed it on the back of her chair. At least my chair is more comfortable, Magnus thought.

"So Magnus, the cause of death was asphyxia due to strangulation. No newsflash there. There's the substance under the fingernails. That's been sent off along with his blood for analysis, but I'm sure you knew that already. Sorry Magnus, but there's bugger all else that I can tell you."

"How long until we get the results from the lab?"

"I have a friend at the NFC who usually tries her best to speed things up for me. I'll try and push for it as quickly as possible. I know she said to me last time they were behind with all the work they have on their plate. So I don't know, hopefully, a week or so."

"They are always behind," Magnus said curtly.

"I'll be off then. Call me as soon as you have the results," Magnus added.

Magnus and Kerstin said goodbye to each other, and Magnus left.

Magnus walked out of Kerstin's office and closed the door behind him. Once he got outside, he wished he was back inside. The heat is getting ridiculous, Magnus thought to himself. He then started thinking about the National Forensics Centre in Linköping. They better bloody well hurry up, he mumbled to himself. Unfortunately, there wasn't much of a way to get them to hurry up. Varberg wasn't exactly the priority when it came to cases. Kerstin's friend was the best bet for help. Magnus also needed to hurry up. He had somewhere to be.

The office air conditioners were going great guns to keep things inside cool. Stina Wahlgren sat at her desk, which was next to Eva Lindqvist's, just a few metres away. They both had run of the mill work desks in an open-plan office. Magnus, as well as Rosenberg, were the only two who had offices. The rest worked in the middle of the room. It was generally a messy environment, except for Stina Wahlgren's desk. She had a desk planner on her desk, with post-it colour notes placed all over the calendar, with things she needed to do. She had pencils, pens, colour markers, three of each one. There was a glass of water on the side, as well as her laptop on the left-hand side of her desk. Stina Wahlgren scanned through the tire database with her blue eyes. The partial print had been added to the database, and now it was up to Stina to find some matches. With only a fragment of a tire print to work with, it was not going to be challenging to ascertain possible hits. Possible matches would be plentiful. Stina would have to narrow these plentiful possibilities down. Stina was optimistic about her chances as she sipped her water, and then placed it down and picked it up and tapped it down again for no apparent reason. She then picked it up and tapped it down again. Eva had been at her desk but had since made an exit to the bathroom, and was seated in one of the toilet stalls on the floor, next to the toilet. She was sweating profusely, more than you could give the weather credit for. She was trying to take slow breaths, and even though she did, she still felt a tightness in her chest and that feeling of being out of air like an unfit person sprinting a hundred metres. I can't let this get to me, she thought. These things happen. That phrase of these things happen didn't help her relieve any of her anxiousness. She didn't really believe that these things happen was even close to a reasonable explanation of what had occurred, did she? She sat with her eyes closed for a while, a good ten minutes, and slowly she started feeling better. Her confidence was particularly fragile at this point. There was a gentle tap on the stall door.

"Eva. Are you all right? You've been in there for a while."

It was Stina.

Eva got up off the cold cement floor and opened the door.

"Yes, I'm all right. Just having one of those days. You know. Still got this shooting in my head."

Stina looked to the ceiling for a second, knowing exactly what one of those days was like as well as knowing about things going around in one's head.

"Can I make you a cup of coffee? Maybe that would help you to settle down a bit."

"The machine is broken, remember?"

"Oh, yes, of course. Silly me. I think I will nip out just now and get us a cup."

"That would be nice."

They both gave comforting smiles to each other. Eva then asked Stina the reason she had come looking for her.

"You didn't look well. I thought I better just check up on you," Stina said.

"Thank you. I think I will be alright."

Stina looked directly at Eva.

"You can't let it beat you, this stuff about the shooting."

Stina gave Eva a gentle tap on the shoulder and exited.

She's right, Eva thought. You can't let it win.

While Magnus had been speaking to Kerstin Beckman, Rolf Jonsson had the very unpleasant task of visiting the Julin residence. He had taken his time to get there. Even though Rolf didn't show emotion often, he sure as hell would find it tough not to in this situation. He rang the doorbell outside the Julin's home, a pleasant enough looking house, but not one of significant size. Rolf gathered the impression of the family being middle of the road financially as he looked around. A good example of Sweden, he supposed to himself. A figure opened the door, but not entirely, the door extending only a few inches. The voice that came through the door was a weak, mild one.

"Can I help you?" uttered the voice.

"Good Morning. I'm Rolf Jonsson, a detective from the police department. I have to come to see Mrs. Julin." Rolf showed his identification.

"I'm Alice. My mom is lying down upstairs. But please do come in," Alice Julin said, looking completely out of energy. Her blond hair looked untidy, her face dull. She looked around twenty-one years old if Rolf had to guess. Rolf shuffled in through the door staying to one side almost as if he was going to break something if he walked straight in. Rolf gave Alice Julin a consoling smile as he made his way through. He was shown into the living room and took a seat on a red couch that was quite comfortable, although he was hardly going to mention that. Alice Julin asked Rolf if he wanted coffee, and he politely accepted. He always accepted in these situations, in a way to try and alleviate the grief the person was feeling by them doing something else. Even though it probably made no difference whatsoever, Rolf thought at least he was trying to make things a bit easier. Rolf looked around the room while he waited. The house was modest, but the warm colours combined with family pictures gave it a homely feel. Alice Julin returned with Rolf's coffee and a cup of tea for herself. She then excused herself for a second and went to see if her mother, Viveka Julin, was ready to join them. Alice returned alone. Would it be all right if she answered Rolf's questions instead of her mother? That was the query she raised. Her mother was fast asleep and had taken the news very badly. After bouts of crying, she had finally fallen off to sleep, and Alice thought it would be best to let her sleep a little. Rolf didn't have a problem with that. After some rather lengthy condolences on Rolf's part, he finally had begun to tackle more investigative questions. He started with the standard questions and left the dreadful discussion about coming to see the body to the end. He tried to get to know a bit more about Sven Julin. What was he like? What did he do? His relationship with Alice's mother Viveka, as well as if he had any enemies. Alice had been quite helpful, certainly in Rolf's estimation with nothing to hide. Her father was a kind man, and for him to have any hint of an enemy was out of the question, in her opinion. He had run a restaurant previously in Gustavsberg, but his main passion was the piano, and they had moved to Varberg because he had wanted to open up a piano school. Sven had been an outstanding pianist in his day, and after opening up his school in a small building in town, he had scraped off his rustiness and impressed all his budding students with his high level of play. Rolf had wondered if there had been a market for that kind of thing. Nothing massive apparently but enough to live reasonably well, although the family couldn't spend frivolously. Sven Julin had good repeat business with his clients really liking him. The marriage had always been a good one. Of course, they had their quibbles, but in general, it was a loving and happy marriage. Rolf came back to the point regarding enemies.

"I'm sorry to ask again, but are you certain no one had it in for your father? Even a small argument, an unhappy client, that kind of thing?"

"I'm certain."

"How was your relationship with your father?"

"I loved my father dearly. He always bent over backwards to help me. He did everything a father could do. He was also very nice to everyone he met." Alice's eyes began to well up, and she went and opened the window in the living room and took some deep breathes out into the summer air. Rolf was happy she did. It was starting to upset him as well.

"It's all such a — such a shock," Alice said,

sobbing softly as she looked out the window. Rolf was all but finished with his questioning. He did have one more question. When had they last seen Sven? He had gone to work that morning. Alice had popped in for breakfast, as she didn't live with them, she had her own small apartment not far from them. He had gone to work as usual. He had walked to work as it wasn't far away, and he had chatted with Viveka midway through the afternoon. Sven had mentioned he was going to be late due to composing a new piece. He, in the past, had on occasion come home late, so Alice told Rolf that Viveka was slightly concerned he hadn't returned home, but it hadn't raised any alarms that he may have been in danger. He sometimes got stuck on his piano, composing, deliberating, experimenting. Viveka had fallen asleep and was awoken by that phone call. Her husband was dead.

"Thank you for speaking with me. I know how difficult this must be for you. Listen, I have enough to work with for now. If I have anything else I need to speak to you or your mother about, I will contact you. The other thing I have to ask you is when you would be ready to come and see the body?"

Alice's eyes grew twice the size. The little colour she had in her face disappeared, making her as white as a sheet.

"I don't know how either my Mom or I will

be able to do it," she said. Tears were taking residence in her eyes again.

"It is a terrible thing to have to do such a thing. However, I think if you do it sooner rather than later, you can then grieve in peace."

"It's going to be hard to grieve in peace when you know someone murdered your father. You know two weeks ago when I broke up with my boyfriend, I thought *that* was upsetting. Then my father gets murdered. Dear God." Alice burst into tears.

Rolf went up to Alice slowly and gave her a friendly hug. All the pain and anguish came out of Alice. It was, in a way, a nice feeling for Alice, even though she felt slightly embarrassed that she was balling her eyes out on a policeman's shoulder. Once the crying stopped, Rolf tried to offer some words that would console Alice even though Rolf knew there wasn't anything he could say that would help.

"Our homicide division is very good. We will find who did this."

Rolf gave a polite nod and started for the door. Before he was out the door, Alice said she and her mother would come to view the body as soon as possible. Rolf gave a smile. Just before Rolf left, he turned and asked Alice something.

"Would it be all right if I went to your father's workplace? There might be something there that would be helpful."

"Yes, certainly. I have a key. Let me get it for you."

Alice Julin went to find the key, and Rolf waited with strange thoughts going through his mind. Maybe Camilla can go to piano lessons with Sven in heaven? He then gave a type of frown. What's going through your head? Rolf had always been unsure about if there was a heaven or not. Then images of Sven Julin and Camilla falling love in some sort of other universe. He needed some air. Luckily, Alice Julin returned with the key quickly, and Rolf was able to be on his way.

It was now back to the drawing board for Rolf. He got in his car, which was rusting, and on occasions not getting into gear smoothly. The gears would grind, and sometimes Rolf would shift from first gear to third as second gear was the problem. The steering wheel was also becoming a problem. Turning corners was like a daily gym workout because of the stiff wheel. Rolf would have to have his grey Kia Ceed serviced properly. New EU rules had come into place recently where every fourteen months, your vehicle must be inspected to evaluate its roadworthiness. And Rolf had six months left when the besiktning [inspection] had to be completed by. Rolf proceeded to make his way towards Sven Julin's workplace, hoping that he may find something there.

8

Magnus sat at a plain white table inside the ATG horseracing betting shop. He had already purchased some coffee as well as a cinnamon bun from the little kiosk inside the store. Currently, he was alone, but a couple of his friends said that they would be coming down later. Rolf Jonsson had tried to call Magnus, but he didn't answer and would not be taking calls from anyone apart from Lena. Now that Magnus had an idea about the case, the rest of the team could work on getting more evidence. He didn't need to be there to hold their hands. Besides, he could have a little think during the afternoon as to what was going on. Others may not see him sitting having a bun and reading the race form as being anything other than lazy, but Magnus didn't care. It was all about the final result. He wasn't going to sit all day inside the police department when his team was busy gathering material. There wasn't much he could add being there anyway. Of course, there was other work and cases—all in due time.

Sweden's horseracing is virtually all trotting, in which horses pull a two-wheeled cart with a driver in it. There are around 1000 race meetings a year with massive pools and interesting bets. Magnus was a regular. The meeting he was watching wasn't a big one, but there was still plenty to win. There were many bets you could take. Today he was going to take the V64 bet, which was over six races in which you needed to pick the winner of each race in order to win. The more horses you put into the bet, the more it cost. There was a consolation pay-out if you got five, or even four right, however, it usually amounted to peanuts. Even for this small race meeting, there was five million kronor in the pool. Magnus began working out his permutations while taking a big bite of his bun and slugging down some coffee. It was pleasantly cool inside the betting shop. Magnus had an important text to send to his friend Kristoffer, who he had known since school. Kristoffer worked at one of the stables and always provided helpful information.

"Working out a V64. Anything worth noting today?" Magnus punched send.

Magnus continued to fiddle with his bet until he had finalised what he wanted to take. He had around twenty minutes before the bets were closed, so he would give Kristoffer a few minutes to reply. In that time, he decided to think about the case in a relaxed fashion. Sven Julin. Hung from a tree. Magnus liked to start with a bare plate. Discount all the evidence found and try and form a basic idea of what had happened. Why didn't the killer just shoot Julin or do something along those lines? Why be that specific? It was a little concerning. The next question was, why Sven Julin? Was it a random act by a deranged killer? Or was Sven Julin the target? That was the place to start. Start to establish if Sven Julin was the intended victim. Because if Sven was the intended victim, then there must have been a reason the killer went after Sven.

Magnus's phone beeped. Kristoffer.

"Fourth leg of V64. Jackpot Man. Everyone thinks the favourite will win, but I know for a fact Jackpot Man is much much better," was Kristoffer's reply.

"Awesome," was Magnus's reply.

Magnus put his phone back in his pocket. He changed his bet slightly, and also decided he was going to have an individual bet on Jackpot Man.

This could be quite the afternoon, Magnus thought.

By the time some of Magnus's friends showed up, the fourth leg of the V64 had come and gone, with Jackpot Man winning easily and Magnus picking up about 3000 kronor in winnings. Magnus's other bet fare didn't nearly as well, with him collecting 52 kronor after it cost him 250. Magnus bought his friends who had showed up — Henrik Gustafsson, Claes Winterqvist, and Alan Pettersson — a round of drinks. Magnus declined on any drinks himself as he was driving. When asked about his day at the races, Magnus said he had broken even. Magnus never passed on any information he got from Kristoffer to anyone else. It was very enjoyable to spend some time with the guys, and after something to eat, Magnus went home. Driving back in the car after his leisurely outing, he had an idea regarding the case. I need to go to the campsite near where the body was found, he thought.

9

Someone must have seen something, thought Magnus the following afternoon as he was on his way to the Läjet camping site. The campsite was a big one, certainly not some rinky-dink setup. The reception was a quaint little red brick building that had a small snack bar inside, with a seating area outside where you could sit and enjoy your food and beverages. On the left was a miniature golf course in immaculate condition. Nine holes. It was in a smallish area, but they had used the space well. Magnus parked at the reception and got out to have a closer look at this course. Magnus walked to where the first hole began. A narrow straight hole with a tree stump in the way. The tree stump had a thin gap intricately carved out through the middle of it, so if you wanted, you could putt straight through the stump. If you didn't fancy your chances, you could always take a more cautious way and go around the stump, but it would usually cost you an extra shot. Magnus found himself thinking strategy and how he would approach this hole. He was not a good golfer, and only played on occasions, but he loved a game of mini-golf. The next hole Magnus peered at was a double story hole. You putt towards a massive hole, in which the ball goes down and pops out of a pipe towards another hole on a level below and to the right. The walkways around and through the course were beautiful pine boards. There were a few holidaymakers busy playing, and they all looked relaxed. For a while, Magnus forgot about why he was there in the first place. He peered over to another hole that had a little walkway bridge in the middle of it. It was still hot, but settling into the late afternoon, the temperature had declined, so it was probably close to an ideal temperature. The air felt cleaner — a Swedish summer in all its splendour. Usually, the Swedes couldn't wait for summer to come. After the snow and the darkness of winter, summer was a welcome sight. Although this summer, all that could be heard was complaints. Everybody had been whining about the heatwave. Magnus had also been guilty of this, swearing many a time as would wipe sweat from his brow. Maybe I should stop moaning about the heat, he thought. Magnus's gaze returned to the reception, and then he realised he was there to ask about a murder just on the outside of the campsite. So, there would be no sinking putts and attaining glory on the miniature course. Jumping back to reality irritated him. Then he began a rant in his head about his working environment. Would there be an acknowledgement from any of his superiors for his efforts? Not even a pat on the back. Well, maybe the salary made up for this lack of praise? Not exactly. He received the same mediocre salary regardless of the outcome. Not that he was saying he needed a big bonus or anything like that, but he had said for a long time, a sort of performance structure would be a good idea. Rosenberg naturally disagreed with that. But Rosenberg didn't have to worry. He got a decent cheque for doing sweet nothing. Lunches. That was his thing, lunch with Mr. So-and-So from such and such a district. Magnus knew it was just an excuse for a nice meal on the house. Travelling and entertainment. That's what it was coded to in the monthly accounts as far as he knew. Whatever! Rosenberg wouldn't know what an investigation was if it hit him in the face. Magnus then realised he had been standing overlooking the miniature course and stewing.

Magnus needed to get a move on now. Magnus shifted quickly, and he lumbered into the reception area. The man at reception was attending to a customer, so Magnus had a look around the reception area while waiting.

There was a big calendar on one of the

walls with all the activities lined up for the rest of the month. Movie nights. Yoga. Disco. Children's club. His eyes veered to another wall, which had an advertisement of what else was available in the way of facilities. There were tennis courts. Magnus was an avid tennis fan, having played at a club through school, and being rather good as well. There was a BMX track. Giant Chess. There were a host of other things which Magnus stopped looking at, as he became aware that the receptionist was now available out of his peripheral vision. Magnus had thought it best to start at reception, and then maybe take the side closest to the woods and ask some questions to the folk staying in that part of the campsite.

"Magnus Markusson, Chief Superintendent, Varberg Police. I want to ask you a few questions," Magnus said.

"What's this about?" The young male receptionist replied. He looked a little nervous. He had a name tag on. Kurt Johansson.

"I take it you are aware there was a murder in the woods next to the campsite?"

"I read they had found a body, but the paper had only speculated murder. I wasn't sure if it was actually a murder," Kurt Johansson said, his voice unsteady. He swallowed a heavy swallow after replying. There had been various papers that had something on the case, although it wasn't easy for most to get anything ready for print for that morning, and what had appeared had been vague and small, and as Kurt Johansson had said, speculative. There was bound to be a lot more media attention in the next twenty-four hours, where more details would emerge. Whether that would affect business at the camping site was another question, but it probably would to a degree.

"Well, I can tell you that it was a murder. Could we perhaps chat somewhere? In a spare office, perhaps?" asked Magnus.

Johansson quickly asked a lady at a desk nearby to please watch the front while he took Magnus into an office to chat.

"So, there was a murder in the woods next door to your site. With everything being in such close proximity, I think maybe someone staying here could have seen something or heard something. Were you working two nights ago?" Magnus asked.

"Me? Well, yes, I was here until 8:15 pm. I certainly didn't hear or see anything out of the ordinary while I was here."

"What about anything funny within the site? You know, anything unusual."

"No, nothing like that. Everything was as usual here. Just another day, as they say."

"If you don't mind, I may want to have a word with some of the people on the side of the campsite closest to the woods."

"That's no problem with me, but I don't know if the boss would like you pestering our guests. I would have to call him and get the all-clear."

"Well, if you prefer, I could roll in some squad cars, and bring in a host of detectives to question everyone?" That did not sound good to the receptionist as he swallowed with some difficulty yet again. So, he was caught between a rock and a hard place.

"I think it would be fine if you asked around by yourself. I've only been working here a week and a half, so please just take it easy. I don't want to be fired."

"Just help me with my questions, and I will take it easy," Magnus said.

"So, you can't think of anything else that would be useful to me?" Magnus added.

"No, no, I really don't think so."

As Magnus got up to leave, Johansson started to wag his finger, slowly with a bit more conviction as he went along.

"You know, just thinking about it, you should have a bash with Linus," Johansson said.

Who the fuck is Linus, Magnus thought.

"And who is that?"

"He's this guy. A homeless guy. Totally harmless. He hangs around here sometimes. We usually give him food once a week. We all feel a little sorry for the chap. I've only met him once, but he seems nice enough. The others here told me all about him."

"So, when did he check-in for his last meal then?"

"Two nights ago in actual fact."

Magnus thought for a second, looking curious as well as concerned. Although Sweden had homeless people like other countries, there weren't many, so it was a bit unusual.

"Can you give me a description of this guy?"

"Well, I think I have a picture here somewhere. We had a bingo evening a while back, and they let Linus stay and have food here and play the bingo. One of the staff wanted to take a picture of a few of them, and thought it would be nice to take a picture with Linus as well."

"Are you in the habit of letting people in off the street like this, and letting them sit and eat here and play games, and then have them included in pictures?"

"No, it was just the one time as far as I know. As I mentioned, he's no trouble. He wouldn't hurt a fly. He's quite smart, but at the same time, he's not quite right."

"Can you elaborate a bit?"

"Well, for one thing, he always carries around this book. Always scribbling things down in it. Won't let anyone near it."

"Can you find that picture for me?"

"Yes, just give me a minute."

While the picture was being attained, Magnus thought about this. Could this Linus guy have seen something? He needed to find him. A minute later, Johansson returned with a picture that he had found under some papers on a desk in the other room. He pointed Linus out to Magnus. Quite a dishevelled looking individual, a typical look for a homeless man.

"Thanks for your help. As soon as this Linus fellow comes back here, please call me right away."

Magnus handed him his card and left. He gave his red soft collared shirt a pull, trying to fan himself. He took one more glance at the mini-golf as he got into his car. Magnus sat there for a second. He wanted to follow up on this strand of information first. Better that than going through the whole blinking campsite and wasting time now that he had acquired this new person of interest. Magnus started his car and left.

With being it fairly late in the afternoon, Magnus decided to carry on straight home. His mobile phone made a loud ping. A WhatsApp message. It was Lena. *Please go to ICA and buy some dog food. The dogs don't like the new food you bought.* So, the trip going straight home had been rerouted with Magnus having to go via ICA because his dogs weren't happy with the food that was in supply at home. "Un-be-lieve-able," Magnus said slowly and loudly with a heavy snort and then began speaking to himself in a very sarcastic tone. "I'm so sorry dogs, how rude of me to purchase such cheap shit. What should I get for you this time? Seared Tuna? Duck, perhaps?" By the time Magnus arrived at the store, he was still mumbling things to himself. His mood improved a touch when he realised he was already there. ICA, the leading grocery retailer in the country, was certainly a favourite of Magnus's. That didn't mean he liked to go there because the dogs didn't like their food. There were four ICA stores in Varberg, and the giant one, ICA Kvantum, was 650 metres from Magnus's home. Hardly out of the way, but when Magnus wanted to go home, next door would have been out of the way. Once he walked in the doors, he felt much happier. ICA was always clean, tidy, and extremely well organised. The staff was always working, packing, doing something. The food was always great. Well now that I'm here, I may as well take a snack or two home, Magnus thought. He grabbed himself some bread with some ham and cheese, along with a slab of Marabou chocolate. Let's take an extra one, he thought. Two for thirty kronor deal. You've got my money. He remembered the dog food as well and bought some that were pricier than his previous selection. Well if they don't like this, then they can come and buy their own. Magnus got to the counter and paid for his things, packed them into a packet, and left. He pondered to himself on the short ride on home about the victim, Sven Julin. So, Mr. Julin, he thought to himself. What did you do to get yourself killed?

10

Two men struck up a conversation in a local hotel bar. During their discussion, they both learnt that they were in town for the same reason. Business. Not the same type of business, but business nonetheless. Both were in town for a very brief stay, with both parties due to stay until the next morning. With that in common, they continue a relaxed chat. They decided to have a quick bite to eat and order some food. They decided to eat together. During the meal, one of the men caused a real commotion regarding the slow service. After things had settled down, and he apologised to his new acquaintance about getting so angry. He also added that he was right to be angry with such poor service. He then followed up with a question about the evening.

"So, have you got any plans tonight?"

"Well, I thought of just sitting in my room, having an early night."

"Why don't we meet up later, you know, a one for the road type of thing?"

"Sure, why not." He was a little uncertain

when he agreed.

"There's a club nearby we could go to. I heard it's more of a cocktail bar, so we wouldn't have to worry about young riff-raff puking their guts out."

"OK, so what time should we make it? Should we meet down here at the lobby?"

"Eight-thirty. Down here. Man, there should be some great women around. Wouldn't mind finding a good lay."

"You go right ahead on that front. I'm happily married, so I won't be joining in with that."

"Suit yourself. More for me."

11

Eva Lindqvist had been on the phone with her sister, Malin, for quite some time since getting home from a rather unproductive and distressing day at work. A gentle call to her sister would have been nice and calming in a way. However, now the standard type of argument had ensued. The topic for the fight was Malin's boyfriend, Jonas Langberg. The relationship had been going on for around nine months, and for the last six months, Eva had not seen hide nor hair of her sister. She had never liked Jonas Langberg. That slick backed hair smooth-talking son of a bitch. Malin found the look classy. Eva found it slimy and sleazy. She couldn't put her finger on it when she had met him. There was just something, something she instantly didn't like. Didn't like had been ramped up to couldn't stand.

"I don't think you can see how controlling Jonas is. It's ridiculous," Eva said in a sharp tone.

"Why do you always have to be like this when I'm happy?"

"Because you *aren't* happy!"

"Says who? The frigging expert on relationships. The divorcee herself."

"Well, at least I got out. Maybe you should do the same."

The conversation was getting out of hand.

"There is nothing wrong with Jonas being protective of me — It's quite charming in a way."

"Oh, cut the crap, Malin. Stop defending him. You never do anything; you never go anywhere. You do what he says. When was the last time you visited me or vice versa? That's right, a few months back. But wait, didn't Jonas put a stop to that? Hmm, yes, as I recall, you were coming to see me, and the evening before, he just cancelled your plans for you."

"Something came up at home, actually!"

"You keep telling yourself that."

"I don't need to listen to this shit."

"Well maybe if you opened your —." Malin hung up with Eva in mid-sentence, trying to hand out a few more home truths.

The dialling tone rang in Eva's ear like she had a case of tinnitus. Eva let out a long breath, the wind going out of her sails. There seemed to be no way of talking sense into Malin. Malin had gone for the low blow as well, bringing up Eva's divorce. Could it be that Eva was just jealous? Malin had less time for her now because of her new man. She also was in a relationship, something that Eva was not in. After a brief ponder over those things, Eva came to the definitive conclusion that jealousy was out of the question. Jonas was just a manipulating swine. Not another thing to worry about, she thought. Eva had enough problems of her own that were causing her sleepless nights. The worst thing was that she had no idea how to solve her own problems. How could she help her sister when she couldn't help herself?

Eva went to make herself some dinner. She whipped out some pasta, an easy microwaveable dish, and got that going while she opened a bottle of red wine. Try and relax, she thought as she sipped the wine she had just trickled into her glass. She liked that taste of this particular bottle from her pantry and commented to herself about the subtle fragrance and the more sophisticated taste. Well, it tasted sophisticated to her. Then she started wondering about people and their wines. Are these so-called wine connoisseurs just that? Would they know a cheap wine from an expensive wine if they didn't know which was which? An interesting question. She just tasted the wine, and if it tasted good, it was good, and if it didn't well, then it was crap. Price had no outcome on her critique. Apart from wines, a similar thing could be said about many subjects or people. How many people liked or disliked something because of what other people said, the price, or the name? Eva felt it was always good to be yourself, and if that meant you didn't like the latest trend on social media, then so be it. Too many children nowadays followed the flock like lost little sheep.

Eva's food was ready, and she went to sit in front of the TV, on her soft white couch. It was the most comfortable couch she had ever sat on. She sat down and then got up again, deciding to get a small blanket, even though it was still warm outside. She flicked around channels until she found a cooking show to watch, something easy where she didn't have to concentrate a great deal. After a decent meal, and two glasses of wine later, Eva felt very tired, and decided to take a nap on her couch, hoping that she would be able to sleep. Thankfully, she passed out in a flash and began snoring gently.

Malin Lindqvist had gotten off the phone with Eva and was furious. Eva didn't know anything about Jonas! Eva just liked to be negative. This whole shooting thing has gotten to her, Malin thought as she put some dishes away. Jonas Langberg had gone out for a beer with the boys and had said he would be home later. Malin had found his comings and goings slightly strange of late. Going out at odd times and coming home at all hours. He was "letting off some steam," but still, Malin found it odd.

Malin went to take a shower. With the house to herself, she could take a long one. Malin hopped into the shower and looked up at the showerhead. She turned the valve for the water, and it took her a couple of minutes to find a suitable temperature. Back and forth, adjusting from hot to cold and back again. Malin started thinking of her and Jonas's relationship while the water cascaded onto her back. Every relationship has ups and downs, she thought. However, they were still going strong. They loved each other. At the same time, she was thinking this, Malin looked down at her rib cage for the first time since taking off her clothes and going to shower. She had been avoiding looking there. Now that her Nordic blue eyes had peered there, Malin saw the dark black bruise that covered a rather vast majority of her ribcage. She grabbed a forest green body wash and began scrubbing at that part of her body, in a furious motion. Tears started to venture from her eyes when she saw that no amount of body wash would take it off. Her previous thoughts of her and Jonas loving each other had dwindled. Was it love when she had black bruises after she and Jonas had an argument? A few tears started to form from her eyes.

12

The new morning had an uncomfortable air to it. Viveka and Alice Julin had contacted Rolf Jonsson late the previous evening and said that they were ready to see the body. From there they could make the necessary arrangements for the funeral and so forth. So, it had been arranged that the Julins were going to see the body that morning. Rolf had got up a little earlier in anticipation of this event he was undertaking. Sylvester, his cat, was lying on top of Rolf's stomach and looked quite perturbed that he had to be moved because Rolf had to get up. In all eventuality, it wasn't a big deal because Sylvester reconstructed his plans. He went and whined for breakfast while Rolf was making his own and got a generous helping of his favourite cat food. He then went back to bed afterwards. It's good when you can adapt to the situation. Rolf wanted to crawl back into bed too, right under the covers and not come out for a few days, but instead, he was off to the morgue. When Camilla had passed away, Rolf also had made these same arrangements that the Julin family were going to have to make shortly. His heart went out to them. To organise a funeral was as unpleasant a task as he could think of. You see people at the funeral that were also grieving about the person's death, and they wanted the same thing as you. For that person to come back. Like magic. Magic that would bring them back. No one would understand, but no one would have to. All they would need to know is that it would bring back people. Of course, the reality was that the funeral was a farewell. A most concrete farewell. Not a goodbye or a see you later. This was a farewell forever. Then there would be food, tea, and coffee afterwards. What on earth on for? Why stand around more and bathe in the surrounding morbid atmosphere? Also, most of the time, everybody would comment on how the particular food they were eating was nice, and the coffee was good because there was nothing else to talk about. Rolf had a friend who said he didn't go to funerals. Out of respect for the deceased. An interesting way of looking at things.

Rolf's way of preparing to see the Julins, who had explicitly asked him to be there when they came, was to have a decent-sized breakfast. A decent size was a lot bigger for Rolf than it was for other people. Rolf had been on a diet. This diet of Rolf's, another one in the many he had tried, was portion control. The keyword was control. Rolf was having a tussle with that. This diet had been underway for a week or so, and it had already hit a few speed bumps. Rolf would allow himself a few indiscretions based on the kind of day he had or was going to have. To get through a viewing of a body, he would have to ready himself by having a more casual menu. He would also up the portions. Today the portion he planned was going to be big. Back in the day, Rolf had been fairly sporty. He was no superstar, but he was decent at a variety of sports. His weight had never been a problem. Now, weighing 108 kilograms, his weight was definitely not good. Then it dawned on him. Camilla's death. He thought hard about it. And that was it. He had been eating ravenously more or less just after Camilla had died. Rolf wondered why he had never thought of that before. It must be some type of comfort eating then. However, he got no comfort. And to try and stop was going to be a challenge. Rolf got himself some coffee while he started on his breakfast. He wondered if that coffee machine at work would be fixed soon. It would be fun to see what Magnus would do if the machine wasn't fixed quickly. Rolf finished off making his breakfast and went to sit down at the breakfast table.

Rolf managed to fit his breakfast all onto one plate. Three eggs, five streaks of bacon. Three pieces of toast. Baked beans, almost a whole tin. Pork sausages. A whole string of them. The plate looked like a busy day at Arlanda Airport. A traffic jam of various foods bumping into each other, each trying to find their spot on the plate. Unlike Arlanda, the traffic eased quite quickly as Rolf polished off his food in short order. Rolf cleaned his glasses and prepared to get ready for what he had been dreading.

The body lay there on the metal slab, almost as if it was just a piece of meat, devoid of feelings or thoughts. Rolf stood outside, waiting for Viveka and Alice Julin. Rolf had been distraught by how Camilla had died of cancer and knew what it felt like to lose a loved one. He did not, however, understand what it must have been like to have a family member murdered. Strung up in a tree, left to hang there, swaying left and right. In all these cases, the family, the public, the police - they only had one question they wanted answering. Who did it? That was the resounding question everyone was trying to arrive at—all except the killer.

Alice Julin tried to show a polite smile when she arrived. Viveka Julin was sobbing already as she approached the entrance to the door. Time to enter and see the unseeable. Kerstin Beckman waited inside by the body, with her being the one to make sure that Alice and Viveka saw only what was required. The face. Kerstin said nothing at all as the Julins entered alongside Rolf. She thought to herself that Rolf's stomach looked huge, a lot bigger than usual. Heart attack material. When everyone was close enough, Kerstin pulled up the lifeless white sheet as far as necessary, to which everyone saw an equally lifeless face. Viveka's hands were trembling badly, while Alice held her, tears coming down steadily. Rolf now regretted eating that much breakfast. It felt as if all his breakfast was sitting in his throat region. Kerstin was the orchestrator of this viewing, deciding when enough would be enough. After a few more seconds, she placed the sheet back over Sven Julin. Alice asked Kerstin if she could see her father's face once more to which Kerstin nodded and rolled the sheet back so Alice, as well as Viveka, got one more look. Alice touched Sven's cheek with her hand. Viveka, very slowly, leant in and kissed Sven. So that was that. Kerstin nodded to Rolf that he should start to help the Julins out to which he did, ushering them to the door slowly. There was nothing else to say to them. He still needed to chat with Viveka, ask her some questions, but now was not the time to bring that up.

Viveka said nothing as she left. Alice gave Rolf a half-smile.

"Thank you. You have been very nice to us. Thank you ever so much."

Rolf reached into his pocket. He took out the key for Sven Julin's piano premises.

"Here is your key back."

"Did you manage to find anything?"

"There was nothing of interest, I'm afraid. Not to worry, our team is busy with many different things."

Alice Julin thanked Rolf again, and she and her mother left.

The two Julin's moved out of the building and went slowly to the car. Rolf's mind was all over the place. It was only 8.30 am. He had the whole day ahead of him.

The press conference began on time at 9.00 am, in which the district police commissioner, Erik Rosenberg, ran through some details of the current case, as well as field some questions from the journalists that had arrived. Everyone was gathered in the designated conference room in the police station.

"A couple of nights ago, namely Tuesday the fifth of July, we responded to a call we received about a dead body in the wooded area next to the Läjet camping site. We found a dead male, who has been identified as Sven Julin, fifty-two years old. He was found hanging from a tree, and our preliminary investigation of the scene suggests he was murdered. Based on this, we have launched a homicide investigation and are currently in the early stages. We hope to have this resolved as quickly as possible."

Pens clicked, and most of the journalists in the room made notes of the statement Rosenberg had given. Rosenberg continued.

"I am available now for a brief period to answer any questions anybody may have." Erik Rosenberg rubbed the right side of his face, the site of some very rough and bad looking skin. He put his hands on the desk and awaited questions. Hands went up quickly. The room had become stuffy, as yet another sauna of a day was brewing outside.

"Have you any suspects?" a lady at the front asked who had large circular earrings.

"At this time, we are still gathering evidence and are following a few different lines trying to link things together. So, to answer your question, no, there are no suspects at this time."

"Who made the phone call?" a short, rather chubby woman asked.

"It was a tip-off made to our offices. The caller didn't leave his name."

"Is suicide out of the question?" a male correspondent queried.

"Yes, it was definitely murder. No doubt about it."

"Varberg is a particularly safe town. Now we have someone hung from a tree. What are you people going to do about it?" another man said in a slightly aggressive tone.

"Look, let's not panic. We have our best people on this case, so we, just like the public, want a speedy resolution."

"Is it a serial killer?" the same man questioned again.

"We have yet to ascertain that."

"Oh, come on. Is that the best you can do? So, in a nutshell, you people know jack-shit!"

"Listen, I am doing this press conference to fill everyone in. There is no need for that type of abrasiveness."

"Well, you have filled everyone in. We know now the police are incompetent idiots!"

Before Rosenberg could say anything, the man got up and stormed out.

When at the exit, he added, "Look forward to my report on the case." He then left.

Order was resumed, and questions continued for a short while, with just generic queries, along with generic responses. Rosenberg wasn't prepared to give much away, primarily because there was not much to give. He did point out that to be on the safe side, the public should stay vigilant at this time, and if anyone had any possible information, to please ring the police. Rosenberg called the press conference to a close. Almost simultaneously, everyone got up from the plastic chairs, creating a unified dragging sound. Magnus better hurry up and find something, Rosenberg thought as he gathered up his notes.

"Linus who?" Rolf asked Magnus, sitting opposite him in Magnus's paper-strewn office.

"How the fuck should I know? But be that as it may, this guy is always by the campsite, looking for food, and generally just sitting outside there or walking those roads. The campsite gives this guy food once a week to help him out, and they gave him his latest food package the day of the murder. Maybe he saw something," Magnus replied.

Shit, Rolf's stomach is huge, Magnus thought.

"Yes, I suppose it's possible," said Rolf.

"I need you and Alexander to find this guy. I have a picture of this bingo evening where he was in a picture." Magnus fished out the bingo picture he had obtained at the campsite.

"The guy there at the back, the scraggly looking one," Magnus added.

"We will get right on it."

"Before you go, how did your talk with the Julin family go? And Sven Julin's work? Did you find anything there? Should I get some forensics to go there?"

"Nothing useful at all at his work. No signs of any struggle or anything out of place. Nothing at all. As far as the chat went, there wasn't much either I'm afraid. The wife was too distraught to even come out of her room, so I spoke to the daughter. They also came and saw the body this morning. It was terrible." Magnus nodded, having forgotten that Rolf had done that this morning.

Rolf had a small folder in his hands. He put it on Magnus's desk.

"Some notes about the talk I had with the daughter." Magnus flipped through it casually and chucked it on his desk.

"So, you didn't speak to the wife at all?" Magnus asked.

"I had a good chat with the daughter, and I mentioned I would return to speak to her mother if necessary."

"I think you need to do that when you get a chance, we can't leave people out because they are distraught. But first things first. This Linus guy needs to be found."

"I'll get Alexander, and we will head off."

"Excellent."

Rolf pushed his glasses in and had one more question for Magnus before he left.

"Could Linus not have been the killer? I mean, he was in the area. He's always there. So, he knows his way around I'll bet."

"Do you think a homeless guy would go to that type of trouble to kill someone? And how did he do it? He would have needed a vehicle. I think we can rule him out. But one thing is for sure; we need to talk to him."

It couldn't be that vagabond, Magnus thought. No way.

With Rolf out of the way, Magnus decided to check what had happened with the coffee machine. He had been too busy when he had walked through the door first thing to even think about coffee or checking if the repairs to the device had been carried out. He got to the machine, and someone had attached a note on the side of it. A pink post-it note stuck to the white appliance with the words "out of order." I can't believe this, Magnus thought. I just want a cup of coffee. Is that too much to ask? Magnus stamped his way back to his office, his black shoes thudding on the way there, indicative of his mood. He sat down at his desk and brushed his brown hair out of the way. Eva appeared at the wrong time. She had an update for Magnus, but Magnus first had another agenda to discuss. Eva could not get a word in before Magnus got going.

"I thought this damned coffee machine was supposed to be fixed."

"Rana said to me that Rosenberg said to get someone out to look at it would be a waste of money for an old machine," Eva said.

"That son of a bitch. Him and his fucking budgets. I'll speak to Rana about getting someone in."

"Don't you think you are being a little petty about this machine?"

"Petty! We are all entitled to a cup of coffee." Magnus was even more annoyed now, but when Eva said nothing and just looked at him, he decided to continue.

"Now, what is it you wanted me for?"

"Just a quick update with the tire tracks Stina's been busy with. She has managed to find 284 possible matches to our partial tread. The hard part is now to isolate the tread further."

"Well, it's a start. Maybe ring the car dealerships and see if any particular models are discontinued. See if there are any models that aren't readily available in this area. I'm sure we can narrow it down further."

"Will do. I'm still working on Sven Julin's personal details. I haven't had any luck thus far but will keep you in the loop."

"Great. Alexander is out with Rolf, so you can help with some of his work as well."

"Yes, no problem."

"Great. Please make sure to close my door on the way out. I have lots of work to do."

Eva Lindqvist left the room.

Now I can get down to business, Magnus thought. He turned to his computer and went straight to the ATP tennis website. So, who's in action this week, Magnus thought to himself.

Eva went and put down Stina Wahlgren's documents about her tire tread analysis back on her acutely organised desk. She probably hadn't put them back exactly how Stina wanted them, but hey she had covered for her. Stina wasn't at work yet, and Eva had updated Magnus on her findings to prevent the off chance of him asking and finding Stina, not at work. Magnus wasn't impressed when his team was late, which was odd, considering Magnus got to work late regularly. Stina was usually at work at the same time every day, to the second. Where on earth was she this morning?

Stina was already sweating from her frustration at trying to leave for work. She knew she was late, and that only made things worse. It was quite warm already, and that, coupled with her annoyance, had caused her to break out sweating early on. Stina's face had a long frown on it. She went to lock the door again. She turned the key, and the door clicked closed. She started to walk away from the door, and for some reason, as often with other things at non-specific times, she got a feeling that it wasn't right. She got this "not right" feeling frequently. The door not locked right, the pens not in the right place, the TV not turned off right. She went back again for what may have been the fifteenth time, her usual alert blue eyes looking at the door with torment. What the hell is wrong with me? Why do I keep going back when I know I'm being stupid? You close the door, lock it, and leave. It took ten more minutes before she managed to lock the door without going back. She started her vehicle, a Volvo as well; however, compared to Magnus's model, a lot more economical and diminutive. Stina rested her head on the steering wheel, feeling mentally exhausted. Now she was late for work, which only added to her problems. Once she arrived at work, Stina tried to slink in quietly, which succeeded until she bumped into Eva.

"Where have you been?" Eva whispered in a concerned fashion.

"I'm so sorry I'm late," Stina said sincerely and continued.

"I woke up feeling dreadful. I managed to eat something, and I'm feeling much better now. I don't know why I felt so sick." Stina didn't want to tell Eva why she was really late.

"That is strange. Listen, I covered for you and updated Magnus on your tire tread news. Next time phone me and let me know what's happening."

Stina assured Eva she would do that, and smiled gratefully, to which Eva returned a smile. Just then, Magnus walked past in a hurry and towards the entrance to the building.

"Where are you off to?" Eva enquired.

"I need to ask the Julins something."

Alice Julin let Magnus into the house, and she asked Magnus whether he would like some tea or coffee, clearly lacking energy. It hadn't been long since she and her mother, Viveka, had gotten back from seeing Sven Julin's body. Magnus unusually turned down a cup of coffee as he didn't envisage his stay to be extended.

"I may need to ask your mother for some help regarding something."

"She's still really devastated after this morning. Maybe I could help you?"

Alice Julin seemed sincere, so Magnus decided to ask her instead of her grieving mother as long as he got what he wanted.

"In some notes I received from my detective who was here previously, it says your father ran a type of piano school. Is that correct?"

"Yes, that's correct."

"I wonder, did he have a client list of his customers somewhere?"

"Yes, yes, he did. I remember him having a weekly sheet of who would be coming for tuition as well as their personal details."

"Would it be possible if I could have a copy of his contact list?"

"Why? You don't think someone he taught could have killed him?"

"I need to gather evidence to find the person who did this, so I need to check up on his clients. I'm sure you understand this is something I'm experienced in."

"I see. Yes, I can find a copy for you if you don't mind waiting two minutes," Alice Julin said after a slight pause.

Magnus waited on the edge of one of the sofas until Alice Julin returned a few minutes later with a contact list of anyone that had come to piano lessons with her father. All in all, there was a list of some forty-six people who had received piano tuition at some stage from Sven Julin. Magnus thanked Alice very much and bid her a good day. Magnus got up to walk out the door and then saw something that made him stop suddenly.

"Is everything OK?" asked Alice Julin.

"Who is that?"

"Who?"

"That guy, in the picture there? Who is that?" Magnus said loudly.

"Oh, that. That's my ex-boyfriend. We broke up about two weeks ago." Alice pointed to a picture of a summer barbeque with her parents and her ex-boyfriend.

Magnus was trying to remember the name of a person he had seen recently. Then it came to him.

"Is his name Kurt Johansson by any

chance?" Magnus remembered him from the campsite.

"Yes. Do you know him?"

"On second thoughts, I will have a cup of coffee. We have a bit more to discuss."

Magnus sipped his coffee and wanted some details from Alice Julin regarding Kurt Johansson, who was now working at reception at the campsite. Alice had a puzzled look on her face as to why Magnus wanted to ask about him. Alice said that she and Kurt had gone out for about eighteen months, and she had ended it because it just wasn't working out. She couldn't see a future with him. Kurt had been a little too carefree and a little too "chilled" for Alice's liking. Kurt had seemed to have no goals and was just happy to goof about. Alice said Kurt had a good heart and was kind, but it just wasn't going to work. It hadn't ended well. Kurt had been angry with Alice, saying that it was her father, Sven, who had caused the breakup. Sven would regularly call when Alice was out to check in all was well. Kurt had taken these calls to mean he was checking up on him. Alice told Magnus that was nonsense, and she had told Kurt that too. Kurt hadn't believed it. Alice told Magnus that even though she had ended the relationship, it was still sad as at one stage, she and Kurt had been very much in love. She had cried about it for a good few days after.

"Do you know where Kurt is working now?" asked Magnus.

"No, I don't. He tried to phone me once or twice, and I didn't answer. He then messaged me, saying he was working now. I congratulated him but told him it didn't change anything. I haven't heard from him since."

"He works at the Läjet campsite. Right next to where your father was found murdered."

"What are you implying?"

"You date this Kurt guy. You break up. He blames your father for the break-up. The next thing is your father is found dead right next to Kurt's new place of employment. That's a little odd, don't you think?"

"Are you suggesting *Kurt* did this? No, no, there's no way. He might have blamed my father for the break-up, but he would never do anything like that."

Magnus downed the rest of his coffee and thanked Alice Julin for it and for answering his extra questions. He needed to get a move on.

Magnus hopped in his Volvo and sped off. He was going straight back to that campsite to speak to Kurt Johansson. The connections between Kurt and the victim made Kurt a definite suspect. The only thing that didn't fit is that the killer seemed to be very clever in how the murder was set up. Would he be dumb enough to work next door? Kurt would have surely known his connection to the Julins would have been noticed very quickly. In any event, a more forceful chat with Kurt Johansson would help answer a few of these questions. Magnus got out his phone to call Eva, but as he did this, he saw that she was ringing him.

"Eva, I was just about to call you. What's up?"

"I can't do this anymore. This shooting is destroying me," Eva said, her voice weak.

"Stop being stupid, Eva, and listen to me. I'm coming past the office to get you. We need to go and speak to the person at the reception at the campsite now. He used to date Alice Julin and get this—Alice said he blamed Sven for the break-up. Break-up was two weeks ago."

"I don't know if I'm up to it. I'm not feeling good."

"We can talk in the car if that would help. I'm on my way. This is important. Think of the case."

Eva rubbed her face.

"I'll be waiting."

Eva hung up the phone. Magnus's face had concern all over it. Eva's apparent unravelling was a problem. She didn't want to come along to question a suspect. Things couldn't be good.

13

Rolf Jonsson and Alexander Holström sat parked in Kungsgatan with both having their windows wound down. The temperature had hit thirty degrees centigrade. Where they had parked on Kungsgatan was nearby a Thai restaurant. Both Rolf and Alexander had ordered a takeaway lunch and rather enjoyed it, with Rolf's order a bit more sizeable than Alexander's. They had decided to park at their designated spot for a while, and with it being a reasonably central spot, they were hoping a few hours in the same place would result in Linus walking past them or at the very worst, near them, enough for them to spot him and have a chat with him. How hard could it be to find a homeless person? There were not too many around. They both got into a conversation regarding each other's trials and tribulations. Rolf chatted about how he found moving forward in life without Camilla quite an arduous and downright sad task. Alexander recounted the issues he was having with women. He had all the charm and good looks the women loved. Alexander's woman problems had become quite complicated. Alexander was keen on Liza. No big deal in of itself. However, he also liked Stella. Also, Trina. The next issue is that Alexander wasn't too sure how keen he actually was. Was he looking for sex only? Was he interested in settling down? Alexander didn't know what he wanted. Maybe he should just carry on as he was for now and see what happened.

Another issue was that these three women had all made it clear they were keen on him. His life had been a juggling act; Alexander had been seeing them "casually," so, in his terms, that meant he could sleep with all of them while he decided if he wanted to pursue the more formal arrangement. A more monogamous one. Rolf laughed at this.

"When they find out, and they will find out, you, my friend, are in deep shit."

"That's where you are wrong, Rolf. I'll just work out which one I want to see more seriously and ditch the other two."

They both chuckled. What was no laughing matter, was truth be told, Alexander felt claustrophobic after saying the word seriously. That seemed a big leap. Alexander was always happy to jump right in and chat about his personal affairs with women and virtually anything else for that matter. However, whenever someone asked him about his family, he would give a generic response and answer and behave awkwardly. No one knew anything about Alexander's parents other than that they "were fine" and that they were "busy with this and that."

In the rear-view mirror, Rolf, who was looking around, saw a man coming towards their car from behind. The man looked dirty, and his clothes were in lousy condition. He had an old light blue button-up shirt on, with the one arm slightly torn. As he got closer, he looked a lot like the man in the bingo picture. Linus. Rolf prodded Alexander and, without ushering a single word, pointed his index finger towards the man just as he walked past the car. They both stared intently for a second. Then they looked at the bingo picture which Linus had been in. Then they looked at the man again, now in front of the car and heading down the street. They looked at each other.

"It has to be him," whispered Alexander.

Rolf said nothing. He nodded back at Alexander, who started the car. They began to follow the man. They followed the man down another street, and into a busier one. The car was slowly creeping towards the target. Alexander didn't want to startle the man.

"As we get to the corner, let's quickly pull over and grab him," said Rolf.

"Sounds good. Our first day looking for him

and we find him. Are we good or what?" said Alexander.

Magnus had collected Eva from the office,
and they were headed towards the campsite.
Magnus had clarified all the points regarding Kurt
Johansson, and Eva had agreed that they needed
to have a serious talk with Johansson.

"You feeling better now?" Magnus asked.

"What do you think? I haven't been sleeping—anxiety attacks at work. Maybe I should just
quit, you know. Get out of this work completely."

"Eva, what good do you think that would
do? Quitting is not the answer."

"So, what on earth am I supposed to do?"

"How about starting with acceptance. Accept you killed this guy. And also accept you did
what you had to do; otherwise, his wife would
have been killed."

"I just don't know. Maybe I should go and
talk to someone about it."

"Eva, listen. You are a great cop, and what
you did was right. You *had* to kill that guy."

Eva felt better temporarily. Maybe Magnus
was right. She had heard of the saying, "time heals
all wounds." Maybe that was true in this context.
She was really hoping it was.

They arrived at the campsite, and Magnus
didn't have a look at any miniature golf this time.
He and Eva went straight into the reception and

found Kurt Johansson at the counter. Johansson saw them and gave a half-smile.

"Hello, Kurt. Could we have a chat in private?" Magnus suggested.

"Well, I'm quite busy."

"Find someone to look after the front. We need to talk *now*." Magnus said, his voice raised.

"Umm, give me a second."

Kurt Johansson went to a back office and managed to find someone to look after the front for him.

Johansson showed Magnus and Eva into a spare room.

"I've only got a few minutes. What's this about?"

"I think we will be the ones who decide when we are done," Eva said.

Johansson said nothing. He started fidgeting with his hands, moving them around constantly. He moved his long hair around while he chewed on some gum. He was in a type of work uniform, but his shirt was untucked.

This guy is a complete goofball, Magnus thought.

"Right. So, Kurt, you didn't mention to me in our last talk you knew the victim," Magnus said.

"Well, I did know him. But he was just my ex's father. It's not like we were mates or anything."

"I still find it strange you wouldn't mention it."

"Well, it's not a big deal. Me and Alice, we're not together anymore."

"What happened with Alice?"

"She just like ended it. Said it wasn't going anywhere, and there was like no future."

"Well, Kurt, your ex's father, is found murdered next door to your work. And according to Alice, you thought Sven was the cause of the break-up."

"I did say that. He was always phoning her when we were somewhere asking how Alice was. Alice used to say he liked to check in here and there and see how she was, and I was like whatever. He was doing that because he wanted to check up on what *I* was doing with Alice. I think he thought I was a bad influence."

"I remember you said you were working on the evening of the murder last week. Can you confirm what time you finished?"

"Yes, I was working. I got off at 8.15 pm."

Magnus heard a bunch of beeps, and Johansson took out his phone to check his messages or whatever else was going on.

Not another one of these phone fucks, Magnus thought. Who would want to be on their phones all day, hoping for messages every two damn seconds?

"If we can get back to the real world now,

Kurt," Magnus said and continued.

"The murder happened around 9.00 pm, so things don't exactly look good, Kurt."

"What? You think I killed him? No way man. I did nothing."

"Where were you between 9.00 pm and 10.00 pm?"

"I always go shopping afterwards and then I go home."

Surprised he doesn't get lost on the way to the shop, Magnus thought.

"You stay with anyone?"

"My flatmate, but he has been away for the last week or so. Come on man. I didn't do anything. I'm not going to kill a guy because he was overprotective of his daughter."

"Have you got anyone who can vouch for your whereabouts?"

"Well, I always go to Lidl on the way home. They know me there at the store. I always go there. Cheap prices."

Magnus and Eva headed back to the office after concluding their talk with Kurt Johansson.

"What do you think?" Eva asked.

"We will check out his alibi, but I can't see how that buffoon could have done it. Alice was right about him. Said he is just too laid back and messes about. Let's check his alibi and go from there."

"I'm with you. Unless it's all an act. Maybe the guy is some type of genius."

"Well, then he has us all fooled."

Magnus's phone started ringing. It was Rolf Jonsson.

"Rolf, what's happening?" Magnus asked.

"You aren't going to like this," Rolf muttered.

14

"You lost him? Oh, for fuck's sake!" Magnus said in an angry tone.

Eva was listening intently to the call, trying to fill the dots in as to what was going on.

"So, did you tell the guy you were in the process of trying to bring in a possible key witness before he cut you off?"

More talking on the other side of the phone.

"He can do what he likes. Tell him to come to the station. I'll tell him to piss off. He's stuffing up our investigation."

Rolf spoke a bit more.

"OK, you ring me right away if you see him again."

Magnus hung up.

"What's happened?" Eva asked.

"That Linus guy. They lost him."

Just before Rolf had rung Magnus to tell him the bad news, they had planned to pull over at the corner of the street and quickly stop Linus in his tracks. Both Rolf and Alexander agreed that Linus might be spooked and run for it. Gone were the assumptions that maybe this was Linus. It was Linus. Stopping or cornering Linus would have to be a quick operation. They had to cross a lane to get to the vacant space on the curb. Alexander Holström, who had legendary status for his slick driving skills, was about to get across when another car came up from behind them and cut them off, ignoring their indicator and went past them. Alexander managed to swerve back in his lane. As the other car went past, Alexander hooted aggressively, causing the man to brake and delay other vehicles behind him after Alexander had returned to his lane. This little scene startled Linus, and he started sprinting down the next street. With the driver who cut them off halted and making other cars wait behind him, and with Rolf and Alexander still in the lane across from the turning, they could kiss finding Linus goodbye. Alexander drove up beside the man in the car and started yelling at him, who was sporting a sleek dark blue Mercedes. Alexander's first impression was this man was pompous, who probably thought he could as he pleased.

"Don't you know how to drive? Bloody idiot," exclaimed Alexander.

"Fuck you." A very aggressive reply.

Rolf then joined in.

"We are police trying to bring in a witness,

and with your unruly driving, you have messed up any chances of us getting this witness." The argument had spilled out of the cars, and now all three were standing arguing while cars behind them tried to make their way around the argument. As cars passed, many had a good stare at what was going on. As in any country, there would be accidents or issues on the road, but it was unusual in Sweden to see people stopping their cars and getting out to have a go at each other.

"Let me tell you cops something. I'm going to go straight to your offices to speak to your boss. I don't have time to be messed around with little traffic cops."

The well-dressed man, probably around sixty in age, got in his vehicle and sped off. Rolf and Alexander resumed their journey in search of Linus, both furious. Linus was long gone after the interruption the pair of them had with the man in his fancy car. That was when Rolf had made the call to Magnus to inform him of what had happened.

15

The two men met at 8.30 pm, as they had discussed earlier. They both were on time. Both had chosen a smart-casual ensemble. The venue was picked out through a consensus. A local pub was the choice. They arrived at the venue and got the impression of a jovial atmosphere as they entered through the door. The pub had a traditional pub type feel to it with big varnished oak tables. A long similarly coloured bar counter with many beers on tap. There was a games area, with the usual array of pub type entertainment. Darts. Snooker. There was also a separate part of the pub devoted to those who wanted to dance. Disco lights. Music.

Both men decided to have a few drinks at the bar and would see how the night went. They got to know each other a little better, with discussions about business, politics, and, more specifically, the Swedish immigrant laws and the tightening of them, as well as hobbies. There had been a tightening in these laws in the last few years. With so many immigrants fleeing to Sweden and seeking asylum, the government had put the brakes on this to due to such an influx. It was still possible to come to Sweden and settle; however, the requirements laid down by Migrationsverket were much more stringent, much more specific. Both had slightly contrasting views but nothing too contrasting to cause any type of argument. The beers were going down very well, and the topic changed from immigration to more relaxed discussions. One of the men was not a big drinker and found himself feeling a little tipsy quite early on. He certainly had not had any big "benders" for many a year, and even then, they had been very rare. The other man, smelling of a cavalcade of aftershave and deodorant, had made his way to the restroom to relieve himself. He shut the stall door, urinated, and then proceeded to pull out a bag of something white and powdery. Cocaine. After snorting a sizeable dose, he left the toilet area invigorated and thought to himself that one woman he had seen by the bar was ripe for the picking. He would have to get in there tonight. Really bang her brains out. He would start working on that in due course, but first, he needed his white powdered friend to kick in and give him some bravado and smooth-talking skills. An hour or so later, this particular lady's entourage of friends left while she decided to remain at the bar by herself. Now's my chance, the cocaine man thought. What a bit of luck. She's obviously staying because she's looking for some action. He went up to her while his acquaintance had become drunker and was staying put swirl-

ing his beer around in its glass, with his head also swirling around in all directions. He did not feel very well. He did not know why he had so much to drink, although it hadn't been much to get him pissed.

"Would you like a drink?" the man said eagerly to the woman, a big smile on his face.

A moment of deliberation.

"Yes. OK. That would be fine. Thank you.

What harm could a drink do? She thought to herself.

16

A week later, with time ticking by, Magnus Markusson was sitting in his office with the contact list that Alice Julin had given him. Two and a half pages of contact details in a nice tidy Microsoft Excel format. Magnus stared at the names for a while, readying himself to set about this mundane task. Phoning all these people was going to be tedious. He decided that he better get going. The case had been dragging along, with the team no further than they had been the week before. The weather was still very warm, while Magnus looked out his window at what he could see of Varberg. Magnus had a deep affection for Varberg. He felt privileged living in this charming city. It wasn't a big city, but it was big enough to have everything. They had beautiful beaches, which made this a popular tourist destination, even though Magnus didn't like all these blasted tourists. Magnus didn't like all the extra Swedes coming down for a break, either. Varberg had many relaxing elements about it, and interestingly enough had a tradition of being a health resort town dating back to the 1800s. It really was a great and relaxing place.

Magnus picked up his office phone and started phoning. While he was listening to the sound of the ringing tone, he heard some commotion in the main reception foyer. Magnus, irritated, had to hang up because the disturbance had become quite raucous. Before he had gotten to his office door, he heard some of what was going on.

"Excuse me, sir, but you can't go in there. As I said, if you need to speak to a detective, I can find out who is available to see you," said the Iranian born receptionist and admin clerk Rana Zia.

"I will go where I please. This is Sweden, not whatever country you came from."

The other voice was that of a man, and he got to Magnus's door before he began his next tirade.

"Who's in charge?" he screamed.

"That would be me," Magnus replied and came out of his office and closed the door.

The man's suit looked expensive, he had a bald head, except for a little hair on the sides which were Winter white.

"About a week ago, I was in town when two police officers, or whatever you want to call them, started swearing at me and abusing me because I wouldn't let them in my lane. The one flipped me off as well."

He's come in here looking for a fight, Magnus thought. And this prick is going to get one if he doesn't calm down.

"Firstly, sir, you need to calm down. I heard about the incident, and the two officers you mentioned were in pursuit of a witness. So, they may have been a bit flustered."

"The big fat one, he flipped me off. What are you going to do about that?"

Magnus was sure that was a lie. Rolf, who must have been the "fat one"— as Alexander was as fit as a fiddle — would have never behaved like that. Magnus had hardly ever heard Rolf raise his voice, let alone show someone a middle finger. Nope, entirely out of the question. Alexander, on the other hand, well he wouldn't have been surprised had he raised his finger in annoyance at this man, considering he had a bit of a chip on his shoulder.

"I will speak to the officers in question and contact you once I have done that," Magnus said.

"And you *will* discipline them."

"I don't think we need to go that far. As I said, the two detectives were in the pursuit of a witness. I'll have a good talk to them about their conduct."

"I'm sorry, but that's not acceptable. Something better be done or else."

The "or else" at the end of the smartly dressed man's sentence irked Magnus.

Who does this arsehole think he is, Magnus thought.

"Or else what?" Magnus questioned.

"Or else I'll make some real noise. Go to the papers, phone someone higher up."

"Well, if you don't mind, I have a lot of work to do. I don't have time for this crap."

"You police. You are all useless, and now you have to resort to getting immigrants to help. I won't let this rest!"

"Get out of here now before I throw you out!"

The man's face went extremely red when Magnus told him to leave in that manner. Magnus found it amusing. The man left in an almighty huff, reminding Magnus that he was going to take it further. Magnus fiddled with his brown and grey beard and then snickered to himself.

You go higher up. Go for it, Magnus thought as he adjusted his faded jeans and fiddled with his dark red t-shirt.

Magnus went to Rana Zia at the front desk of their department.

"I'm sorry you had to listen to that rude man," he said to her.

"It's all right. I know there are some that don't want immigrants moving here."

"Well, those few that think don't like it are

idiots. You do a great job here. Keep it up."

Those words got the customary smile out of Rana Zia, and her rosy cheeks lit up. Rana always tried to do her best, and her work was excellent. Organised, a fast worker, and polite. Her Swedish was also outstanding, so the language was never an issue. She had been to SFI, the Swedish for immigrants course — fully funded if you had been granted residency — to learn Swedish and had come away being one of the best students by the end of it. Swedish was not an easy language to master, but Rana had worked very hard at it. Also, when Magnus said he was going out to important meetings — when in most cases it was either a trip to the horses or power nap at home — Rana would make sure no one would bother him. Magnus appreciated that.

With Magnus back in his office, he sighed at not having started any of the contacts on his desk. He sat down and started ringing the first number on the list, a Mrs Andersson. How unique, he thought. After two rings, his mobile started ringing. It was Kerstin Beckman. He hung up the office phone and answered his phone.

"Hi, Kerstin. I hope this is good news."

"Hi, Magnus. My friend has done a great job. I have the results of everything we sent off for analysis."

Still took a bit more than a week, Magnus thought.

"Excellent. What have we got?"

"I have a meeting right now, so I'll send through all the findings. Then you can call me with any questions."

"Will you send the email now?"

"Yes. Of course."

"Great. Enjoy the rest of your day."

"You too."

Magnus checked his email and found Kerstin's report a couple of minutes later.

He clicked on the report attachment which Kerstin had done in .PDF format. The attachment opened, and Magnus went through the report. The red substance that had been found was red paint. Standard red paint. The toxicology report that had been conducted had found mild levels of a Benzodiazepine that was commonly known as Midazolam, Versed, or Dormicum. Nothing ground-breaking had been found in these reports. Magnus didn't bother phoning Kerstin about anything. A pretty self-explanatory report. He instead went to Rana and asked her to do something for him.

"I need you to send a press release to the papers. Just a small note about the evidence I have just read through," Magnus said.

"Sure thing. What would you like me to say?"

"Say we found a red substance under the

victim's nails. It was found to be red paint, and that we are moving forward with this evidence."

"Hold on a second," Erik Rosenberg appeared and interrupted from behind. He had heard the conversation, and it seemed like he did not like the idea.

I wonder where he came from, Magnus thought. Probably back from twiddling his thumbs somewhere.

"Why do we want to reveal this to the press?" Rosenberg then queried, looking annoyed.

"No concrete reason other than a gamble. Ruffle some feathers. If the killer happens to read this, maybe he will get worried and panic. There's a good chance he is checking the papers regarding the progress. He may well do nothing, but it's worth a try. It may rattle him."

Rosenberg thought about it for a second.

"Well, all right. Send it off."

"Great. Rana, just the big papers please."

Finally, the village idiot has backed off on something, Magnus thought. Rosenberg proceeded to leave for the day shortly afterwards as it was late afternoon.

The day was winding down. Magnus got ready to leave. Magnus powered down his computer when the phone rang. Usually, Rana manned the phone, but she was probably busy with the press release. Magnus contemplated letting it ring but decided to pick it up.

"Hello, Markuson."

"Just the man I wanted to speak to." The voice on the other end was distorted. It sounded like a voice processor of some sort was being used.

"Who is this?"

"You police really have no idea, do you?"

Magnus picked up a pencil and flung it out his door, as to attract someone's attention. Eva saw the pencil hit the floor and got up to see what was going on. Eva walked into Magnus's office, and as soon as Magnus saw her, he started scribbling furiously on a notepad. He ripped the piece of paper off the notepad while talking on the phone, being quite aggressive towards the caller. Eva read the paper.

The killer is on the line. TRACE.

Eva sped out of the office and found Alexander, who was now back at his desk after a fruitless day outside. She asked him to trace the call as he was the accomplished one in the office with that type of thing. Alexander got onto it right away. He told Eva to tell Magnus to keep the caller talking while he found a location. Eva raced back and did just that.

"Keep him talking," she whispered.

Magnus continued talking and nodded his head all over the place as if to say "you don't say."

"Why don't you turn yourself in? It will spare you being *hauled* in."

"Detective Markuson, I have a better idea. Stop wasting your time. Let the case go."

"No can do I'm afraid."

"Suit yourself. You haven't a clue what this is about, do you?"

Alexander signalled to Eva, who signalled to Magnus. They had the caller's location.

"Thanks for the call. Have to run now." Magnus hung up.

"Where is this bastard?" Magnus shouted.

"Just off the sports hall on Snickargatan," Alexander replied.

"Eva, you stay here and see if the location changes. Alexander let's go. You drive," Magnus said.

The location was nearby. It was a three-kilometre drive. They took Alexander's car. A red BMW.

Magnus told Alexander to floor it. Once again, Alexander made driving look easy at such high speed. They arrived at Snickargatan to find a small warehouse, that was dilapidated. Abandoned. Magnus had been on the phone to Eva, and she had said there had been no movement. The trace pinpointed that the killer's location must be inside. Magnus and Alexander got out of the car. Both assumed the warehouse hadn't been used for anything in ages. They reached the warehouse entrance and got ready to enter. Magnus peered into the warehouse and saw a wide-open space except for a chair right in the middle of the space. Magnus went forward. Cautiously Alexander followed. Both had their guns at the ready. They saw no one and proceeded to check the perimeter of the run-down premises to make sure they were not about to be ambushed. It was soon clear there was no one else but Magnus and Alexander in the warehouse. Both were frustrated. They put their weapons away and continued towards the chair. Underneath it was a phone. On the chair was a piece of paper. Alexander was sweating. Magnus picked up the note. It was an A3 page that was completely blank.

"Dammit!" shouted Magnus.

"What's going on?" asked Alexander.

"I mean, why is it blank?" he added after Magnus refrained from saying anything.

Magnus looked like he wanted to throw the chair across the room.

"Nothing," Magnus said.

"Nothing what?" Alexander said.

"It's a message from the killer."

"What, a blank piece of paper?"

"He's telling us we have nothing."

17

After an unsettling time at the warehouse, Alexander was almost ready to leave to go out. He wasn't going to change his plans because of the day he had at work. He applied some gel to his jet-black hair. Aftershave. Cologne. He left and headed for the restaurant, a popular place that he had to book two days in advance for. He got in his car and sped down the road. Alexander really looked after his car. A massive chunk of his pay went towards his red BMW, but he was fine with that. Black leather seats, tremendously comfortable, many gadgets on the dashboard - GPS, climate control, auto volume up and down - and the actual driving experience was unparalleled. This car could seriously move. Even though Alexander loved to put his foot down, people at work had noticed his imperious driving skills, whether speed was involved or not. Eva always remembered Alexander sliding into a tight parking spot on one occasion with such ease and precision. One another occasion, with Magnus in the car, and with them in pursuit of a fraudster who had run to his car and decided to gap it, Alexander had again been awesome. He had needed to turn the car around and chase the man, but from where Alexander and Magnus were parked, they would have had to have done a three-point turn. Instead, Alexander reversed out the parking, and continued up the road in reverse at high speed, then with sufficient space available, he pulled up the handbrake. The car spun around, and with perfect timing, Alexander dropped the hand brake and accelerated. Even while the chase was on, Magnus had remarked: "how the fuck did you do that?" Alexander tried to not use his car much at work. While himself and Rolf had been looking for Linus — which was still ongoing — Alexander had driven Rolf's — in his own words — piece of tin and had still shown off his talent behind the wheel, managing to avoid being rear-ended by that stuck up man, although it hadn't been too difficult. That afternoon Alexander had been in action behind the wheel again, flying to that warehouse. Alexander had been reflecting on the warehouse incident with the killer leaving that message for them. It had scared him if he was being honest with himself. Alexander felt the case was a ticking clock. They needed to do something fast. Hopefully, the phone left at the warehouse could give them something. Alexander's thoughts wandered to a familiar place. His father. Alexander's throat felt restricted. There was nothing he could do that could help. His mother had said to remain positive, but she knew just like him that the situation was awful.

Alexander arrived at the restaurant, named John's place, and managed to find parking. Alexander had invited Liza Holmgren to dinner. Liza was one of the trio of women that he had kind of being seen without any idea whether he was keen on them or not. There was always a concern that maybe the three would be furious if they found out, but hey, no one had said they were exclusive. John's place was situated right atop the beachfront, and during summer, the look was breath-taking, hence the difficulty to get a table. Alexander stepped inside and was promptly helped to the table he had reserved. Liza was already seated. The atmosphere was excellent. Just the ticket after a day like this, Alexander thought. Liza was an attractive lady, and Alexander liked her company most of the time. She was funny and entertaining when they were alone. Often though, in public, he found she could be extremely false. Instead of just being herself, she would try to be the centre of attention and behave differently. What for? He didn't get it. They both ordered some wine and were busy deliberating what meal to have. Alexander hadn't been to John's place for a while and looked at the menu prices and thought they were on the high side. 389 kronor for a pepper steak. That's pushing it, he thought. Alexander made up his mind and then glanced around at the other patrons in this pretty laid-back atmosphere. Then sitting by herself, with what looked like some documents, he saw Stina Wahlgren. She had the look of having just come from work. This was a pretty casual place, but even so, people usually didn't sit and work. Stina had a natural type of beauty, but here she looked very ragged. She wasn't one for worrying about what people thought about how she looked, which differed from some other things of hers that had to be exact. Stina's hair was out of place, and her clothes looked scruffy after a long day's work. Liza peered over in that direction; her mind made up on what she would order. Once she saw Stina, she became very condescending. As if she was old garbage that was stinking out the place.

"You know they shouldn't let such common people in here," she said to Alexander.

"I don't quite follow," he replied, now looking outside at the spectacular view, with the sun still out for a few hours to come.

"That lady over there. Look at her. I mean seriously."

The way Liza said the word seriously felt like someone had run their nails down a chalkboard. Alexander felt himself getting worked up but avoided saying he worked with her or that Liza should not be so damn critical of others. Alexander liked Stina. Sure, she was a bit eccentric, but she was very good at her job. He always remembered being lectured once by her for moving her "phone pen." Her phone pen was the pen that stayed next to her phone at her desk to take down phone messages. It had to be that pen. You couldn't take messages with another pen as far as Stina was concerned. Liza rolled her eyes and gave a click from her tongue against her teeth and then groaned as if to add an exclamation point to what she had already said. That was enough for Alexander. He couldn't take it another second.

"Oh shit. I just got a text — a break-in. I have to go," Alexander lied through his teeth while looking at his phone's home screen.

"What? We've just got here. Why do you have to go? We had to book for such a nice table."

"I'm sorry. I know - its ridiculous. I'll be sure to have a word with my boss. I'll have to make it up to you."

Liza was very unimpressed but accepted there was to be no dinner, as Liza would hardly sit by herself in the public eye. Alexander said for her to go to her car, while he would sort out the payment with the waiter.

He did no such thing. He just waited two minutes after Liza went out the door, then went to where Liza had parked and said goodbye to her. He ran to his car, trying to play the part of the "rushing cop" like he was in The Bridge TV series. Alexander got in his car, and drove off, deciding to go around the block. Once, he got back, his parking was still there, and Liza had gone. During his excursion around the block, Alexander decided that he was wasting his time with Liza. He got out of the car and went back inside, with the waiter giving him a curious look.

"Could you move me to this table, please? The lady with me had to leave," Alexander said.

"Certainly sir."

Alexander went to Stina's table.

"Hi, Stina."

"Oh, hi, Alexander. What are you doing here?"

"Here for dinner. How did you get a table?"

Stina looked at Alexander a little strangely.

"I booked."

"Ah, yes, right. Can I join you?"

"Sure. However, I'm looking over the case. I heard about your chase to the warehouse earlier."

Alexander sat down.

"I'll just order, then I'll tell you about it." Alexander felt very comfortable.

Rolf Jonsson was busy with dinner. He had put a roast chicken in the oven and was walking around the house aimlessly, waiting for his dinner to be done. Sylvester was asleep on a chair, curled up in a ball. However, Rolf had no doubt when his timer made that ding sound, Sylvester would get up. Sylvester would have a stretch and come and ask for chicken. Rolf started thinking with regard to his living situation. Did he need to stay in the house anymore? Rolf could get a smaller apartment. Rolf had a decent house so he would undoubtedly be able to be left with some change if he bought an apartment and sold the house. Rolf was walking through all the rooms in the house and stumbled on an old closet. Even though old wounds may become reopened with this, he decided to satisfy his curiosity. He started looking through the clutter. The closet indeed had accumulated some dust. Rolf hadn't taken a look in there for quite a while. Most of the items were precisely that - clutter; however, he saw an old cardboard box and decided to see what it contained. There were some files, which Rolf took out. Before he peered into them, he noticed a small little photo album. It was labelled "Photos USA." Rolf had a look of excitement but also worry. How did this album get here? It was an album of the trip himself and Camilla had taken to America around seven years back. He hadn't seen this album for ages. He forgot about the files and took out the photo album — which was a little flip-file type of book — and closed the closet and went to the dining room table. Rolf got

a rag and wiped down the album. Rolf seated himself to take a trip down memory lane. He began
flipping through various pictures and as he did
each page began heavier to lift. Rolf looked at a
picture of himself and Camilla at the end of going
on the El Toro rollercoaster in Jackson, New Jer-
sey. He had told her there was no chance of him
going on it. She had coaxed him into it by saying
she had read it was mild, and with it being a
wooden rollercoaster, she had added that being
wooden made it slower. It was all a pack of lies.
On the ride, he hadn't known if he was coming or
going. The one thing he had known was that he
was petrified. What a way to go, he had remembered thinking to himself then. And then Camilla
had asked one of the staff to please take a picture
of them, with Rolf still looking bewildered.
What the people must have thought. Rolf went
through some more pictures. The Grand Canyon.
Golden Gate Bridge. Yellowstone National park.
They had packed in everything on this trip. Rolf
looked towards the ceiling and remembered
those times so very fondly. He then closed the album up. It was back to reality. Reality hit him
like a sharp stinging jab. Camilla was never coming back. There was still some peculiar part of
Rolf that had hope of Camilla arriving back home
one day. Rolf took off his glasses and rubbed his
eyes. He suddenly felt extremely tired. He was
tired of living without his wife. Why did it have

to be this way? Why, for goodness sake, why? There was no answer to that question. Tears started trickling down his face. A combination of sadness and fatigue. His tears were stopped by Sylvester putting his bum into Rolf's face and arching his back. I better check on the roast, Rolf thought. He made his way to the oven with Sylvester darting in front of him energetically.

18

The weekend had come and gone, and mid-way through the following week, the case was dragging. It was nearing a month since the case was opened. A murder investigation usually had a few pieces of adrenaline-soaked moments. But the vast majority of the time the work was bland. It was time-consuming, and most information didn't yield anything, but a person had to go through everything as you just didn't know where evidence would be found. The proverbial smoking gun could be somewhere. The biggest piece of news that week had been negative. Forensics had reported that the phone, as well as the letter from the warehouse, had nothing at all that was of any use. There had also been a newspaper article from the journalist who had stormed out of the press conference, which had been extremely rude. He had called the police force bumbling fools and was particularly severe on Rosenberg, stating that he was clueless and that he would struggle solving the daily newspaper crossword, let alone a homicide investigation.

Magnus had enjoyed his weekend. Himself and Lena had spent not one, but both days at the picturesque Getterön Nature Reserve. On Saturday, Magnus had told Lena it would be nice just to go down and bird watch with some nice food and drink. Magnus wasn't an avid bird watcher by any stretch of the imagination, but it was a nice change. The nature reserve was an outstanding one, with many things to do and see. Magnus always found it very tranquil. Magnus and Lena started with the nature trail, and thankfully it was a cooler day than during the week. There were blue skies. However, they had white puffy clouds as guests helping to cool things down as the sun would disappear behind them. The temperature was around twenty-three, making it virtually ideal. They walked briskly, and at the top of the trails hill, they enjoyed a little water and a few biscuits they had brought with. After the sprightly exercise, they grabbed the rest of the things from the car and went to spend most of the day at the observation hut. The hut gave off a great view of the whole reserve. It was quite spacious, and this particular Saturday there were not too many visitors, so Magnus and Lena had ample space. Lena sat, legs stretched out on the long wooden bench, while Magnus leaned on the also wooden railings and surveyed the lay of the land. Lena's mood became a bit more jovial the more wine she drank. After a long day, they both left in high spirits with Magnus having seen a wide array of bird-life, and Lena, well, she had eaten the snacks, and drunk the wine and provided a useful extra set of eyes as far as she was concerned. They had gotten home, and just after walking in the door, Lena had gone into the bedroom and called Magnus to join her for a second. Magnus had stepped in, and Lena was lying stark naked on the bed, with her legs spread wide apart. Magnus felt himself respond. He felt a powerful surge of energy through his body. Lena, who was in an extremely provocative position, motioned for Magnus to join her. The sex went on for a while, with both embracing the moment veraciously. Finally, after they had both experienced their respective jubilations, they just lay in bed and drifted off to sleep. The following day, they were off to the reserve again, with a barbeque on the cards. They had taken their time getting up and had ended up getting to the reserve at around 1:00 pm. Magnus had brought various meats to barbeque, and after getting annoyed at the soot from the charcoal getting all over his hands, himself and Lena parked themselves on a chair each, and let the cooking process begin. Magnus wanted to have another enjoyable day, but while he was cooking, he found himself thinking about the case. The adversary they were up against bothered Magnus. Firstly, the killer had been very careful. The scene had yielded very little. The killer also had gone to quite specific lengths. It wasn't a question of the killer murdering the victim in any fashion. It looked clear that the killer wanted to kill the victim this way, and this way only. Were there more people the killer was lining up to murder? Or was this the end of it? Then the killer had pulled the little stunt of phoning the police station and sending them on a wild goose chase. But why do that? The team really had to find something sooner rather than later with someone like this out there. Magnus didn't like the fact that this bastard thought he could outsmart him. Magnus's approach was pretty casual, and certainly never bombarded himself with work; however, he didn't like someone thinking they were brighter than him. And he especially didn't like the arrogance of someone phoning him and playing silly little games either. I'll show you, you fuck, he thought.

As the afternoon progressed, Magnus began to forget about his case troubles. Lena got busy with some wine but was more reserved than the day before. Magnus and Lena enjoyed their grill fest immensely, which consisted of salmon, vegetable skewers, and some lovely sausages. By the time they both trundled in their front door, they were both exhausted. The dogs had been left at home, and all of them were full of boundless energy. "Let's go then," Magnus had said to them, and gotten their leashes and taken them for a walk. All of them had done their business a little out of the way from a dog poop bin, so Magnus had to extend the walk further. So, he collected their business, walked on and deposited it in the bin. As soon as the walk was concluded, Magnus sat down on the couch, and when Lena came into the room, she found him fast asleep and snoring. Lena nudged him into a position where Magnus stopped his snoring. When Magnus awoke, at around midnight, he quickly realised that Monday was around the corner and wondered why weekends had to go by so damn quickly. His lip dropped at the thought of it. Magnus was nearing fifty, and now would be the time to start looking to pass the torch so to speak. He could take more of an observant role, which meant more days for horses, more afternoon naps, earlier dinners; however, he wanted to structure his days. He would still clear the cases, and hopefully, the others would take the reins more. After all this pondering, Magnus found something to sleep in and rolled into bed next to Lena who had gone to sleep. The dogs had all made some spots either in or around the bed, and Magnus had very little space in which to get comfortable. We need a bigger bed, Magnus thought.

Everybody continued their tasks. Rolf Jonsson and Alexander Holström were attempting to locate the rugged street-goer Linus. The rest were all in the office, and not having much luck. Eva Lindqvist had finalised checks on various things and had come up short. Firstly, the rope that had been used to hang Sven Julin. It had been a type of hiking rope. That sounded encouraging until Eva had started digging further. This rope was particularly popular, and available readily online, so to narrow it down wasn't going to happen. Julin's bank accounts and cell phone records. All painfully normal. Steady income, nothing flashy, but steady. Cell phone records showed nothing unusual at all. So, two colossal dead ends there. Eva was waiting for the owner of the Lidl store to come back to her about Kurt Johansson. They had a camera near the checkout counter so the owner was going to check if he could find Kurt Johansson on camera.

Stina Wahlgren had made moderate success with her tire tread, being able to eliminate a further 103 possibilities thanks to help from some manufacturers leaving 181 possible tread matches. Magnus was in his office, and his day wasn't going well. The coffee machine hadn't been fixed, and it was proving impossible to find someone to come and look at the one in the office. The solution was obvious. Get a new machine. However, Magnus knew it would be a bun fight in trying to get a new machine out of Rosenberg. A coffee machine was a perfectly reasonable requisition. A cup of coffee would have been nice while he was having to sift through and call the rest of Sven Julin's client list. Magnus got back to the list, ringing the parties following the alphabetical order that was neatly in front of him on the excel worksheet. It was after finishing the K's, that he needed a slight break, not that he was lethargic, but because he was getting the same answers over and over again. In short, every person he had called had said that Sven Julin was a lovely man. Very kind, very patient. Most were quite stunned that someone had done this to him. A few had chipped in with their own analysis of the case. Because suddenly everybody was a detective. The consensus was this had to be some sick person who had done this, because Sven Julin was such an excellent human being, that it must have been a random act. Magnus pushed his hair back and felt his beard, which was getting ragged and untidy. He needed to shave soon. So, what did Sven do to get himself killed? Magnus thought. That was the number one question he wanted to be answered. Magnus pulled out a book. A Mons Kallentoft novel. He had been a bit annoyed that he hadn't read much of it lately. Magnus went and closed his office door completely. He then spread papers all over his desk to look really busy if someone had decided they needed to see him. Magnus enjoyed Kallentoft a lot and decided after reading ten pages that another half hour of reading would be perfectly fine. After another four pages, and nearing the end of a great chapter, Magnus heard and then saw his door handle being opened. Rana popped into his office, and Magnus put his book on the side of his desk. He looked at the papers on his desk and pretended to be in deep concentration. Can't people just leave me alone at work? He thought to himself while trying to look busy. Rana smiled and left a copy of Hallands Nyheter for Magnus to read. Mons Kallentoft, Rana thought to herself after closing Magnus's door. I like his books too.

Magnus had expected a bumper story to arrive at some stage, and now the paper had put out a big spread. Unlike the rude journalist who had written an article at the beginning of the week, this article was from a much bigger paper, and with reputable journalists. This paper was also one of the papers where Magnus had offered up a bit of information some time ago, which was why he was keen to read the article. Big headlines on the front page.

Hallands Nyheter

Does Varberg have a serial killer?
Police in the dark.

The full story on this tense case on page 4.

Magnus flipped onto page 4.

Case hanging by a thread.

I see what you did there, Magnus thought.

The murder case involving a man being found hanging from a tree has the police clutching at straws. Last Month, Sven Julin, a piano instructor in Varberg, had been found dead and hanging from a tree just off the Läjet camping site, in the nearby woods. The investigation thus far has made it clear that this was a homicide. At this stage, the manner of the homicide is interesting. Some information from the police is that after conducting some analyses on evidence found at the crime scene, is that there is a good lead. Some red paint was found on the victim's fingernails. With this clue, a prominent detective has told us the case has moved forward well. There have been suggestions of a possible serial killer, but that has not been confirmed at this time. With only one victim, that does seem unlikely, but members of the public are advised to be vigilant and remain calm.

Magnus sighed and tossed the paper onto the floor. There was still another page or so of the story, including a diagram of the scene that some bright spark at the paper had drawn up.

Magnus had seen enough. His idea about sticking the paint in had been included. However, the newspaper had put their spin on the whole story. Typical. The headline of there being a serial killer was just pure guesswork on the paper's part. It was possible, but no one had discussed anything of the sort. The paper did go on to say it was unlikely, but they still got in the big black headline of questioning if a serial killer was lurking in Varberg somewhere. That would worry the residents, a definite negative.

Magnus's thoughts then veered to his son Sebastian when he saw a file on his desk regarding a closed drug case. Where was he? What had gone wrong? Magnus thought back to Sebastian, playing sport as a ten-year-old. Sebastian had enjoyed that. He had played a wide variety of sports and had done well in all of them. He enjoyed helping with things at home too. He would ask intelligent questions about various topics. How did Sebastian then go from there, to getting into a gang-type group and being involved in drugs, and who knows what else? Magnus doubted that Sebastian had ever been on any substance that was really dangerous, but he was sure Sebastian had been peddling them.

What a disgrace. And how truly sad. Magnus and Lena had sat and spoken on many a day, about what had they done as parents, and what could they have done better. Then the decision of telling Sebastian to leave their house had been a drastic call. However, what choice had Sebastian left them? Would it have taken someone to get killed in the house before something changed? This hadn't been Magnus's and Lena's first move either. They had tried all kinds of things at home as well as going to speak with a few teenage counsellors — a waste of time. They had tried a psychologist as well. It made no difference. Sebastian's behaviour went from worse to even worse. Magnus and Lena had sat with guilt for quite a while once Sebastian was gone and out doing who knows what, but with time they had come to terms with the whole situation. Also, Magnus had told Sebastian that one day he could come back if Sebastian had gotten back on the right road, and he would help him further sort out his life. Sebastian had been aggressive, saying he hated them both and it was all their fault. Anyway, he had close friends. Felix. Now that was someone who was always there for him. So, Sebastian had been defiant. He wasn't coming back. Magnus had given Sebastian some money to which Sebastian had snatched and mouthed off some foul words and that had been that. Four years later, Magnus nor Lena had heard from Sebastian. Magnus suddenly came back to reality. He looked at the time. Better check in with the others, he thought.

Magnus had assigned Eva the task of digging into the paint and went to Eva and wanted a progress report. Also, it was time Eva looked into the sedatives too. Maybe the paint could be narrowed down to a store? Perhaps the sedative could be placed back to a prescription? Eva undid her hair, redid it in somewhat of a slapdash fashion, and said she was still busy with the paint and she would get to the sedatives when she had a chance. Seconds later, Erik Rosenberg flung open his office door, his face showing anger.

"Markusson, my office *now*!"

19

The smartly dressed man that Magnus had told the previous week to get out had been on the warpath to get Magnus, as well as Rolf and Alexander into very hot water. The man, who was fifty-nine years old, was a Mr Kjell Sandell, apparently a big shot at the IKEA in Göteborg. He had gotten around to calling the National Police headquarters, and after constant attempts, had gotten through to the NPC, Mikael Andersson. How he had managed this was quite a surprise. Possibly, his constant pestering was the key to getting put through. Kjell Sandell had told a slightly slanted story in which he had been the victim, and the cops had been rude, obnoxious, and totally unprofessional. Coupling that with Mikael Andersson being in a foul mood with many other pressing matters, Andersson had taken Sandell's side and had apologised and explained he would see to sorting out these unruly Varberg cops right away. Andersson had called Erik Rosenberg and had displayed his fury in no uncertain terms.

"Erik Rosenberg," Rosenberg had said when answering the call.

"Erik. Mikael Andersson. What the hell is going on in that circus down there?"

"I'm sorry sir. I don't quite follow. What is this all about?"

"Allow me to elaborate. I had a gentleman call me this morning. Mr Kjell Sandell. He had some miscommunication on the road or something with two of your detectives. I don't know exactly what happened, but apparently, someone cut into someone else's lane. The point is your detectives then were so rude that this man went to the station to complain and your head superintendent told him to get lost. He has then phoned here constantly until he managed to get me on the line. So, Rosenberg, *you* better sort this out right now. Markusson is treading on thin ice, and for that matter, so are you! You are supposed to be in charge there dammit. I want this resolved by 5.00 pm today."

Before Rosenberg - who had been wiping his forehead constantly during this barrage - could say anything, the NPC had slammed the phone down. Now Rosenberg was waiting for Magnus in his office. It's about time he got what's coming to him, Rosenberg thought. He walks around here like he owns the place. He thinks he knows everything too. Always an answer to everything. Its time to realise I'm the boss, not him! Magnus entered the office and took a seat.

"What can I do for you?" said Magnus.

"Do you know a Mr Kjell Sandell?" Rosenberg barked.

"Should I?"

"Let me jog your memory. Mr Sandell was the man that Jonsson and Holström were extremely rude to, and the man you told to get lost when he came to complain. Maybe that rings a bell?"

Here we go, Magnus thought.

"Oh him. Well, if you would care to hear my account of things, it may help to clear up the whole affair," Magnus said.

"I'm all ears."

"Well firstly, Jonsson and Holström were in pursuit of a witness. A homeless guy we think may be important in our murder case. Secondly, this guy ignored their indicator and them turning into his lane. He just carried on, paying no attention to what on earth was going on. So, it was his fault. Suffice to say, the witness disappeared. Holström told him he didn't know how to drive, which he shouldn't have done, but that's no big deal. The guy then yells "Fuck you" back, and that's where all the fun started." Magnus had managed to speak to both Rolf and Alexander about what had happened to have his facts ready in case a problem arose.

"You see, this man now somehow managed to get on the phone with the NPC. The NPC then called me and made it clear that this needs to be sorted out immediately so I'm going to call this man and you, Jonsson, and Holström are going to be here and apologise to him."

"I don't see why we must apologise. That's totally wrong."

"Look, it doesn't matter. The NPC said that's the way it is, so it has to be done."

"This is *bullshit*!"

"I'll tell the gentleman to be here at 1.00 pm."

Magnus got up and slammed the door as hard as he could. Typical Rosenberg behaviour. He will call up and kiss this guy's backside so he can keep his job nice and secure, Magnus thought. I mean he's never here. We are the damn ones busting our backsides.

He got on the phone and called Rolf on his cell and explained the procedure. Rolf, as well as Alexander — who was mouthing expletives in the background — were utterly unimpressed, but Magnus said they should all just get it over with. It's not like they mean what they would have to say. A quick apology and they can get on with work. He told the two, who had made no inroads in locating Linus's whereabouts, to be at the office at 12.45 pm as this IKEA bigwig would be arriving at 1.00 pm. Rolf confirmed they would be there. With that, Magnus could get back to work, and finally continue calling these clients of the victim, Sven Julin. He sat at his desk and took out a toasted cheese and bacon sandwich he had made for himself at home and had a bite or two during his call intervals. Magnus was finally getting something done without any interruptions. He continued and made his way into the T's. Next to call was a Mrs Hilda Thoren. As, what was by now routine, he was told by Mrs Thoren what a lovely man this Sven Julin was. Hilda Thoren was another who was stunned that Sven Julin had been murdered. She had learnt how to play the piano very well thanks to Julin, and that helped her a great deal at the time.

"Did Sven ever seem worried or anxious about anything? Any problems or altercations you may have seen? Did anyone ever come in while you were there and have a heated discussion with him?"

"Dear me, no. Nothing like that."

"Anything you could think of that might help me?"

"No, I don't think so, detective. I wish I could help."

"Well, thanks anyway. Please take my number down and call me if you remember anything that could help. Even if it's something small."

Hilda Thoren took down Magnus's number and said she would phone if she remembered anything.

Magnus hung up. Yeah right, he thought. She ain't phoning back.

Magnus continued these monotonous calls until he reached the end of the client list. Nothing. He had thought on the weekend that the killer was a dangerous adversary, but now Magnus started to think he was even more dangerous. They needed to find something soon.

Midway through these thoughts, and others which included Magnus wondering about what was for dinner and what was on TV that evening, Rana Zia knocked on the door and walked in without waiting to see if she could come in.

Why does she knock if she's going to barge in, Magnus thought.

"That man, Mr Sandell, he's here."

"Is it that time already?"

"Yes. The time has flown today."

"Are Rolf & Alexander here?"

"Yes, they got about fifteen minutes ago. I've just told them."

"Right let's get this over with."

20

They used the conference room to conduct what would be best described as a very forced apology. Kjell Sandell, dressed in a maroon suit, with matching coloured tie and pants sat down.

Just add some sawdust, and we've got a circus, Magnus thought.

The metal chairs broke the silence. Magnus decided to go ahead and speak first.

"Thanks for coming in Mr Sandell. On behalf of the three of us, I'd like to apologise for what has transpired. My two detectives were in the middle of pursuing a person of interest in a, particularly important case. They reacted in the heat of the moment, and even though it was a volatile situation, they shouldn't have done so."

"What will the police department be doing about them? I hope you will also be given a good wrap on the knuckles." Sandell gave Rolf and Alexander condescending looks and stuck his nose up towards Magnus.

Don't say anything, Magnus thought. The

quicker we get this done, the quicker we see this prick get in his car and trundle off to IKEA.

There was a pause. Magnus then replied.

"These two have already been spoken to and reprimanded. They have received an official warning for their behaviour, and this will be noted on both their records which makes it difficult to move up the ranks unless they make a vast improvement on what has transpired here. As for myself, I received a caution for my manner when you came to complain."

"I see," Sandell said.

Both Rolf and Alexander looked stunned but said nothing. They hadn't heard about any official warnings. Surely a warning was only official when the person in question signed the documentation? Both Rolf and Alexander chose to say nothing about this.

"I hope you will accept our apologies," Magnus added.

Magnus stood up and stuck his hand out in the direction of Sandell, who stood up and accepted his hand.

"Thank you. I'm glad you can all see the error of your ways."

What a rip-roaring idiot, Magnus thought. The error of our ways. Get fucked.

Magnus escorted Sandell out of the room and saw him to his car. They amicably parted ways, but Magnus was left annoyed at Sandell's smugness at what obviously Sandell considered a victory.

You know what they say, Magnus thought to himself. Payback is a bitch.

When Magnus got back inside, Rolf and Alexander were waiting for him.

"What's this about an official warning?" complained Alexander.

"I think it grossly unfair," said Rolf.

"If you two would let me speak," said Magnus.

They both quietened down.

"Nobody is getting any warnings so relax. That was the quickest way to get all of this out of our hair. I would have liked to have told him to go to hell, but that would have completely gotten in the way of this case, and this is high priority at the moment."

"Oh. Good one," said Alexander.

With the pesky, and unreasonable Kjell Sandell out of everyone's hair, normal work could resume. Magnus felt quite hungry. That toasted sandwich hadn't filled him up at all. With Alexander and Rolf heading back to their desks, Magnus asked them if they wanted to pop out and get a quick bite near the office. Have a nice little sit-down and chat a bit. They both were very keen for some food. Magnus, Rolf, and Alexander had all made their way out the door when Rana

Zia came running after them. Rana, who had been inside the whole day, had the heat hit her right in the face. She called Magnus, who was going towards his car. He turned around and gave her a bothered look. Rana said there was an urgent call for Magnus. There was a detective on the line from Luleå.

"Can't it wait? I can call them back," he said.

"She said its extremely urgent," Rana replied.

"Oh damn it! All right," Magnus said as he went back inside to his office, telling Rolf and Alexander to wait at the car.

Rolf and Alexander did just that with Rolf leaning his hands against the windows in an attempt to do some sort of a stretch. His round belly was touching the windows. He looked at the ground while leaning, the heat affecting him.

"What do you fancy for lunch?" Alexander asked.

"I don't know really. A steak would be nice."

"Come on man. That will slow you down, a big steak like that."

"Hey, it's been a busy morning. I need a decent meal." More excuses when it came to food.

"Hey, do what you want," Alexander said, a hint of disappointment in his voice.

The eating habits and styles of these two

were completely different. Everyone knew about Rolf's diets and excuses. The popular one was always that he needed some extra "fuel." You know, tough day, stress, running around all over the place. The problem was that the fuel tank was now huge. Alexander was a healthy eater. He liked his veggies. He always brought Tupperware with food for the day, and unless there was a rare occasion, something like this, for instance, then he would eat that and nothing else. And if he did pop out like they were about to do, you could rest assured that he would make a healthy choice. No rubbish.

Alexander had chipped away at trying to get Rolf to eat better, but these bad habits of Rolf's were difficult to change. Alexander wiped his brow, sweat already having formed after being outside for just a few minutes. What's taking so long, Alexander thought. He then saw Magnus approaching the car, but with his hands gesticulating for them to return inside.

"Sorry guys. There's been a development. Lunch is off."

"What development?" asked Rolf.

"A big one. Inside. Now."

21

Everyone gathered in the small, colourless boardroom for the emergency meeting that had been called just ten minutes earlier. Rosenberg was the only one not coming as he was in another meeting in Göteborg. That probably would have suited most of them anyway, and most certainly suited Magnus. Magnus wasted little time in getting started. He stood in front of everyone and began. "A Mrs Monika Ranström, a detective from Luleå, called me just now with some very interesting news. She said to me that, just over a year ago, she had a case that bears some striking similarities to our case. A lady was murdered and left hung in some woods next to a school. She added that what struck her was that in her case, there too was red paint under the nails. They had also gotten a DNA sample for fragments of skin under the victim's right middle fingernail, which yielded no hits and they had no suspects to match it too either. She happened to read that newspaper article and called us right away."

Good call putting that paint info in the paper, Magnus thought to himself.

Magnus was quiet for a second, letting everything digest this as if everyone were having that first taste of a meal at a restaurant. He then continued by saying that the detective from Luleå had organised Postnord to collect and courier down the case files of this particular case to them once she put the relevant information together.

"This is all we have so we need to look sharp," said Magnus.

"Surely this murder up in Luleå is connected then?" said Rolf.

"I'm not so sure," Eva then chimed in.

With much conjecture going around the table, Magnus let them throw around their thoughts. Maybe someone would say something helpful.

In the middle of this debate, Stina managed to forge in her speculations.

"I think the biggest question to ask is what the odds are of finding two murdered people with paint under their nails, both hung in a tree? I don't know the specifics how the person in Luleå was murdered, but not even taking that into account, the odds, in my opinion, are maybe somewhere, I don't know, let's say one in a million. These cases are linked." Stina said this with complete certainty.

When it was described in that way, Magnus was now sure that there was a link between the two cases. Some of the others still weren't sure, but the immediate plan of action was to carry on with what everyone was doing and see if anything else could be turned up. Once they had more details of the Luleå case, everyone could reconvene. Magnus went back to his office, and while walking, he got a phone call. His friend Henrik Gustafsson. He had known Henrik for about six months and hadn't seen him since Magnus's big win at the horses.

"Henrik. How are you?" Magnus said exuberantly.

"All good. Your side?"

"Well up to my ears in work, but hey, the usual."

"I called because I have some free time later. I thought we could meet up for a beer later."

"Yeah, that sounds great."

"Perfect. I have a great story for you."

"Do you think we could have a beer at my place? It doesn't look like I'll be getting out of here till quite late. You are welcome to have dinner too. I'm sure Lena would like to see you as well."

"Its a deal. See you later. What time should we make it?

"Oh, what about eight?"

"Eight it is."

After Magnus had left at around 6.15 pm, as well as the rest of the team, Eva Lindqvist decided to stay on for a while. It wasn't because she wanted to get extra things done, but because keeping her mind busy might stop her unwanted anxiety and panic in her estimation. It was working to a degree although she was now exhausted. Maybe exhaustion was good. Then maybe she could sleep. She had been busy with the paint. She had gotten the specific shade of red paint that had been found on the nails of Sven Julin, and she had tried for hours to gain some insight if there was something that stuck out about this paint. A few places of inquiry were now closed, but Eva found out enough from those she had managed to contact. Eva had gained a bar code for the type of paint, but that hadn't helped much. The paint was freely accessible from a wide range of stores, as well as online. The online part made things a lot more difficult. You could order from pretty much anywhere. It would be possible to go to various paint stores in the vicinity and try and get receipts for that type of paint. One could try and do a follow up from there. So, in theory, you certainly could gain knowledge of those who bought the paint. The next point was if the Luleå murder was, in fact, connected with the same paint, which was still to be confirmed but pretty likely, then to try and go through each paint store from Varberg to Luleå — which was a whopping 1300 kilometres — was absurd. Eva thought of all these things over and over in her head. She felt her face and was astounded it felt as it did. She went to the bathroom to wash her face and freshen up, and she didn't like what she saw in the mirror. Bags under her eyes. Dry, wrinkled skin. She looked as if she was ten years older than she was. Her hair looked greasy. Maybe it *was* about time to go home. She wondered how her sister was. It was a while since she had heard from her. Maybe the leash doesn't reach the phone, Eva thought to herself. Eva laughed to herself and then became concerned. It really wasn't a laughing matter. Maybe worrying about something else was a positive? Was that what it had come to? Was that now considered a positive? She gathered some things and decided she could review a bit of the case at home. The medication was another thing on her to-do list, although Eva feared a similar outcome to that of the paint. Eva started thinking about Sven Julin's wife. Eva knew that Rolf had not spoken to her as yet. Maybe a discussion with her was in order quite soon. Eva could always chat with Rolf so he could be made aware she was going to speak with her. She knew he wouldn't have a problem if she went to chat with Viveka Julin instead of him. That was the way forward. Getting to know a bit more about Sven Julin. As Eva began driving home, her worries got going again, all of it to do with that same question that had been bothering her nonstop: Was shooting that man right? Was it justified? Until she could work out how to move on, the uneasiness was not going to let up.

Magnus handed his friend Henrik Gustafsson a beer. A Stigbergets brewery creation called West Coast. It had a fruity taste to it, but the funny thing about the beer was that it was particularly difficult to ascertain which fruit it tasted like. Magnus often referred to the beer as "tropical" when he was asked about it. Nonetheless, the beers were going down very well indeed as the two sat and waited for dinner on the couches in the TV area while watching a program discussing the Allsvenskan football league which was fourteen games into the season. Henrik had always supported AIK, a Stockholm based side, even though he wasn't from Stockholm. Magnus had wondered why he didn't support a local team from the place he had grown up in. Henrik had said they had moved around a lot due to his father's work and besides he liked AIK anyway. During this football program on the TV, Magnus and Henrik were mainly chatting and would occasionally peruse the program. Henrik's story he wanted to tell Magnus was to do with football as well.

"So, this story I had to tell you. I've become quite a fan of using twitter now. There is so much news when it comes to football on there. I can get all the latest on AIK. Plus its quite nice to converse with fans and see what they think."

"I'm not into all that stuff. By the time I get home, I'd rather converse with no one," said Magnus.

Henrik laughed and then carried on with his caper.

"Well, I posted that AIK are starting to run into form. Have you seen Larsson lately? He's on fire. He's had like five assists in the last three games with his crossing. Just whipping them in. Anyway, with us only two points off the top, I tweeted that AIK has hit form at the right time and they would be crowned champions come season end. Some user then replied to my post and said there was no chance of that happening. I had no idea whom this person supported and didn't feel like arguing, so I just posted back "We shall see."

"I'm assuming it didn't end there?" asked Magnus.

"Oh no, it didn't. This user replied to that by saying and I quote "We sure will. Fucking cunt.""

"What? That's ridiculous."

"You know I'd read about these people that spew all sorts of rubbish and think they won't be caught," said Henrik, who was a computer IT expert. An expert's expert in fact.

"I was so mad I quickly set about tracing him. I got his IP address quickly enough and fiddled around, and presto I found the address," he added.

"Where? I hope you didn't drive across the country."

"Actually, no. Just to Apelviken. It took me about ten minutes to drive there. Fancy that it was so close."

"Well, what happened?" said Magnus, interested.

"I knocked at the address, and a nineteen-year-old pipsqueak opened the door. I asked if anyone else was home to which he replied no, so I gathered he was the one. I decided to give him a piece of my mind. Anyway, if it wasn't him, I wasn't leaving until the culprit came back. I grabbed him by the collar and asked him if he sent that message, and he was so scared he admitted it on the spot, and I kid you not, at the same time he started to wet himself. I told him not to do that to anyone again because people can get worked up about that sort of thing."

Magnus found this very amusing and let out a large laugh. He wasn't surprised the offender was scared. Henrik was around six foot three, six foot four, in the region of 220 pounds, muscular, and had big bear paws for hands. Magnus had often thought about how far someone would fly if Henrik gave them a crack. The topic then changed to a more serious note with Henrik enquiring about what he had read in the papers about the murder in the woods. Magnus had responded by saying things were moving along well, which was a bit of an exaggeration. Henrik was relieved because a couple of friends had made him feel a little unsafe, as they had thought a maniac was on the loose. Magnus said they were on the right track. As they moved to the dinner table, Lena started asking Henrik how things were in the relationship department, to Magnus's chagrin. Who gives a fuck, he thought, but after all, Lena had made such a nice dinner, so she might as well ask away. Henrik answered Lena's cross-examination. He said that he had been so busy, so he hadn't really gotten into anything, nor did he want to. He didn't mind taking something slow, but he wasn't looking for any serious stuff. Magnus thought to himself that was a wise idea of Henrik's. Just take your time pal, he thought. The evening began drawing to a close. The dinner - which had been marinated salmon with dill potatoes - had been world-class. Lena had made homemade ice cream for dessert, another winner. Henrik thanked both Magnus and Lena for a great evening. Magnus saw him out and was glad Henrik had decided to go at that time because he was getting very sleepy. All three dogs looked at Magnus as he closed the door, expecting something for the excellent table manners they had displayed having not barked or yelped for food. There was some leftover salmon and Magnus, who was a complete pushover when the dogs eyed him out, gave them all a bit of the salmon, and watched them devour it while their tails all wagged happily. Magnus gave a contented smile and was particularly happy that Chloe (that had been the name decided upon of the new dog), who had not long ago been sleeping in some dreadful abode outside of the place Magnus had found her, was looking great. Her coat was shiny and clean, and she had taken to everyone in the family and played with the other two with such enjoyment. Magnus crawled into bed, feeling relaxed. It had been a delightful evening. As he was about to drift off to sleep, his phone rang. Who is phoning at this hour?

"Hello," Magnus said, half asleep.

"Detective Markusson. I'm so sorry to bother you. It's Hilda Thoren. You said for me to call if I remembered anything that could help the case."

"Ah, yes. How can I help you?"

"Well, I've been sitting around the last few hours trying to work out if I should call or not. That maybe it's nothing, and I shouldn't bother you. But then I thought I better call in case it's important," Hilda Thoren said, sounding worried.

"What is it?"

"Well, I did remember something about Sven Julin. The one day we got into a bit more of a personal chat. I had been struggling with a few things, and that was actually the reason I started the piano. It had made a world of difference and Sven, and I spoke a bit about that. Then he mentioned something about his life and that he had also struggled with things."

"OK, and did he mention what it was?"

"No, he didn't. He just said something along the lines of all of us having our problems, and by always pushing forwards, we can overcome them."

"Thank you for calling. That information will help us get a better picture of Sven, so it was good of you to call."

Magnus and Hilda Thoren said goodbye to each other, and once Magnus had hung up, he started thinking about what he had just heard. It took him another hour to fall asleep.

22

Another week came and went. The oppressive heat had stayed. Upon the beginning of the new day, the weather report on the local radio station noted that this day would be close to the hottest day in history and there was also zero chance of rain. This possibility excited some residents, the thought of being part of a record. The predicted maximum for the day was 34 degrees Celsius, which if the temperature did reach that, would eclipse the previous high which was 33.4 set in 1901. When Eva walked in the front door of the police station that morning, she gulped down two glasses of water. The early heat already had her feeling a bit off-kilter. As she sat down, Rana Zia came and found her and gave her a friendly smile.

"Morning Eva, a Mr Arne Eriksson from the Kungsbacka precinct called just before you got in and was looking for you. I told him you would ring him when you had a spare moment. He said it was quite urgent."

"Thanks, Rana. I'll phone him now."

Eva didn't have a clue who this policeman was, but was concerned as her sister stayed in Kungsbacka, which was fifty kilometres away. Eva wondered if it was related. She decided to call him right away. Arne Eriksson answered the call very readily and then went on to explain that a police vehicle had been up to her sister's residence the evening before as a neighbour had been concerned. The neighbour said it had sounded like an almighty fight was going on. She had told the police that there was screaming and shouting loud enough for the whole street to hear.

"Anyway, once the vehicle got there, your sister's boyfriend opened the door and laughed at the insinuation that a big fight had been going on. He said there had been - in his own words - "a little tiff," and that is was a minor misunderstanding. Your sister then came to the door with a towel drying her hair, so it seemed as the neighbour had been exaggerating. We left it at that. We informed the neighbour of this, and well she was still adamant that there had been a full-scale war going on. Maybe you should check in with your sister, see if all is well," said Arne Eriksson in a calm and friendly manner.

Eva's cheeks went bright red.

How embarrassing can you get, Eva thought.

Eva thanked Eriksson for all his help. She

hung up and put her head on her desk for a full minute. Gently patted her head against the desk several times to which the desk made a small clunking noise.

More trouble with Malin and this slime-ball, Eva thought.

Eva got back to work. She checked her emails, and there was one of definite interest regarding the case. The manager of the Lidl had finally got back to them with an answer regarding Kurt Johansson. The manager had checked the cameras and receipts for the night of the murder, and Kurt Johansson had definitely been there that night. The teller had become quite chatty with Kurt and was able to confirm to the manager that it was definitely him. She also remembered him coming in. To solidify that, Kurt Johansson was seen on camera at 8.49 pm. The approximate time of death was around 9.15 pm. There was no way Johansson could have done all that in twenty-six minutes. Cross that suspect off the list. Eva got up and felt a cup of coffee would at least give her some temporary respite. Only when she got in view of where the coffee machine was supposed to be, did she realise it wasn't there, and there was not a replacement. She had forgotten all about that. Mid hallway on her way back to her desk, Eva bumped into Alexander and Stina, who looked to be in a frantic hurry. Stina filled Eva in on what had transpired. Rosenberg had caught wind that the case files from Luleå were supposed to be delivered to them via Postnord. The commissioner at the Luleå branch, who had found this out when a detective had mentioned it to him a few days later when she was putting together the information to send, had called Rosenberg about this arrangement. The Luleå commissioner didn't like this whole idea of sending down files of their cases, and he thought it best Rosenberg send someone up for a few days to look at the crime scene and go over the case files in their offices. Rosenberg had then told Stina and Alexander when they came in they would go up to look into this whole affair. They were to leave that day.

"I told him I didn't want to go," said Alexander.

"I've got work to do down here. And Rosenberg just went off about how I must wake up and do as I'm told. He said we need to stay for a week and cover the case properly," Alexander added, not amused.

"I'd rather stay too, to be honest. I think it benefits the case more of us staying put," Stina said.

"I'm sure we will manage. Hopefully, you can find something up there. Anyway, I need to get a move on," Eva said and went and sat down at her desk, not taking much interest in these proceedings.

Stina went home to go and pack some things, while Alexander went outside to make a phone call, a last roll of the dice. Maybe Eva was disinterested at the whole affair, but Alexander was sure there was another person who would be very interested. If Alexander played his cards right, maybe he could stop his little trip up to Luleå. He dialled the number, and it rang. Magnus answered. Alexander gave him a rundown of the Luleå situation. Before Alexander could voice his discontent, Magnus went mad.

"*What? A week.* Fuck that. No one's going anywhere," said Magnus and hung up.

Alexander had a grin like a Cheshire cat as soon as he hung up. He flicked his black hair and went back inside.

23

Magnus had been enjoying a slightly longer morning at home until he had received that phone call from Alexander. He hung the phone up and went from a leisurely pace to a breakneck one. Once again the police commissioner was interjecting himself in matters of Magnus's that were all in order. Magnus said a grumbled good-bye to Lena and the dogs and was already mouthing off things when he did so. Lena knew best not to ask what the problem was. Besides, she had a lot of work to do on her website today. Once he stepped outside, the heat didn't deter him. Sweat started forming quickly all over his face as he hopped in his Volvo and got his air conditioner going once he had driven off. The cold air that started to come through eased the sweating.

I wonder who filled in Rosenberg about the files? Magnus thought.

Magnus was vehemently against this little excursion for a variety of reasons. Firstly, there was a lot to be done *here*. Anyone could see that.

The Sven Julin case had been progressing slowly so to send two of the team to Luleå sounded ridiculous. Secondly, if the cases were linked, then they could do the work right here in Varberg. The files could be sent down and used in conjunction with this case. In turn, that would help solve both murders. Also, last but certainly not least, why the hell did Alexander and Stina have to check out the crime scene again? Some woods, around thirteen, almost fourteen months later. How could that remotely offer up any more evidence? The winter, as well as the changing seasons and weather, would have destroyed any trace evidence. Magnus got out of his car and slammed the door. He found Rosenberg sitting in his office reading the paper. His desk was neat and tidy, virtually spotless.

He doesn't know where to start, Magnus thought.

"I hear you want Alexander and Stina to go down to Luleå? I'm sorry, but that's ridiculous."

"Well good morning Magnus. Before you go on, do you know that the police chief in Luleå was very aggrieved that you had arranged with a detective of theirs to have those files sent down? Those files are theirs. There is paperwork as well as correct etiquette when it comes to transferring of files."

"Well, they can have them back. Alternatively, they can make copies for us."

"Well, I spoke to Arvidsson about it, the commissioner up there. I know him well, and we both agreed to send someone up there."

Magnus was silent for a second. Arvidsson. Arvidsson. Where did he know him from?

While Rosenberg continued explaining the ins and outs of routines and procedures Magnus wasn't listening. In one ear and out the other. Magnus was trying to place this Arvidsson fellow. And then he remembered.

There had been a golf event for all of the higher-ups two years back. A two-day event, where everyone could play some golf and get to know one another. A nationwide team morale exercise. A fruitless gathering really, but the food was free, and it was a few days off work. It had been played in Stockholm. Mildly competitive. Magnus's golf game was mediocre at best. In the four-ball on the first day, in his group were himself, a detective from Kiruna, Jarvi Jarvinen, another detective from Malmö whose name he could not remember, and Arvidsson. Within about four holes, Magnus had hit it off straight away with Jarvi Jarvinen. He had also summed up Arvidsson as being possibly the biggest imbecile he had ever met. Arvidsson came equipped with expensive clubs, pristine golf attire; you name it he had it. In the first few holes, Arvidsson went on and on about his equipment, with the only break being when he wanted to critique all the others. The funny thing was Arvidsson was absolutely useless, and every time he shanked another ball into the bushes or the bunkers, he had a new finely tuned excuse. Jarvi Jarvinen had told Magnus he had an English friend who had taught him an English saying which he told Magnus in his clear Finnish accent. "All the gear, no idea," is what Jarvi had said. Magnus had chuckled for about three holes. Magnus now imagined what Arvidsson must be like as a Commissioner.

"This all makes no sense. You and this Arvidsson dickhead are doing a great job. Bravo on that! Alexander and Stina don't have a week to go up there when they could just get the files and incorporate it into our current case," Magnus said.

"Magnus, you need to watch your tone. I'm the boss, and this stands. They are going. Now get out."

Magnus accepted the invitation to leave Rosenberg's office, and he harrumphed on his way out, to emphasise his discontent. Would Jarvi's little saying be appropriate for Rosenberg as well? All the gear and no idea? Probably not, because Rosenberg didn't have the gear either. He sat down back in his office, angry. As he was calming down, a thought set off in his mind, the wheels rolling in that skull of his. Had that blinking coffee machine been replaced? He went out of his messy office and walked straight to the device. He saw quickly that the machine was gone and there was no replacement. Magnus kept on walking, out the front door, and mentioned to Rana he would be back just now. She smiled and decided against asking anything as she could see he was in a mood. Magnus then called Alexander and told him staying was a no go.

"That fucking Rosenberg won't change his mind, so just go and get it over with."

Magnus got in his car and put his foot down. Magnus reached his destination rapidly. He got out and started walking. Magnus made his way into Elon, an appliance store chain. As he walked through the automatic sliding doors, sales attendants came scurrying like vultures. He asked one of them to direct him to the coffee machines and then said that was all the assistance he required, and he didn't want to be bugged. Just let me shop in peace, he thought to himself. Usually, Swedes are quite unassuming; they mind their own business. Not the ones in this store. He started browsing through the different machines; his attention was directed to a Nespresso machine that was pitch black in colour and compact. On a huge special as well, 499 kronor instead of 999. One of those pod machines. Magnus's mind was made up. He added two boxes of sixteen pods per box to his purchase, paid and left. He made sure to get a receipt because one way or another, the department was paying for this. Budget or no budget. A lot of people, including his wife, would have said Magnus's behaviour was incredibly petty. Magnus didn't care. Magnus put the machine as well as the pods on his front seat. He imagined how the conversation with Rosenberg might go and blurted out his response aloud. "Get stuffed," Magnus said as he drove out of the parking area having won the conversation in his head.

Eva knocked on the door of the Julin residence. Alice Julin answered the door promptly and let Eva in. Eva was offered some coffee to which she accepted. Eva said she wanted to speak to Viveka Julin. Viveka came down the hall while Alice and Eva were talking and introduced herself. Viveka seemed better, but Eva could still see the sadness in her blue eyes. Just by looking at Viveka, Eva felt deflated. All three of them sat down in the living room once Alice had returned with the coffee.

"I'm sorry to have to intrude like this. If I could ask a few questions, it would be a great help," said Eva.

"It's perfectly fine," said Viveka, who nodded to Alice that she would answer the questions.

"I just wanted a bit of background. Hopefully, that would help us along in our investigation."

"Have you any idea who did such a terrible thing?"

"No, unfortunately not yet, but we are working on it."

More wind out of Viveka's sails.

"Anyway, I wanted to know a bit more about you and Sven. How long had you been married?"

"Well, we had been married for a good long while. Nineteen years. We got married, and then Alice was born about two years later."

"How was your relationship?"

"Very good, in fact. Sven was a kind soul. Always went out of his way to help people. Helped us with everything."

"Have you always lived here?"

"No, we moved here recently, around ten months ago."

"And before that?"

"We used to live in Gustavsberg."

"What did both of you do there?"

"Well I worked at a stationery company, you know a typical bookkeeping kind of job, and Sven was the manager of the Mat och Prat cafe."

"Did Sven ever have any issues with anyone? Anything of that nature?"

"No, I don't recall anything. I'm sure Sven has had his share of disagreements, but even those would have been mild. Sven was always a non-confrontational person."

Eva could see Viveka Julin was close to becoming emotional and that this was still very hard for her.

"I just have a few questions left, I promise," Eva said in a friendly way and took a sip of her coffee.

Bang average coffee, Eva thought.

"Why did you move?" Eva continued.

"Well, Sven just decided that one day. He had always wanted to do something with pianos. That was his real love. So, one day he just said we should pack up and move, get some new scenery, a new house, more time for the things we wanted to do. Because of Alice's study plans, we decided on Varberg as it was close to Göteborg University. Alice had a friend who was going there, and she wanted to go there too. So, I thought about it, and decided it was a great idea."

"So, he never had Varberg in mind?"

"No, he wasn't sure, he just wanted to move."

"Was Sven prone to decisions like this? To just up and move?"

There was a slight pause.

"Well, I suppose not really, but Sven did want to pursue this piano idea of his so he may have been planning to move for a while."

Eva took out her small book and jotted something down.

"The next few questions may be difficult, but please understand this will help us if you could answer them."

Both Viveka and Alice took big gulping swallows and prepared for the questions. Viveka was more nervous as she was the one who had to answer.

"We found some paint under your husband's fingernails. Did he paint much?"

Viveka held herself together, although a very tough task.

"No, not really. Certainly not recently."

"Was he on any medication for anything?"

"Not that I was aware of. No, No, I don't think so. I would have known about something like that."

Viveka then burst out crying. A horrible sounding gut-wrenching cry too. It was all just too much for her.

"I don't understand why anyone would kill him," Viveka managed to squeeze out.

Eva decided to be on her way. She thanked both Alice and Viveka for their time and promptly exited. What a horrible atmosphere, Eva thought as she left.

Eva got into her car and before she drove off, took one more look at her book with what she had written and mulled it over.

Why did Julin get everyone to pack up and move in such a hurry?

Magnus and Rolf pulled into the Läjet camping site car park.

They both got out of the car and headed towards reception. At the reception, they found Kurt Johansson at the counter. Eva had briefed everyone that Kurt Johansson was no longer a suspect, along with what she had found out.

Kurt Johansson looked worried.

"Don't worry Kurt. Your alibi checks out. I needed to ask you something else."

"What would that be?"

"Has Linus come to collect his usual food ration?"

"No," Johansson replied.

"However, he isn't that routine. He does come around randomly quite a bit, but he usually doesn't go too long without making an appearance. And he knows we give him food once a week," he added.

"OK, well as I said before, as soon as he comes here again, then you ring me right away," said Magnus.

"Certainly. You got it."

Magnus and Rolf then moved to the side while Johansson attended to another customer. They were contemplating whether they should go back to work or have a coke outside when Johansson stopped serving the customer at the desk and quickly walked over to them.

"He's outside. Linus, he's outside. I saw him coming this way," Johansson whispered loudly, trying not to get too excited.

They asked where Linus usually went when he went to get food and were told to go out outside the reception, go left and from there they would find the back of the kitchen. Linus usually went there. They bolted outside. As they went around the corner, they caught sight of a scraggly man, with greasy clothes and hair.

"That's him. The same guy we saw in town," Rolf whispered as they stopped running and started a tiptoeing on eggshells type of walk.

Linus was greeted by a friendly man, who then saw them as well and greeted them as they were nearing Linus. Linus turned and was decidedly startled and didn't hang around to find out who these men were. With a scared look on his face, Linus darted off as fast as he could go, round some buildings and out of sight. Magnus wanted to go and crack the guy that greeted them but had no time for that.

"The car," Magnus said assuming Linus would end up down the road somewhere, and both him and Rolf ran back to hop in and make this chase to their advantage, as Linus seemed to know his way around the area. Linus was fast. He sprinted through nooks and crannies, and shrubbery and bushes.

Magnus got back to the car, waiting for Rolf

to get to and open the doors of his rickety Kia, which they had gone in.

"Hurry up," Magnus ranted.

"I.... I can't find my keys!" Rolf said, who was panting after his moderate jog to the car.

"What do you mean you can't find your keys?"

"They must be inside."

Before Magnus could say anything else, Rolf ran inside to look, panting heavily.

This can't be happening, Magnus thought.

After several minutes, Rolf came out, the jogging now more like a trundle, and the stomach was wobbling from left to right in quick movements. Rolf had found the keys, and they were in his left hand. I should have run in, thought Magnus.

"Let me drive," said Magnus.

Rolf didn't say no, but at the same time, didn't want Magnus to drive either.

Magnus started the ignition and set off at his desired speed which was as fast as possible in search of Linus who couldn't have been far away. The Kia was nothing like Magnus's Volvo. It was as if the vehicle had a cold. Sputtering. Battling to pick up speed. Linus's experience of this area was invaluable. After fifteen minutes of looking for Linus, and not even a glimpse of him, both Magnus and Rolf resigned themselves to the fact that Linus had evaded them. This was the second time

Linus had gotten away from Rolf. On the way back, Rolf recalled that Linus had been carrying a book in his hand. A quite dilapidated one. He mentioned it to Magnus and asked if he thought it was important.

"I was told the first time I came here that Linus keeps some book with him. Some type of logbook. He won't let anyone see it. My bet is that's why he made a dash for it."

"I don't think he's quite all there," said Rolf.

"No, probably not."

Magnus and Rolf continued back to the office.

"Another thing," Magnus said.

"Hmmm?" said Rolf.

"Get yourself a new car."

24

Alexander Holström and Stina Wahlgren had driven up to Göteborg to get a direct flight to Luleå. They had both brought a small amount of luggage. They checked in, and once the usual formalities were done, they had about thirty-five minutes to spare before departure. Both decided that coffee was a good idea. Alexander, however, had been concerned with Stina's body language. She looked worried and was very fidgety. He chose to say nothing and be a calming influence instead. Maybe she was just worried about the case. She was relatively new in this division, and you didn't want to drop the ball in a case such as this. They ordered coffee, and waited for their order, with the talking limited. Stina was not saying much in reply to Alexander's attempts at a conversation. Once they had got their coffee - a mighty good cup, Alexander had thought - Stina continued her panicky behaviour. She was looking in different directions regularly while tapping her cup constantly. She kept rubbing her eyes as well. Finally, Alexander decided he had to ask Stina what on earth was wrong. Stina replied, saying nothing was the matter, and that she needed to pop to the toilet. Alexander finished the coffee, sorted out the bill, and waited near the restrooms for Stina to appear. Stina came out looking quite pale. Maybe she's not feeling well, Alexander thought. With a couple of minutes left to board, they waited in line. Just before they got to the front of a pretty small queue, Stina asked Alexander if she could chat with him and motioned towards a free area out of the line about twenty metres away.

"I don't think I can get on the flight," she blurted out before Alexander could say anything.

"What do you mean you can't get on the flight?" he responded.

Stina started to tear up. Alexander hadn't seen Stina show any emotion before, so he was not sure how to handle this. He felt sorry for her.

"If...If I get on the plane, If I get on, then my mother will die."

Alexander didn't understand what was going on.

The last call was made for anyone boarding the flight.

Eva decided that it was time to make the phone call she had been dreading. The call she felt she ought to make. Eva thought she probably didn't have to make it, but she felt obliged to. Obliged. What did that mean anyway? That she was making the call out of public service rather than compassion or love? Even though her sister had been giving her uphill, she always felt responsible for helping her with things. Surely her sister was capable of sorting out her own mess? Speaking of messes, her life was nothing to write home about. The bullet she had fired to kill that man still rung in her ears. She picked up her Samsung mobile and dialled. It was answered after about seven or eight rings.

"Hello."

"Malin, what the hell is going on?"

25

The pain of what happened is still etched in my memory. It will not go away. Each day is a battle. What keeps me going is knowing I'm not far from completing my goal. My quest. One down, one to go. The one left to go is the real bad apple, and he will be paying soon. I need to be quick about it. At the same time, I can't be stupid. The police seem as if they are working hard on this case. I can't see how they would be at all close; however, it's best not to take chances, so time is of the essence. My little diversion was something I would rather have not done. I would rather have gone on about my business in the manner I had been doing, but I had to muddy the waters. Again as a precautionary measure. So now I sit here in my abode, with the time drawing near to the finish. Once this is over, maybe the sickening feeling in my stomach will relent somewhat. A normal life is out of the question; however, maybe I can regain something? I can move far away and start again. But not before justice. Our justice. That is the very least we deserve.

I am not a lunatic. One of these deranged killers. I am merely writing a wrong. I am enjoying a good breakfast as I write this in my journal. Bacon, eggs, a cup of coffee. I may have a cinnamon bun afterwards as well. I am a pretty ordinary person, except for the tragedy that befell me. I'm not looking to involve anyone else or kill anyone else, just the two. If someone gets in the way, well then they may become a thorn in my side too, because they are impeding my writing of the wrongs. And then they might have to be taken out as well. I read a quote once about revenge. It goes like this:

Weak people *revenge.*
Strong people *forgive.*
Intelligent people *ignore.*

I suppose that makes me weak. And I'm fine with that. There's no going back now. I can forgive them once they are dead. Actually, I can't.

26

Rolf Jonsson went straight to see Camilla after work. The cemetery looked beautiful. The grounds were pristine. There was a marvellous array of flowers blossoming all around, and all the individual gravesites were superbly maintained. There were a couple of staff who worked there, and Rolf had often seen them scurrying about with rakes and watering cans. There was a man who was always giving orders, so Rolf safely assumed he was the head groundskeeper. He seemed perfectly pleasant, a thin man, with a smile on his face. His staff too seemed quite happy with what they were busy with. They were still working energetically at the end of the day. It felt a little odd to Rolf. Such cheerfulness in a cemetery. He wasn't sure why it was strange. Did he expect people to be moping around, hating their arduous chores because it was a cemetery? Did he expect the place to be falling apart? He didn't know. He went to stand next to Camilla's grave and pulled out a small spade, as well as a box of six flowers that were in a black tray in a white packet he was holding. He started to dig just around the perimeter of the gravesite and plant the flowers he had brought, one by one. Sharp-Lobed Hepatica. They were in the early stages of blooming, so before long they would look amazing. Rolf sat next to the grave for a while, having a coke after his gardening efforts. Rolf would still chat with Camilla about things.

"This case has everyone a bit on edge, you know. We haven't gotten anywhere. This Linus I told you about, we had a chance to get him today, and wouldn't you know it, I forgot the keys at the reception desk of the campsite. That wasted valuable time, and he disappeared. Magnus was not impressed."

This talking did ease some of the pain. Rolf found it comforting. Being at home in the evenings was a lot less encouraging. At least Sylvester was good at helping lift his spirits. Rolf got up and just stood for a while in front of the grave, chatting a bit more about this, that, and the other thing. The thin smiley man, the boss of the place, was now in his vicinity and approached him to say hello. Although Rolf had regularly seen him, usually the man was way too busy to chat and exchange pleasantries.

"Hello," the man said, sticking out his hand.

"Hi," Rolf said in return and looked at his

grubby hands.

"I'd shake, but my hands are dirty from planting," Rolf pointed out.

"I see. Well, I'll make sure your new flowers are looked after, and we will make sure the gravestone has a good clean too."

"Thank you. That's most kind."

There was silence for a bit before the man asked Rolf a question.

"Your wife, I presume?"

"Yes," Rolf replied.

"It's a horrible thing, death."

"Yes. Yes, it is," replied Rolf.

There was more silence then Rolf continued.

"How are you supposed to cope? I mean, it's so final. No one ever comes back."

"Good question. I don't think there is an answer to that. However, I will say when it comes to life; I have a motto I try and always remember."

"What would that be?"

"While you are living, its good to be alive while you are doing it."

"But it's hard to live life when you have lost someone."

"Of course it is. However, you can live and remember fondly and miss while you are living, doing things you have always wanted to. I'm sure the person you love would have wanted that."

"I must be going. Lots to do here, but it

was nice chatting to you," the man added and left with a smile and wave.

"Likewise," said Rolf.

Rolf thought it was time for him to head home as well. He walked out of the cemetery, feeling a bit strange. He felt as if that talk had done him a world of good. Be alive while you are alive. Hmmm. Rolf decided he really should try and do just that. Who would have known he would have got such sound advice from the thin man who was in charge of the cemetery's grounds.

Stina and Alexander were about three-quarters of their way through their SAS flight to Luleå. The estimated time was expected to be an hour and forty minutes, but the pilot had sent a friendly message to the passengers and said they were around ten minutes ahead of schedule. Regardless of this, Stina still felt tortured. Alexander had managed to get her on the plane by saying he would listen to what this problem of Stina's was all about once they had taken off. Up to this point, Stina had closed her eyes and tried to sleep, but was having no luck on that front at all. She was sweating. She was having thoughts racing through her head of her mother collapsing and dying on the spot and her father running to check on her. He would be too late. Why had the thought hit her just when they had gotten to the airport? She had a few fleeting thoughts about the flight earlier, but it had not bothered her. Alexander decided not to poke the bear unless Stina wanted to talk. Besides, Alexander was enjoying a thoroughly excellent crime novel called Woman with birthmark. Just as he passed the 200-page mark, Stina interrupted him.

"I have magical thinking," she said.

"Excuse me?" Alexander replied. What is she on about? He thought.

Alexander listened while he closed his novel and put it on his lap.

"Magical thinking. It's this type of OCD I have been told. Had it for as long as I can remember."

Alexander had a vague idea of what OCD was.

"Magical thinking is these horrendous thoughts that if you do or don't do a certain thing, then something bad will happen."

"But that isn't true. It's not logical. We're detectives. We're logical."

"The thing is I know that it's nonsense. However, I get such high anxiety that these thoughts maybe could actually happen. You get such an overwhelming terrible feeling that you don't know what to do."

"So how do these thoughts pick which things cause bad things to happen?"

"Beats me. They just come up from time to

time. The aeroplane one I've had a lot."

"But your mother didn't die the last time you were on a plane, so why is it bothering you?"

"It's the thought of well, maybe it will happen this time."

"Have you seen someone about this?"

"Yes, I know what to do. However, it's hard. You are supposed to do exposure therapies."

"What are those?"

"You are supposed to ignore the problem and what's bothering you. The anxiety will begin on a level of ten, the ten being very high, and while you sit it out, the anxiety level then begins to drop."

"Does it help?"

"Well it does, but all of a sudden I'll find it tough to do. Like today, the plane thing just freaked me out. All of a sudden."

"Sounds horrible this thing."

"Sometimes I do checks too."

"Checks?"

"Like I'll shut the door to go to work, and I'll have these thoughts that maybe it's not closed properly. So, I'll do it again and again. The other day it took me about forty minutes to close the front door. I know its stupid, but it's the anxiety that bothers you so much, you start thinking if you do it again, the anxiety will go away."

"For what its worth, anytime you want to talk about it, let me know."

"Thanks."

"You know I wear dark blue socks to work every day. Same colour and brand. Think I'd lose it if they were, say black ones," said Alexander, trying to lighten the mood.

"Very funny," Stina laughed and gave Alexander a gentle tap on the shoulder. She smiled.

Alexander was happy to have listened to Stina. Maybe she would listen to his story about his parents, well his father really. No way, he thought. I can't talk about that.

A message broadcast to the cabin. They would be landing soon.

27

Lena Markusson's evening had begun poorly. Her husband, Magnus, had come home from work in a foul mood and had gone on another very detailed rant about everything that the police commissioner Erik Rosenberg had been messing up. On and on and on. Eventually, Lena decided to tidy some things up around the house while replying "yes" and "I know" as Magnus continued to run down his boss.

"Maybe you should sit down and relax," said Lena. "Put the TV on. You and I can watch a movie."

Magnus seemed to nod, but then moved his already dishevelled hair around and carried on. Messy beard and hair as well. Casual work attire. What a catch, Lena thought.

"Who the hell does he think is going to do their work while they are gone? And they are gone for what? A bloody wild goose chase. A year-old crime scene in some woods. Ha! Its hardly like that scene has remained untouched, out in the open. In the wind, sun, and snow. What a waste of time."

"I get that, but you have already told me this. So maybe its time to settle down?"

"And as for that fucking NPC, he can go to hell too. Maybe he should listen to us for change, and not some suit from Ikea. And I'm telling you now; I'm *not* going back to Ikea. You can count on that.

"Ah Magnus, stop being silly now. You love Ikea."

"No. That's it. I *won't* be going back. I can go to Jysk from now on."

Magnus was a big fan of Ikea, as was Lena. Their house was decked with many Ikea items.

The next half an hour was more of the same: Rosenberg this, Rosenberg that. Screw the NPC. Stuff Ikea. Finally, Magnus sat down.

"What are you cooking?"

"I was going to start something soon."

"I have an idea. Let's get some pizza. It's nice and easy. I'll pop off to ICA and grab one quick. I'll invite Eva over and tell her to bring what she was working on in the case and go through it. While we are busy with that, I can chat with her about Alexander's and Stina's work as well."

"It's unusual for you to do after-hours work."

"I know. But I'm worried. We need something. After this case, we are out of here for a week or two. They owe me leave."

Magnus darted off to buy pizza, and once he returned, he called Eva and told her that he would appreciate it if she came over to work on some things with him. Eva agreed somewhat hesitantly and said she would be around in about three-quarters of an hour. She was very accurate with her estimation, arriving virtually when she said she was going to. Magnus was already busy eating a slice of pizza when the doorbell rang. He wasn't the first one to go towards the front door. The dogs beat him to it. They raced to see who the guest was — barking from all angles. Magnus let Eva in and tried to calm the three down. Eventually, Eva managed her way to the couch. She noticed Chloe. Eva felt a wave of happiness to see how Chloe was thriving in her environment. From the night when Magnus had put her in the car to now showed a remarkable difference.

"Chloe is looking great."

"Yes, she's doing very well. She's big pals with the other two now."

Magnus offered Eva some pizza to which she grabbed two slices. There were two different pizzas. A Hawaiian and a meaty salami. Lena got some coffee going for all three of them.

They all gathered around the TV area, with

Magnus and Eva moving a little further away so Lena could watch something and not have their chatter getting in the way. Lena flicked on the TV and found a rerun of Desperate Housewives. Magnus thought Lena should have some standards and not watch such trash. Lena ignored him and carried on. Magnus and Eva got to work. Let's get this over with, Magnus thought.

Malin Lindqvist knew she had to get out. She now knew that was the only possible solution. Pack her bags and get the hell out. After telling her sister on the phone that the lady who had called in the complaint was being ridiculous, she had hung up and thought about what she had said. This quarrel as she had put it to Eva on the phone had in fact been a big fight. And a horrifying one. She had tried to stand up to Jonas. Malin had met a friend in the queue at Coop — another big grocery store — who had said to her that she was attending art classes once a week in Mölndal, which was roughly twenty kilometres out of town. She suggested they go together. Malin loved the idea. She had always been into art; although she was somewhat of a novice, this would be a chance to further herself. When Jonas heard this, he went ballistic. He said that Malin was a cheap whore, obviously going to screw some other guy. He had also wondered who was supposed to look after the house. Malin wasn't aware that a house needed babysitting and wasn't going to give in this time. Malin said she was going, and that's when Jonas grabbed her. Jonas grabbed Malin by her blonde hair tightly. Malin's eyes were looking straight into Jonas's. His eyes looked as if there were no soul in them. No feeling. Like he was a robot. He cracked her across the face, open-handed and she fell to the floor. "You deserve this," he screamed and screamed, getting extremely worked up and stood over her like a predator getting ready to finish off their prey. Jonas then grabbed Malin by the hair again, held her near the top of her shoulder and pulled her towards the bathroom. Inside this pretty bathroom, there was a white toilet, located to the right of a glass shower with beautiful ceramic tiles. Jonas shoved Malin's head into the toilet and flushed. He did not let her up for air; he just kept holding her down. Jonas finally let Malin up, who caught her breath in big swallows. Jonas wasn't done. He shoved Malin down for one more flushing. Jonas yanked her backwards next, and Malin fell to the cold floor, the tiles having that icy touch. Two kicks followed to her stomach area. They felt to Malin as if she had been hit by a car. She just lay there, hoping this hammer like pain would start to subside. Malin also was hoping that Jonas would stop. Jonas then had to urinate, to which he did. But he saved some of his yellow specimen for Malin. He turned and peed all over her just to add insult to the whole thing. Luckily, he walked out of the bathroom after this. This was when he had started screaming.

"No respect. Look at everything I do for you, and you start behaving like a slut. All this is your fault. All of it."

The ranting and tirade continued for a few more minutes until things went quiet. It was an odd feeling, almost as if Malin was in the eye of a hurricane that had just been through and destroyed a village. However, the peaceful part of this eye was lying on the floor, soaked in piss. Malin got up and went to have a shower and was yanked out when Jonas had run into the bathroom and said someone was at the door. He had seen it was a neighbour. He told her to put on her best behaviour, so he could get rid of this nosy old lady.

Going through that hurricane may have been the clarity Malin had needed. Jonas was now out on a "boys' night" again. Malin's mind was made up. The question was, where could she go? The obvious answer was to her sister. But wouldn't that be embarrassing, humiliating, to get the good old "I told you so" thrown in her face? She wasn't on the greatest of terms with her parents. Eva was even on worse terms. As kids, there had been just fighting, both parents guilty of affairs, with each parent almost trying to one-up each other. Boarding school provided some solace, but the bottom line had been that both Malin and Eva had ended up not thinking too highly of both parents, who by now had divorced and wouldn't even be civil towards each other. Sure, Malin could go to one of them, but did she feel like all that again? All that leftover baggage. All the hard feelings both she and Eva had that were never addressed by either parent. Malin had enough problems as it was. As for Jonas, his comings and goings at very odd hours at nights had become more regular, and he always had a story when he arrived home. And some of these stories didn't add up. She asked him once and received a slap for her question. And those pills. Jonas kept taking those pills to sleep. So, when it came time for him to get up, he was in a horrible mood, because he had to go to work, and had trouble waking up. He would then shove down an energy drink or two to try and wake up. What a circle. Can't sleep. Take sleeping pills. Hard to wake up. Energy drinks. In between all this, he would psychically and mentally abuse Malin. Malin had wondered why it had taken so long to realise that the relationship was toxic. But at least now she was leaving. At the end of the week would be when she would leave. That would be the plan. Jonas was quite busy then. Pack up all her things and leave, drive, and never look back. Malin climbed into bed. Only a few nights left.

She breathed a slow, calm breath. Things would turn out all right after all.

Eva had been discussing her various lines of enquiry with Magnus amidst a chorus of loud rumblings from the sky outside. Nothing much had come of Eva's particular enquiry lines. She had told Magnus the paint, and the rope she had been looking into had dead-ended. She had been looking into more pertinent information. Like the medication found in Sven Julin's system. It was also a long shot, but maybe there was some sort of trail there. Maybe Julin had a prescription? Viveka Julin hadn't thought so. Eva had also explained to Magnus that she had checked up on Stina's latest tire tread work. Stina had initially bridged the gap of possible vehicle models down from 284 to 181, and before she had to leave to hop on an aeroplane, she had gotten the list down further. 145 left. An improvement but also something that seemed to be heading nowhere. It was maybe time to try and narrow the scope, and take the 145 partial matches, and try different parameters and see if anything showed up. If only there was something, something tangible that could narrow this down. Finding Linus may be that tangible. The storm clouds opened up outside. At last, some relief from the heat. The rain started coming down in a torrential downpour. The dogs didn't like it, all of them virtually trying to lie on top of Lena, who then got them blankets and organised them, so they were close to her, while she continued to watch TV.

"OK Eva, what do you think is going on? What's your theory?" asked Magnus.

"I had something interesting," Eva said.

"Why do you think Sven Julin was in such a hurry to move to Varberg. From the chat I had with Viveka, he never seemed to be one to make quick, spontaneous decisions. But all of a sudden, he gets the whole family to up and move," Eva continued.

"Yes, but wasn't Alice going to study nearby?" Magnus said.

"That's true, *but* they didn't have to move just because Alice was going to study there. Viveka said Sven just up and decided. It sounded as if Sven wanted to move anywhere. He wanted to start a piano school of sorts."

"Well, maybe that's the reason?"

"Just like that. He's never done any piano teaching until now, but all of a sudden, he decides?"

"Well, if like you said he wanted to leave just like that, what's the reason?"

"I'm not sure," Eva rubbed her forehead.

"Maybe Sven was running away from something."

"He was staying in Gustavsberg. That's got nothing to do with any of the cases though," Eva said.

"We must keep digging. But maybe he was hiding something. Something to do with these cases. I think he saw or did something that got him killed."

"Maybe the other lady that was killed. Maybe she and Sven knew each other. And both got killed because of something they were involved in," said Eva.

"It's possible. Let's carry on going through a few things. I need to think."

After another hour or so, Magnus and Eva both decided not much more could be done as they were both feeling exhausted. It was still pouring, so Magnus offered Eva a long dark brown couch to sleep on and stay the night with himself and Lena. Eva hesitated at first but then agreed that maybe it was best to stay. Magnus went to get Eva some sleeping things and returned with a delicately soft pillow, and a thin blanket. Eva thanked Magnus then asked him a somewhat strange question.

"Does Lena know?"

"Excuse me?"

"You know. Does Lena know? That I killed someone on duty."

"I'm sure I mentioned it to her. But why on earth is that important?" said Magnus.

She sounds as if she's going crackers,

thought Magnus.

"I'm not sure. Lately, whenever I see someone I know, I wonder what they think of me."

"Eva, you can't keep doing this to yourself. You have to stop now."

Magnus went across and woke Lena up who looked a little out of it.

"Must have dozed off."

"You think?" said Magnus.

"Listen, Eva is going to stay on the couch. It's pouring outside," Magnus added.

"With pleasure," Lena said and smiled at Eva who smiled in return.

Lena and the three dogs made their way to the bedroom, as did Magnus behind them.

Slowly all the lights were switched off. Eva's lights were still on in her head, though.

28

Alexander and Stina were onto day three of their trip when Alexander woke up at 6.30 am. His tongue was stuck to the roof of his mouth. He didn't feel at all well. He recalled the previous evening that he and Stina had gone out to a local pub, but the recollections of the rest of the night became difficult after that.

He must have had a lot to drink to not remember much about it. And why did he have so much to drink any way? A few images flickered through his mind when trying to think of what had occurred. There were images of sex. While thinking about this, he turned over to face the middle of the bed, and beside him was Stina, fast asleep, and stark naked. She was lying on her back, her breasts in full view. She had a nice tattoo on her upper thigh. Roses going into a mandala of sorts. Very intricately done. Alexander was naked as well. Surely they hadn't actually had sex? Alexander now remembered the reason for the trip to the bar for some drinks. So far on their trip, Alexander and Stina had gotten almost no help from the local police. The helpful detective, Monika, was away, and all the others had said she would help them, and in the meantime, they could look at some of the files. Not *all* of the files. It was assumed they were on team Arvidsson and considered this visit as stepping on of toes. So Stina and Alexander had thought to get on with what they could and wait for Monika to return. If they told Magnus the local police weren't helping, then Stina had said it would create more problems. Stina had been explaining her personal problems a little more, and Alexander thought that going to a pub for some drinks, and a nice meal may be a good idea. Upon their arrival in Luleå, Stina had frantically called her mother as soon as she had got off the plane. Her father had answered and had said she had gone to get some groceries, which added further panic. Maybe she had dropped down dead in the vegetable section? Twenty minutes later, her mom had called.

Alexander thought best to get up and go and shower. What would he say after he came out of the shower? He bet himself that there would be that uncomfortable silence — what a mess. After a lengthy shower of twenty minutes, he came out of the shower, and Stina had her back to him. She had put a long green t-shirt on, presumably a kind of sleeping top. Stina saw Alexander and smiled, but a half, not too sure type of smile. Alexander quickly just threw on last night's clothes, feeling awkward.

"Coffee?" she asked him.

"Yes. Yes, please."

From there, the conversation was non-existent, each trying to look as if they were doing something when there wasn't anything to do. They mostly spoke about the weather in the north and how the sun virtually never went down during summer. Finally, Alexander thought he might as well come out with it.

"I.... Well....I wanted to ask you something. Did we have sex last night?"

Stina looked a little embarrassed, and her cheeks gave a slight blush of red. She then frowned.

"Uh, Yes, Alexander. Don't you remember?"

"Things, well they seem a bit fuzzy from around when we finished up at the pub. I don't remember everything all that clearly."

"Well, you did have a lot to drink. I had to help you back to my room."

"Oh wait, so this is your room?"

He must still be out of it, Stina thought.

"Yes."

"I see, so you took me to your room?"

"Hang on a second. You weren't doing so good. That was all."

"Then how did we end up.... you know?"

"I gave you some coffee; you were still quite out of it. Then it just happened. You came onto me, and the rest is history."

"My advice is let's go get some breakfast downstairs — apparently it's quite good here. Then I say we forget about what happened and get back to work. We don't want things to be weird. We have a lot to do. We work well together. We shouldn't mess it up. I just need to go and get a change of clothes from my room."

"I agree." Although Stina didn't really agree. Alexander had always come across to her as this sort of flashy guy, but after getting to know him a bit, it seemed more to her that he was entirely down to earth, he just happened to like a few things that people would perceive as flashy. Even though Alexander had been drunk, it didn't detract from the fact that the sex was mind-blowing. Well, it was to her anyway. Stina had also felt a closeness of sorts. Maybe they would be good together? She excused herself to go and have a quick shower, and while in there, she tried to work out her feelings on this matter as a whole. She came up with an apt word. Disappointment. She was disappointed.

29

The morning air felt invigorating to Malin Lindqvist. The day was finally here. Jonas had come home very late, rolled into bed, and had left early again. She had avoided him for the most part and had given him some friendly smiles when necessary. Now that he was gone and not expected home until late, Malin could get to work. She would pack her clothes and some other items, as much as what could fit into her smallish car, a red Skoda, which rarely did any mileage anymore. Well, today that was going to change. Malin had decided that Eva was the best person to go to. Even though she may tell her how Malin should have listened to her earlier, Eva at the end of the day was only trying to look out for her. So hopefully Eva would have enough space for Malin. A little worry — well a big worry — occupying Malin's mind was that of Jonas's reaction to coming back to the apartment minus Malin, and most of her belongings. Malin was convinced Jonas wouldn't take it at all well. Malin started to pack up all her things, and while she was doing this pondered about whether to leave a note or not. Would that diffuse the situation slightly or make it worse? She decided to finish packing before she decided what to do. Once Malin had hurriedly packed up what she could, she decided she would write a short, to the point note, explaining her feelings and hopefully Jonas would let her be after that. She grabbed a pen and a little notepad and started writing.

Jonas,

As you would have seen, I am not at home, nor are most of my things. The reason is that it's over. The way things have been is not good for either of us. Let's face it - this relationship isn't right. I'm going to move on with my life, and I ask you to do the same. Please do not contact me again. My key is under the pot plant near the door.

Malin.

Malin was happy with that note. She didn't want to run Jonas into the ground, even though he deserved it. She thought that might add fuel to the fire. Maybe he would see some sense in the note. And perhaps he would not bother her again. She wasn't sure what she would do, but Malin knew for certain she was making the right decision. Their residence, or Jona's residence now, was more of a townhouse, a modern structure in a complex of more modern structures. They had a month's notice clause in their contract, so if Jonas wanted to leave, he could give his notice. Malin was able to go about her further business at home without bumping into other residents. After loading her things into the car, she knelt down and put the key under the pot plant, took one more look around, and once she had double-checked that Jonas was nowhere to be seen, she hopped in the Skoda and pressed her foot lightly down on the accelerator. Malin was headed towards a new life. Her next stop was Varberg.

Magnus was already onto his second cup of coffee at work, enjoying the coffee pod machine that he had purchased. The weather had been kinder the last few days with a handful of big storms. Things didn't feel as dry as they had done. Magnus got into a brief chat with Rolf and made sure to say very loudly that everyone had tons of work because Alexander and Stina were forced to go and look at an old crime scene. Upon entering his office, Magnus sat down and began by opening up his Microsoft Outlook and going through e-mails. There was one from Erik Rosenberg that caught his attention. It had been addressed to the whole of Magnus's team, as well as himself and the subject read "Private items at work." This ought to be interesting, he thought. He opened up the e-mail with a double-tap with his finger on the laptop touchpad.

Dear all,

This is a friendly reminder that in the work-place, the general rule is not to bring personal appli-ances or pieces of equipment to work. I'm referring to the coffee machine that is now in the coffee area where the other apparatus used to be. While it is a nice gesture to have a communal coffee machine, it may set a dangerous precedent where now other de-partments may start bringing other personal items along with them. Please can this item be removed as soon as possible. An effort will be made to look into the purchase of a new machine.

Regards,
Erik Rosenberg.

Magnus stared at the e-mail for about a minute not sure what to say and then started mouthing to himself. What a load of bullshit. What a *load* of bullshit. Is that the best that goof-ball can come up with? Magnus had no time to do anything about it now. But he had already decided to anyway. How about a nice friendly (and very sarcastic) email back to everyone? That wasn't going to solve the overall problem, however. That problem was Rosenberg working here. Couldn't he see that stupid emails like that dampened everyone's spirits? On top of that, it had to be the dumbest reason to try and get him to take his machine away. And this man was running the Varberg police department. Magnus had arranged a meeting that was due in fifteen minutes with his team, so he needed to get this over with quickly.

Hi Erik,

Thank you for your urgent email, which I think must be addressed right away. The murder investigation can wait. I'm sorry to hear that this appliance is causing such a stir. The problem with removing it is that it is a communal type of arrangement where everyone helps themselves to their coffee requirements when they feel fit. So, in essence, it belongs to all of us. There is no owner. So, in regard to it being removed, it would be an awful bunfight to decide who takes it home. So, I think it needs to stay put. I have a suggestion. I think maybe the department should buy it from me (I used my personal card to purchase it). Then it becomes the departments and no longer a personal item. Everyone leaves happy. Something to ponder.

Your understanding is appreciated.

Magnus.

At this stage, Magnus didn't care at all about the consequences for his sarcastic and in his opinion, quite witty, response. He must try, Magnus thought. I'll take it further. A few minutes later, Magnus strode out to the little boardroom, ready for the meeting. Rolf was already there when Magnus came in. He gave Magnus a wry smile and chuckled once he had entered. Eva followed. It was only the three of them now that Alexander and Stina were in Luleå. The first thing Magnus said was that everyone would have to help with Stina's and Alexander's share of work until they returned. Magnus said he would take care of the tire tread. He asked Eva to look into Sven Julin's old place of employment and follow his quick decision to leave. Did something happen at work? Rolf was to look for Linus himself, as well as go back to the Läjet camping site, and knock on every door, and ask about Linus as well as the night of the murder. Maybe by hook or by crook someone remembered something important.

"Once the other two get back from Luleå with some proper information, then we can reconvene. For now, we carry on this way, and hope something turns up," Magnus said. Eva and Rolf agreed and nodded.

"OK, great. That's settled then. Anything else anyone wants to discuss?" Magnus said.

"No," said Rolf.

"No, no, I'm happy," said Eva.

They were all about to exit the dull boardroom when Rana Zia came into the room, without knocking and looking very bewildered.

What she said was of importance and concern.

"Another body has been found in the woods. Very close to where Sven Julin was found."

30

It was getting very late. The time was just after one in the morning. The two men were talking with the lone lady at the bar. The man who had been eyeing her up was the one talking up a storm, probably egged on by the cocaine from his toilet break. The other man was at this stage very drunk and would make a friendly remark or two, but he was doing more of a balancing act, trying not to fall over. The lady was dressed in a stylish black number.

After two more rounds, a suggestion was made by the insistent gentleman that all three of them should head back to the hotel where the two men were staying. The lady wasn't so sure at first. She thought maybe she should call a cab from the bar. Her friends had been her lift home. The man who had snorted the cocaine said to her she could get a lift with them and come for one drink. She could ring a cab from the room. They could go up to his friends' room — that's what he had referred to him as, even though they barely knew each other — and they could all have one for the road. She asked them to give her a few minutes while she finished her drink. That was fine. The two men left her alone as the one needed some air outside to try and sober up a bit while the other said he would keep an eye on him. The lady had said she would be a few minutes. She thought about this little rendez- vous she had arranged. Shouldn't she just go home? Wouldn't they get the wrong impression? That maybe she was up for more than a drink? She better make that clear from the outset. No, it wasn't a big deal. She liked chatting to people. That was all. Besides, she needed a lift anyway. These taxis were very expen- sive. From the hotel, at least that would be cheaper. And she wasn't going to pester her man at this time and look like she couldn't even get home by herself. She made her way outside and saw the two men wait- ing for her. One drink and I'll be off, she thought.

31

Alexander and Stina surveyed the crime scene in the small set of woods in Luleå where the body had been found. Monika Ranström, the helpful detective who had originally called Magnus, was thankfully back at work and was very helpful. She hadn't understood why no one else had been helpful. Monika put it down to that some of the older cops didn't want to be shown up if the Varberg police solved the crime. "A few past their prime, riding things out until retirement" had been the way Monika had put it. Monika had taken Alexander and Stina to the old crime scene where the murder had occurred. The two of them took turns looking at the crime scene photos. In the notes found in the brown case file folder, the cause of death was a cervical fracture of the neck, more specifically the C1 vertebrae. It had been snapped. The pathologist at the time had ascertained that death would have been almost instant. The victim had been hung post-mortem. It was assumed that the victim,

Miss Maria Ekberg, a thirty-eight-year-old, had received a powerful blow by a hard object at the back of her neck and was brought to these woods to make it look like a suicide. Maria Ekberg's friends had been spoken to, and on the night in question, a few of them had been with her at a local pub. The last time they had seen her was when they were leaving. She decided to stay. No one had bothered Maria that night or hounded her in any way while they had been there. Maria Ekberg had told her friends that she was going to stay a little while longer. She did have a boy-friend, but one of the friends explained, quite oddly, no one knew who the man was. The friend went on to say Maria Ekberg had said they were "taking it slow." Her relationships in the past hadn't turned out too well and had always been littered with heartbreak. Maria didn't want to tell anyone until she was sure that this relation-ship was the relationship. So then why was Maria hanging around in a bar after her friends left? Why wasn't she running to see the boyfriend? Her friends explained that Maria often liked to sit by herself and take in things. She liked to go to a restaurant by herself and sit and enjoy a meal while observing. She liked to chat with people. The neighbours had been interviewed and had said Maria was a friendly lady. They had never thought she was seeing anyone, nor did they see a man visit her either. After reading this, Alexander was convinced they needed to find this boy-friend. Alexander did not know how they would go about it. No one knew who he was except for the victim. A husband and wife, teachers at a school next to the wooded area, were taking a walk when they found Maria Ekberg strung up in a tree, an image hard to etch out of their brains. After the place was then cordoned off, all that was found was some trace elements of a red substance under her nails. The analysis that was done on the substance came back with red paint. Also, a DNA sample had been obtained from some skin fragments. There had been no match in the database. The search into the details of the paint was almost identical to the search in Varberg. There was the same problem, however, regarding tracking the paint. The paint was available from virtually anywhere.

Alexander and Stina split up and decided to pan out and see if there would be anything of interest if their scope was widened. Both were trying to focus on the case, but their thoughts often drifted back to the events of the previous evening. Alexander hadn't remembered much when he had woken up that morning, but now little smidgens of information were coming back to him. Stina, on the other hand, had remembered everything. Alexander had remembering enjoying spending time with Stina. She wasn't fake and didn't show off when they had been talking. She had been funny and honest. Stina had enjoyed how Alexander had listened to her problems and that Alexander was genuinely trying to help, not just saying silly things like "don't think about it." Stina's mind had been racing. She worried about if they started up something what the ramifications would be at work. Was that type of thing allowed? Two detectives involved? She wasn't sure. Maybe there was some type of protocol? But who's to say Alexander had the slightest interest in her anyway. Just because of one night? Stina's head felt like someone had tied an elastic band around it. After spending around forty-five minutes or so basically dithering around, both met back up. Nothing found. No new ideas emerged either. Alexander pretended to look busily at the notes he had in the file he was holding. Alexander's phone rang. Thank God, he thought. It looked like one of the office lines back at their police station. There were so many extensions he wasn't exactly sure who would be calling but guessed it to be Magnus.

"Hello," he answered.

"Alexander, have you found anything?" said Magnus.

"Uh, we're at the scene now. We got the file regarding all the details, but we've found nothing new."

"Enough is enough. You guys are coming

back today. Change your tickets. Do whatever. But you are coming back. And bring that file too."

"What about the people here? I have a feeling that the chief won't be too keen to release —."

"Listen, I'll handle that golfing clown myself. That man can't deny us the case notes that may be linked to our investigation. Even if they are copies, we need that information. I'll make some calls."

"What's going on?"

"Another body. So, you have to come back before the whole city panics. Sort out those tickets."

"Rana organised the tickets, so maybe she can help us change them?"

"Sure, I'll get her to change them now and let you know when you need to be at the airport."

Magnus hung up. Why the hell was he going on about golf? Alexander thought.

"Problem?" Stina asked.

"Another body. We've got to go back. Today."

32

The crime scene in the woods near the camping site was virtually a polar opposite compared to the previous time when Sven Julin had been found hanging. The last time it was dark and rainy and late. Now it was mid-morning and hot. Everybody had something to say about the weather. The heat was back. When the hell was this heat going to calm down? Even though there had been some big showers for a few days, no one had discussed that. The body had been found by two men who were staying at the Läjet camping site next door and were on a jog and had noticed something sticking out of the ground. It had looked a lot like fingers. On closer inspection, they had been exactly right. Both the joggers had been shocked and sickened, and one of them had called the police.

Kerstin Beckman had inspected the body, and the estimated time of death was much more difficult to access as the body was quite far along in the decomposition process. The air reeked of a rotten egg mixed with aged fish. Kerstin had said the person must have been dead around a month. The body had decayed and had started to liquefy. Kerstin had the stomach for this after many years dealing with dead bodies, but even for her, it was hard not to run off and vomit somewhere. Everyone else tried to stay as far away as possible. It was usually the smell that got to you, that sickening smell that would roll around in your nostrils. Breathing through the mouth. That was usually Kerstin's tactic if things were particularly nauseating. Kerstin surmised to herself that due to the extreme heat the body had probably taken longer to break down, because the flies, maggots, and other organisms couldn't act as well in this very warm weather. These insects had been at the face and combined with the breaking down of the body and the liquefaction that was underway, the face was not recognisable. The compelling thing was that if this person had been dead around a month, then it put this death extremely close to another. Sven Julin had been dead for around a month. Certainly, it was possible for the death to have occurred on a different day, but it also could have occurred on the same day. Was it possible to be around the same day and at the same time? That was also possible. Considering both bodies were found so close to each other, could the two people have been killed at the same time? Rain from the last few days had come flooding down, and with the natural soil erosion process, it had caused the body, or more specifically, the fingers, to be noticed. The body, however, wasn't dug very deep. The cause of death was pretty self-evident. There were two gunshot wounds, one on the left side, and one on the right side of the chest. One hung. One shot. Found very close to each other. Time of death very close. This case was quickly becoming a bigger problem.

Eva had remained at the office. She had not been feeling well, so Magnus and Rolf had come down to the crime scene. There were forensic technicians as well, scanning the area for anything of interest. Magnus wanted to know if any evidence had been found. Nothing had been found. Rolf looked at the body, then turned to Magnus who had his hands in his pockets.

"What the hell is going on Magnus?" Rolf asked.

"That's a good question. I have no damn clue."

Magnus and Rolf moved away from the body.

"First someone hung, then someone found nearby shot and buried. Then let's not forget our body in Luleå. Do you think all these are connected? I mean I don't see how they can't be now. Then we have someone who has murdered three people," Rolf said.

"I think we have got to stay focused on the Sven Julin murder."

"Why do you say that?"

"There's something missing in this Julin case; it's my opinion that if we solve that it leads us to the answer to everything."

"I hope so because now the pressure is on."

The usual procedures followed suit, and the next time anyone could expect any real answers was after an autopsy was done. A big concern was that if these murders were linked, the two in Varberg, and the one in Luleå, then three people were dead, and the investigation had yielded very little. It didn't look good from a publicity front. What the hell were the police doing? That would be the question from the public. The papers would have a field day.

Eva was sitting in a toilet stall. Eva hadn't needed to go to the bathroom. Peace and quiet was the reason to go to the toilet and shut the door. Eva had looked in the mirror when she entered the bathroom. Had she been eating properly? Her face looked as if it had lost weight but in an unhealthy fashion. Her skin wasn't a great colour, either. Her head felt like someone had slammed her into a filing cabinet. Eva thought of justice. It must be done in this world. That was the reason Eva had gotten into law enforcement.

So, people adhered to the laws of the country. And once again, Eva had thought back to the shooting. This problem was getting worse. Moving on and letting go was apparently the right thing to do, but it sure didn't feel like it. After flushing the toilet to create an impression she had needed it, Eva came out of the bathroom and walked back slowly to her desk in a big daze. Hair everywhere, her clothes messy. The cracks were starting to get more significant and more noticeable. Rana was at Eva's desk, as always smiling and looking in a great mood.

Nothing seems to get this woman down, Eva thought.

"Eva, I rang your extension, but didn't get you, so I came to look for you."

"Is there something wrong?"

"I have someone here who needs to see you urgently, or so she says."

"Who?"

"She says she's your sister."

Jonas Langberg was on his way home to grab a bite to eat. He wasn't that hungry in actual fact. He used this as an impromptu check up on Malin. She needed to understand that she couldn't leave the house all the time. Malin's latest stunt of wanting to go to art classes had angered him. She would be led astray by her friend. Jonas had never met her but had formed an impression of her as being a tart. A tart that would let anyone take her legs and spread them open. A cheap whore, whom Malin shouldn't be talking to. He at least had got Malin to come to her senses. Some tough love had been needed. Jonas had a busy day but was able to do a check-up on Malin. He would come up with an excuse for why he had time to come home.

Jonas had to blink deeply twice when he saw the driveway minus Malin's car. What the FUCK? His rage boiled over very quickly, and upon parking, Jonas banged his steering wheel four or five times as hard as he could. He picked up his mobile, which had been in the middle compartment between the two seats. Jonas was thinking of what he was going to hurl at Malin while he listened to the phone ring. Just wait, he thought. No answer. Jonas looked at the phone once he had hung up and screamed at the screen.

"FUCKING SLUT."

An angry cry of disdain. Jonas got out and went to the front door to open it. Locked. Jonas unlocked the door and flung it open. He couldn't believe that Malin had the nerve to go out and do whatever the hell she wanted when she should be at home. The disgrace of it all. He's working, and she's having a party. He may have to up the tough love a bit. It was out of love, a method to make Malin a better person. Maybe a belt would work this time. If she didn't exhibit this aloof behaviour, he wouldn't have to do anything. The bitch. It was all her fault. He wagered that was why he wasn't sleeping properly and why he went out a lot. And she had the nerve to ask him where he was on one occasion. She hadn't told him where she was going now, had she? Upon walking into the kitchen, Jonas found the note. He slid down the kitchen wall slowly until he reached the floor, reading how Malin was gone for good. Strangely Jonas didn't get angrier, he calmed down and in a delusional manner thought this was temporary. She would be back. She would definitely be back. In any event, Jonas came up with a backup plan. Two days. She had two days; otherwise, then he would have to go and find her. He could understand if she was stressed and made a knee jerk reaction, even though he couldn't understand what he had done wrong. However, to stay away longer than two days would be unacceptable. That would show that she had scant appreciation for all his efforts. Then he would have to go and find her and make her come to her senses. Jonas made himself a sandwich and was happy with his plan. He had a good idea where she had gone anyway if Malin didn't return on time.

33

They were in the hotel room, having that one drink. However, after that one drink, there had been an offer for one more. The man who had been partaking of cocaine at the pub was at it again, now in the bathroom. He needed a boost. The polite and still very drunk gentleman was sitting on the floor slouching against one of the walls. The lady who had accepted the invitation for the one drink was sitting on the bed, looking at her watch. The chat at the bar had been quite nice, but she was tired and showed very little interest in the conversation in the room. It was time to go. This man keeps insisting for her to stay and have one more. It had gotten on her nerves. The cocaine man returned from the bathroom, ready to make a move. He sat next to the lady on the bed and remarked that this had been a lovely evening. The lady just gave a friendly nod and a bland smile. The man put his hand on her leg softly and leaned in to kiss her. She dodged the kiss, and put her hands around him and gave him a business-like hug, hoping that would send the appropriate message. She wasn't about to do anything with this man, who now seemed like a douche bag. She, at last, had a great guy, one she was going to spend the rest of her life with. The man didn't seem to get the memo that this wasn't going anywhere. As the hug ended, he put his hand on one of her breasts. The lady pushed his hand off firmly and grabbed her bag that was next to her. She was a little worried as well as uncomfortable now.

"I have to go," she said very curtly.

The man was closest to the door, got up, locked it and gave her a stare that turned the slight worry into pure fear.

"Oh, no. You are not going anywhere until I'm finished getting what I want."

34

"This commissioner in Luleå, Arvidsson, he's screwing us around sir," said Magnus who had managed to get on the phone with the National Police Commissioner, Mikael Andersson. Magnus had respect for Andersson. He was firm as well as fair when it came to making decisions. And unlike Rosenberg, he was an old pro in the police force.

"First a detective from Luleå notified us of a case unsolved of a similar nature to the one on our hands now. We arranged that the case files come down to me so we could have a look and see if there was anything worthwhile that could aid us in our investigation, and possibly theirs, which they never solved I might add. The next thing I hear is that it has been changed, and we must send two of our team up there to look at the files and the old crime scene. So, between Rosenberg and this Arvidsson fellow, they are restricting myself and my team members a great deal from getting somewhere in this case," Magnus continued.

"Now Markusson, you do realise that you shouldn't really be discussing this with me. We have a chain of command for a reason," replied Andersson.

"Yes, I understand, but when the so-called people in charge are getting in the way to this extent, well then I thought you should hear about it. Rosenberg doesn't listen to common sense."

"Look, from what you have told me, you do have a point. I'll make sure you get that file for now, but when the case is over, it's to go back."

"Absolutely."

"And don't make a habit of going over the top of your superiors."

"Yes, sir. Not a problem."

The call ended, and Magnus was thrilled with the outcome of the call. Put that in your pipe and smoke it, he thought to himself. Those two buffoons would have to adhere to the NPC now.

The next thing Magnus did was to call Eva and Rolf to his office. Magnus made it very clear to continue on the Sven Julin case until there was some identification made regarding the other body that had been found that morning. Magnus had planned a game of tennis at around 4.00 pm. But he wasn't waiting till then. With it being Friday, Magnus needed to get out of the office and then go home early and perhaps have a little nap before going to tennis. He needed to rest if he was going to solve this case.

"I'm going back to the crime scene by the campsite. There's another angle to this whole thing we are missing," Magnus said to Rana as he walked past her as she was busily tapping on the computer and looking as if she was having a grand old time.

"I won't be back today. Have a good weekend," Magnus added.

Magnus managed to have a good two-hour nap at home, right after he had eaten some beautiful chocolate brownies Lena had made for her new post on her website. Magnus had hoped that he would have been able to have come up with something about this other angle of the case, but he had fallen off to sleep without doing any pondering, and once he woke up it was time to head off to tennis with his friend Henrik Gustafsson at the Varberg tennis club in Simhallsgatan.

Stina and Alexander landed back at Göteborg airport. The near two-hour trip had been tranquil. Alexander had tried to continue his novel but had found it difficult to concentrate. Stina had stared blankly into space, with a million thoughts whipping around in her head. For some reason, her aeroplane thought had not been a problem on the way back. Maybe it was because she was coming home. She had no idea. Alexander had left his car at the airport, and now they had about an hour's drive ahead of them once they had landed. Alexander had been given the case file after a call had come in from the NPC to say the department in Varberg had required these documents to progress. The Luleå chief of police wasn't impressed, but there was nothing he could do. The NPC was to the point. Hand the file over. The trip back was a reticent one. There was still probably something to be discussed, but neither uttered a word.

Maybe I should just say something, Stina thought.

She was interested in testing the waters in this relationship or whatever it could be called. Alexander's phone rang as they pulled up outside the office. As Stina opened the door and got out to say goodbye utilising a wave, she saw that someone by the name of Trina was calling. Even though she didn't quite know who Trina was, she felt a pang of something drop in her chest. Earlier in the drive, a text had flashed from another lady named Stella that Stina had seen pop up on Alexander's phone. That had bothered her a little, but another one was a bit much. She got in her car and shut the door and drove back to her apartment. Stina felt a little tear run down her cheek once she had gotten out of the car. Stina had no idea why she was tearing up. Once she got into her apartment, she was weeping. Why am I crying?

Two sets had gone by, and you would have thought with it being Friday evening and a good nap that Magnus would have been full of energy. The weekend always put a spring in Magnus's step. However, Magnus was tired. He and Henrik played tennis every now and again, and they were of similar strength. The first set had been close on the clay courts of the club. By the second set, Magnus's legs felt like jelly. Changing over, he started mumbling about his play.

The final score was 7-5 6-1 to Henrik. Magnus gave his Red Wilson bag a good crack with his racket before putting it in the bag. Henrik made a suggestion of a beer that sounded really good to Magnus. Maybe that would cheer him up.

"You played well today Henrik," said Magnus, sipping his beer, waiting for a toasted sandwich he had ordered.

"My forehand seemed to be hitting the mark today," Henrik replied.

"My legs just packed up in the second there."

"You did look a little tired. Pressure at work?"

"Things are complicated at work. We are getting somewhere, but I'd like to be getting there a lot quicker."

"Any luck then?"

"Not really, but we will keep chipping away."

"Have you ever thought of perhaps retiring or a career change? It must be a hell of a job day in day out. If I were in your shoes, I'd get out now."

"It's tough, but someone's got to do it."

Magnus didn't really have a problem with his job, considering he made sure to be flexible with his own hours.

"Of course, but you should really think about it. Enjoy life, spend time with Lena." Henrik said emphasising his earlier statement about retirement.

What's he on about? Magnus thought.

"I'll think about it. Now let's have a few drinks and forget about work," said Magnus.

"Good idea. I'll get the next round. This is the life. A game of tennis and beers. Chasing criminals, it's not worth it."

"Henrik, could we not talk about it? I don't really want to discuss my career now." Magnus had a sour look on his face.

"Hey, I'm just trying to help. I mean, there's not many who can do that job year in, year out." Henrik's tone was a little sharp.

"Henrik, I appreciate the support. I'll take it from here. Now let's have a drink and relax."

"Sure. I won't mention it again." Henrik gave Magnus a friendly pat on the back and got up to go and get two more beers.

Rolf Jonsson had lit two candles next to Camilla's grave, one on the left and one on the right of the headstone. After speaking to the groundskeeper the other day, he had felt much better, but now that familiar feeling of despair had returned along with a growl in his stomach. Rolf sat a while with Camilla, then finally said goodbye, and trudged off.

Stuff it, he thought as he drove past a pizza shop.

I'm having a pizza tonight.

He went in and ordered a large pizza. Cheese and salami. He had been to this pizzeria before and knew this pizza was top notch. He got his receipt which had an order number and decided to stand outside and get some air. This case was bothering Rolf. If all these victims were connected, then three people were dead, and the murderer was still out there. Eva hadn't looked well at work today either. She hadn't wanted to go to the scene. Rolf thought to himself that those signs could easily be early stages of burnout. Rolf went back inside and suddenly felt very vindicated at his choice of ordering a pizza. No burnout would befall him. Have a pizza and relaxing was actually really good for the mind. Order 126 was called. Rolf's order. He grabbed his pizza, which had a beautiful aroma coming out of the square box and headed for his car, which was parked around the corner. After a few steps out of the shop, Rolf gasped. A man was looking through a shop window, close to the pizza shop. It was Linus.

35

She had been held down and raped in vile fashion. She had been flung onto the bed, had a knife put against her throat, so close to her skin that she could taste it. She had been told to lie down and shut up. To shut the fuck up to be exact. Anything else from her and she would die. So, she lay there and took it, all of the pain and the anguish, that sick feeling of being violated. She took it all. The man had put the knife nearby her and proceeded to apply a condom and drive himself into her, letting out a sick sound of pleasure. A disturbing sound. He then grabbed her arms and told her to dig her fingernails into his legs. To scratch him. To be rough. He held both her wrists and made sure it was done how he wanted it. She sniffled and wept once or twice, trying to hide the tears due to the fear of what might happen to her because of the tears. The man just told her to grow up. The other man, who was still very drunk, had been looking straight at this act. He knew that this woman was in trouble, was being abused in disgusting fashion. He couldn't act. The alcohol had sedated his mind. So, he had to watch this too. Ten minutes. That was the length of the rape — ten of the worst minutes of the lady's life. The room, which was a pleasant room, had transformed into a dingy twisted place. Once the man had finished raping the help- less woman, he casually said he was going to get his smokes out of the bathroom. He took the condom off and headed towards the bathroom; her dignity shrivelled up in his hand. The man had mentioned the room door was locked, and the woman better not try anything because that would be the end of her. He said he would let her go once they had discussed her not mentioning what had happened to a soul. The woman nodded her head in a very submissive way. Once the man disappeared into the bathroom, a thought occurred to her. Her phone was in her bag next to the bed. If she could just lean over and text her boyfriend the address, he would be here in a flash. Slowly she lent over and in a slow-motion, grabbed her phone out of her white leather bag. She started punching in the message.

been raped help addr

The man was back, and now raged fill his body. He went towards to grab the phone, and the lady had no choice but to send what she had typed down before the phone was flung out of her hands.

At least it would alert her boyfriend to the atrocity that had befallen her. The man grabbed her wrist and squeezed very tightly. The lady writhed in pain, and stood up next to the bed, hoping that would ease the pain, which it did not. The man took the phone and let her wrist go and then switched it off.

"Stupid bitch," he said and gave her a powerful push.

The woman went across the bed, back first, trying to regain some balance. She ended up landing face to ceiling off the bed, the back of her neck cracking a marble coffee table. There was a horrible click when her neck hit the marble table. Instantly her whole body went limp. Her body slumped to the floor, lifeless. The man who had violated her went and checked her pulse. Nothing. Stone dead. The intoxicated man on the floor observed all this and appeared to sober up considerably when the rapist said to him that Maria was dead. Both were in serious trouble.

36

Rolf Jonsson had Linus in his sights. Linus was a thin man, and a stick compared to Rolf. A chase was something Rolf needed to avoid. However, what approach would work? He had another idea. A different type of plan. He went up slowly to Linus, who saw Rolf and looked a little startled. He had surely not recognised or seen Rolf from previous encounters; otherwise, he surely would have run.

"Can I offer you some pizza?" Rolf asked.

Linus looked rather puzzled.

"Why?"

"I'm supposed to be on a diet. And I didn't realise this pizza was so large."

Linus studied the man in front of him.

"OK." Linus sounded uncertain.

There were some tables and chairs inside the pizza shop, so Rolf motioned for Linus to join him inside the pizza shop. Linus surveyed Rolf and the pizza shop and nodded.

People who offer pizza are nice people—no

need to run. Your book is safe. Besides, it's hidden at the moment.

Once inside both sat down, and Rolf opened the box and let Linus help himself to a sliver. Linus's clothes were faded in colour.

"What do you think I do for a living?" Rolf asked Linus.

"Accountant."

"I'm actually....and don't be worried when I say this.... a policeman."

Linus carried on eating his pizza, but his anxiety shot up a notch. Linus was keeping more of an eye on Rolf now.

"I hope you know I haven't done anything. Unless you think I have, and then it would be hard for me to prove I haven't because I'm homeless. I couldn't prove much." After Linus's answer, Rolf set about calming Linus down, who looked at Rolf and took another piece. Rolf nodded happily towards him.

"I actually wanted your help. I know that your name is Linus and you often visit the camping site. My name is Rolf."

"Hi, Rolf."

Rolf wasn't quite sure how to continue. Linus seemed intelligent, but at the same time, also seemed to be a bit odd.

"I am trying to find a person who committed a crime."

"A crime? What crime?"

"A murder."

"That's a bad crime. Where?"

"Near the campsite."

"The campsite is nice. The people there give me food every week, so I often go past there."

"We saw you the other day Linus, and you ran away from us."

"Oh, I didn't see the faces; I just ran."

"Why didn't you run now when I came up to you?"

"You offered me pizza. Only nice people do that. People are always after my book, you know. I don't have it on me now because I'm not working. I'm taking a break, so I have put it somewhere safe."

So, what started as a normal conversation had begun to veer into the bizarre.

What's he on about, thought Rolf to himself.

"What book?"

"I.... I don't know if I should tell you. You might tell other people."

"You can trust me. Why would I want to do that? I could have grabbed you then Linus."

Linus weighed up that statement.

"Well, I don't think you would have let me have pizza if you were going to be mean. That doesn't make sense."

"No. No, it doesn't make sense."

"The book that I have. I have all the cars in

that book."

Here we go, Rolf thought. This sounded ridiculous.

"What cars, Linus?"

For the next fifteen minutes, in between Linus's forays into the pizza box, Linus explained a lot about his mysterious book. It sounded as if he wanted to tell someone about this book of his. Rolf let him carry on and then paused Linus. He asked if Linus wanted another pizza to share with him, and Linus said yes with half a full mouth. Rolf also offered him a drink to which Linus said he would have a Coke Zero. He was trying to stay away from sugary drinks.

Once the food was replenished, and refreshments were on the table as well, the conversation between Rolf and Linus continued. Before the interim, Linus had explained in extensive detail, that he would sit and record makes and models of cars that went past him in the location he was at. He had different areas he would go and sit and write down statistics about the vehicles. With a slice of pizza in hand, Linus continued on and on about his book. More details about records of cars, different brands, all recorded in his book, that he believed everyone wanted to prise from his hands. Rolf was following along but tiring.

"So why do you record all these things

down?" Rolf asked, and Linus smirked.

"To see which car is the best. Naturally," said Linus surprised Rolf hadn't realised this.

"You must have many things written down."

"Yes. I have tons. I have old books too. Lots of them ran out, so I had to buy new ones with some of the money I had."

If things couldn't get any more bizarre, then Linus started explaining "points systems." He would run contests when on certain dates and in certain spots, cars driving past him would collect points, and then after a whole bunch of these "events", you would find out which car was, in fact, the best.

"Why do you record cars?" asked Rolf.

"I like them. They are interesting - all the different types."

After more rhetoric about all these various ways of finding out which car was indeed the best, Rolf told Linus he understood what he was saying, and he didn't have to elaborate anymore.

"So, Linus, in this case, I'm working on I think maybe you have noted down something of interest in your book."

"Not doing cars today," Linus said.

"I realise that Linus. However, I'm not talking about today."

"I know that. I don't have my book on me. I write everything down."

"Do you think I might have a look at that book, to see if there is anything that might help our investigation?"

"I don't know. What if my book got in the wrong hands?"

"Tell you what, how about you come with me to my office at the beginning of next week. If I find anything, I'll make a copy of it and give you the book back. You don't have to decide now. Tomorrow is the weekend, so I'm not working. So, take some time to think, and we can meet up here on Monday, same time. We can have another pizza, and I'll bring some money. If you want to help, then I'll pay you."

"How much?"

"How about 1000 kronor?"

"OK, I'll think about it. I'll meet you on Monday and tell you then. Do you think we could have the same kind of pizza on Monday as well?"

"Yes, of course."

"OK. Good."

Linus got up and walked out, saying good-bye in the process. Rolf sat for a few more minutes. An interesting fellow, he thought. A bit round the bend, that was sure. Rolf got up and walked out of the shop. He was thinking about how to best put across that he was going to need to take 1000 kronor out of the tip-off kitty for possibly one page of Linus's book. Even though Erik Rosenberg had never given him any trouble, Rosenberg was a tight arse when it came to funds and budgets. No doubt, he was going to complain. At least Magnus would support. Not primarily for the evidence, but if Rosenberg moaned, he was sure to counter and back Rolf up. Rolf smiled gently. Could be some more fireworks on Monday, he thought as he managed to put his car into gear and set off towards home.

37

Eva and her sister Malin were on the couch in Eva's apartment. With tacos having become a favourite for Swedes on Fridays, they had followed suit. Eva had seen a Santa Maria tacos advert pop on her phone while she was looking around for news online that morning. What a catchy tune, she thought. Something that had put a smile on her face.

It didn't take long to cook the mince. Once that was done, both Eva and Malin filled their square tortilla tubs with their selection of ingredients, which included crème fraiche, corn, and medium spice taco sauce as well the mince. They each poured a glass of wine and began to sit down and eat. Eva quickly had some food sneak out of the square tortilla when she took a bite, the contents hitting the floor with a plop. Malin giggled.

"Every time I've had tacos that always happens."

"Damned tortillas."

Both laughed a lot about the food mishap,

maybe more than it was worth. However, partly because just being with each other, the sisterly bond on the mend, it made the funny moment that extra bit more enjoyable. The tension was being released. The elephant in the room had still not been brought up. Once the food was finished, Eva brought up the reason why Malin was here.

"So what happened with Jonas? Speak to me."

"I'm going to need another glass of wine."

With both Eva's and Malin's glasses refilled, Malin began to sift through the details of this quite dreadful relationship. The mental abuse, the physical abuse, and all the examples of both were given to Eva. The worst part may have been Malin's denial that all had been fine. Malin often had to pause, with a lump in her throat. She started tearing up but kept on going. She moved onto Jonas's medication problems as well.

"He was also taking so many damn tablets all the time," Malin said taking a big sip of wine.

"He would not sleep properly, so he would take tablets. Then he would struggle to get up so he would then try all kinds of energy supplements and drinks to wake him up. If he hadn't come and gone at strange hours all the time, then maybe that would have helped. God, how could I have stayed so long?" she added. Malin felt like a failure for being so stupid.

"What did he go out all the time for at

funny hours?" Eva queried.

"He would never say. I asked once, and he went mad and slapped me in the face. Asking him that was telling him I didn't trust him in his deluded opinion."

Eva had a thought. Probably nothing but maybe better to ask nonetheless.

"Where did he buy these pills from? Didn't a doctor prescribe them to him?"

"Oh no, he bought them online from some cheap pharmacy store outside of Sweden. He was very lucky he didn't get in big trouble for that."

"What were they called, these tablets?"

"Um, Dorm something."

"Dormicum?"

"Yes, how did you know?"

"Oh, I've heard of them before," Eva said.

Before Eva had time to digest this information further, there was a loud thudding at the door, cutting through the peaceful atmosphere.

Malin gave a start. Eva went and looked through the keyhole.

Two piercing eyes were looking at the door.

Jonas.

He hadn't been able to give Malin those two days to return. He was coming to take her home now.

38

Magnus had just flicked on the television to watch some tennis. He put his feet up onto a soft brown footrest and felt relaxed. He flicked on the TV and found some tennis. Magnus enjoyed watching the tennis pros on TV a lot. It was always interesting to watch the strategies players implemented in matches. He would often try them out. Magnus enjoyed supporting his fellow Swedes. There was a women's WTA tournament on the go, an event in Gstaad, Switzerland. A clay-court event. Magnus's favourite was clay-court tournaments. He felt that it was the ultimate test for a tennis player. Sliding around on red clay for hours. Socks thick with red dust. Long matches. A real mental battle. A Swedish lady from Stockholm, namely Rebecca Petersson, was busy playing Maria Sakkari from Greece.

Magnus quickly rushed to the fridge and got out a beer, and then got a glass out of the cupboard. Ahh. Friday night. Hopefully, Lena wouldn't interject his viewing. He went to see what she was doing as quickly as possible and found her reading a book on the bed, all three dogs joining her there. Perfect, he thought to himself. Straight back to the couch. He took a detour past the pantry and found a half a packet of chips. Magnus felt in a terrific mood. The match was very close and exciting. Magnus had begun watching when Petersson was down one set, 7-6, and also down 3-2 in the second set. The score had progressed from 3-2 to 6-6 — time for a tiebreaker. The rallies were long, with both women crunching their groundstrokes. The score reached 6-6 in the tiebreaker as well, so the match was tense and nail-biting. Petersson then managed to hit a forehand winner up the line, and then on the next point, executed a deft drop shot almost perfectly which Sakkari couldn't run down. Petersson had taken the set, and now the match was going into a final set.

Magnus let out a "come on" of delight at both of those brilliantly played points and couldn't wait for the final set. The standard of tennis was very high. Magnus's phone then started vibrating next to him on silent. Eva. He toyed with the idea of not answering it. Then he decided he better respond to it quickly. He would make sure this was a quick call.

Before he could say anything, Eva started rambling a barrage of words at him.

"Hey, hey, calm down and tell me what the

hell is going on."

"Its Jonas. Malin's ex. He's outside my apartment, and he's losing it. You need to come now. He looks like he might do something stupid."

39

The drive to Eva's apartment wasn't far, around a three-kilometre trip. Magnus was worried at the sound of despair in Eva's voice over the phone. He had heard a few stories about this Jonas Langberg fellow being an unsavoury person. Going nuts outside Eva's door was a touch more than unsavoury. Magnus ripped down the streets at pace. He arrived at Eva's apartment and started heading hurriedly to her apartment on the first floor, where there were already onlookers peering at the fiasco unfolding outside Eva's apartment door. Why hadn't anyone called about a disturbance? It appeared people were too busy watching what was going on or they had figured someone else would phone. Jonas was outside, screaming loudly in a rage, and banging on the door wanting to be let in to talk to Malin. Magnus hadn't realised that Malin was there. Now things made a bit more sense. The onlookers certainly kept their distance as Jonas looked unpredictable and capable of doing just about anything. Jonas peered across to where Magnus had stopped, and where a few others who were surveying the scene stood.

"What are you people looking at? Just fuck off inside," Jonas said and kicked the door leaving a minimal impression on what appeared to be a very resolute door.

Magnus decided it was time to sort this out. He started walking with purpose towards Jonas.

"Hey, hey, just take it easy," he said calmly to Jonas.

"Haven't you gone back to your apartment yet? Hurry up before I beat the shit out of you."

I don't live here you imbecile, Magnus thought.

Magnus looked at Jonas from top to toe. Not armed. No sign of a weapon. That was a green light to go. He was taking this guy down.

"Just go away," screamed Malin from inside, diverting Jonas's attention. That was Magnus's cue.

Magnus ran at Jonas. The next thing they were both rumbling around with each other on the ground. Jonas was a biggish man, close to Magnus's size and weight. Magnus shifted around and managed to land a punch, cracking Jona's right cheekbone. Magnus's ribs were slightly exposed, and Jonas countered with a sharp blow to that unexposed area. Both continued to scuffle, and both tried to get to their feet. The upper-cut sealed the contest. As Jonas went to get up, Magnus took a swing and connected Jonas with a thunderous crack that knocked Jonas right back. He quickly leapt onto Jonas and hit him once more. Jonas was almost out cold and was lying on the ground offering no resistance.

"Eva, it's safe to come out. Have you got cuffs on you by any chance?" asked Magnus.

Eva appeared outside, with Malin staying inside but peering out looking forlornly at Jonas on the floor. Eva did have some cuffs and duly handed them to Magnus. Magnus clipped them around Jonas' hands. Once Magnus's blows had worn off on Jonas, he started to squirm and wriggle.

"You can't do this to me," Jonas said frantically, becoming aggressive again.

"Let's see, disturbing the peace, assault, attempted break-in. A trifecta. A weekend behind bars should do you good."

Magnus gave Jonas a grin, got him to his feet and started walking him to his car, with Jonas swinging his shoulders back and forth. Eva grabbed her leather jacket and followed behind Magnus. Malin went back inside and duly locked herself in the bathroom.

40

A new week began, and Magnus was up early thinking. He was still trying to work out a different angle on this case, and it now had begun to irritate him. After pottering around in the kitchen and making quite a mess to put together breakfast, he had made some bacon and eggs with toast for himself and also thought he would surprise Lena with the same meal. He put Lena's food on a tray and preceded to take it into the bedroom. Lena was still sound asleep, and Magnus gave her a friendly prod to usher her awake. She woke up quite quickly and was surprised to see Magnus with some food in front of her.

"Room service," Magnus said. The dog's ears all perked up, and their noses were quickly drawn to the plate.

"Are you the lady that ordered the continental breakfast?" he added.

I think it's sort of a continental breakfast anyway, Magnus thought to himself.

"Well, yes I am," said Lena playing along.

She gave Magnus a little peck on his cheek and thanked him for breakfast.

"I'm off to work. You have a good day, Magnus said and left with Lena wishing him a good day too.

Better get out of here before I have to clean up the kitchen, Magnus thought.

Upon arriving at the station, Magnus saw Alexander and Stina having a chat outside the reception. Stina seemed to be in quite a jovial mood towards him. Almost like she was trying to impress him, which Magnus thought was odd for her. I'll bet they're banging each other, he thought to himself and gave them a good morning nod and smile. Magnus stepped into his office, to find Eva sitting on his visitor's chair, looking like she had something to say.

"Morning Eva. Time to go and chat with our friend Jonas."

"I've had a good think about something I found out about Jonas. Some information. I definitely think it could be something."

"What's it in connection with?"

"Well, the murder."

"What?"

"Well, Malin was going on last night about what kind of bastard Jonas is. She said something else."

"Can you get to the point?"

"She told me how Jonas was always going out at funny hours. Also, that he had trouble sleeping."

Magnus nodded and continued to listen.

"He was taking pills for this. Dormicum. The same type found in the victim's system. He's also very unstable. Malin said he's been beating her for a while."

Magnus thought about that for a second. It didn't really fit into what he had been trying to figure out, but it was worth looking into. There were quite a few things now pointing in Jonas's direction.

"That could be something. His behaviour would fit someone that could string someone up in a tree."

As Magnus finished saying that, Rolf appeared.

"Good news. I found Linus on Friday evening."

"Great. Where is Linus then?" said Magnus.

"Good job," said Eva.

"Well, I'm meeting him tonight."

"What on earth is going on? We have been bending over backwards to find him, and you just let him go," said Magnus furiously.

Meeting him tonight like two mates, Magnus thought. Come on, Rolf. Are you losing it?

"If you will just give me a chance to explain."

"I'm listening."

"I found him standing outside when I came out of the pizza shop. I offered him some pizza, and we started chatting. It turns out Linus is quite open to discussion with the right food. He's got this book where he keeps records of cars. Very detailed. Quite bizarre really."

"And?" said Magnus hurriedly.

"I offered him money for some of the pages of the book, the pages where he was recording cars on the day of the murder. If he was around the camping site at that time, he might have noted vehicles down that were going past in and around the time of the murder."

"That sounds promising. Well done, Rolf."

"Thanks. As I said, I'm meeting Linus this evening. Then first thing tomorrow I can look into this book."

"Excellent. Do you think he will pitch up?

"Absolutely."

"And one other thing. I need 1000 kronor from the tip-off kitty to pay Linus for his pages."

"1000 kronor?"

I think he *has* lost it, Magnus thought.

Rolf said nothing. He just nodded.

"I know Rosenberg won't be happy with taking that much money out for a hunch, but I think I'm on to something."

Of course, Magnus thought. Rosenberg is

going to hate that. His silly little budget will be thrown off course.

"A good tip-off is a good tip-off. Rolf, you take 1000 kronor, and another 200 for yourself to buy this Linus fellow something to eat as well as yourself. It's no problem."

Magnus stepped into the interrogation room. The weekend edition of the paper had torn the police to shreds. There was now another dead body in Varberg. Execution style, from what their sources told them. Plus there was a link to an old case. What were the police doing about this? The paper had criticised them heavily. Why had they not made further inroads? They had called Rosenberg up to try and get a statement to which he had said: "no comment" adding to the paper's criticism. The room was lit up quite poorly; a single bulb looked down on them from the middle of the room. Two black chairs made up the seating arrangements in the room, and they were hardly comfortable. Jonas had bags under his eyes. His hair was ragged, and he had an unpleasant look on his face. Proceedings got underway, and Magnus quickly got to the point.

"So, Jonas, I believe you have trouble sleeping? I do sometimes too."

"I don't care."

"Well, I do care quite a bit about your sleeping habits. I want to know about where you get your medication from, and I want to know the name of it."

"Why? I haven't done anything wrong."

"It's quite simple. You play the game, and you will be out of here quite quickly. You fuck around, and you are in for a torrid time."

Jonas felt trapped, but he didn't want to answer anything just yet. He had an idea.

"I, I want a lawyer. You can't question me if I don't have a lawyer here."

"Fine. You are entitled to that."

Jonas was left in the room by himself for a while. Magnus instructed that Jonas be able to get a lawyer appointed, and for him to be sent to his holding cell while that process was on the go.

Stina was back at her desk and was busy organising it. She had expected her desk might be a mess after being away. People often had a habit of dumping paperwork and files on it rather than sliding them into the appropriately marked trays. She had managed to negotiate her way out her apartment quickly that morning, having only checked the door three times, even though her head had felt like exploding on the way to work.

At least that is progress, she had thought on the way to work.

Stina's workspace hadn't been muddied by anyone flinging papers on it. However, she still set about tidying it. She moved the items a touch and then repositioned them a touch back. So, after a half-hour of fiddling and with the desk looking precisely as it had when she started, Stina took out all the papers and documents pertaining to the Luleå case and started going through it. The victim had been a Maria Ekberg, thirty-eight years of age. Cause of death had been a snapped C1 vertebrae and death was virtually instant. At the scene, which she and Alexander had visited as well, there had been nothing helpful in the way of evidence. In layman's terms, the case had hit a brick wall. The only bit of evidence found was some DNA retrieved under one of the victim's nails, as well as what had been identified as red paint. Those fragments had also been found under some of the victim's nails. However, as there wasn't even a remotely viable suspect, there was no sample to match the DNA against. Hopefully, Stina could unravel more details.

Eva had been digging deeply into Sven Julin's old employment. She had found out that he was the manager of a restaurant in Gustavsberg called Mat och Prat (Food and talk). Eva had managed to get someone on the phone in Gustavsberg to speak to her about Sven Julin. She got what she already knew. That he was a lovely man, calm, well mannered, blah blah blah. Same old story. Eva had obtained the number from the website, which had all the necessary things a restaurant website has - specials, the regular menu, and high definition pictures of what the food looked like. Eva wondered to herself why the majority of restaurant's food never looked that good when served. A thought crossed her mind. Where she had found contact details for the restaurant, she had recalled there were also details for the other restaurants around the country. Eva went back into the page and clicked the link.

Mat och Prat was a restaurant chain, with quite a few restaurants around Sweden. She had a small hunch about something. She went through until she got to L. There was a restaurant in Luleå. Now that wasn't particularly remarkable as with around 75000 people living there, Luleå was a big city up in the North. But Eva's thinking was maybe Sven Julin could have gone to Luleå on some type of business trip. If he was a manager maybe he went up there for some reason? Maybe there was a connection there. Eva had followed this line of thinking based on the apparent sudden desire for Sven Julin to move to Varberg. So, the question Eva wanted to be answered was whether Sven Julin had ever been to Luleå and if so when? Eva sipped from a glass of water at her desk, feeling happy in her endeavours. This case had been a blur thus far, with more distressing matters in her mind, but at least now she had put two and two together, which hopefully would propel this case forward.

Alexander had been told to find out more about the latest murder, the body in the ground, found in the woods, close to where Sven Julin's body had been found. Magnus had told him to gather information even though he believed this case to be secondary in importance to the Sven Julin one for the simple fact that Magnus believed that Julin's murder was the key. Magnus had offered nothing in the way of a viable explanation other than "an angle" he was figuring out. The first thing that Alexander pondered to himself was that the type of murder was very different. If this was the same killer, why on earth was this murder so contrasting? Sven Julin was a detailed killing, particular. This one was rapid. Gunshot. Dead. A shoddy burial, which was one of the factors why the body had been found. Of course, all three murders, if you include the Luleå murder, could be three different killers. Alexander let out a loud groan. So many damn questions, he thought. So many maybes.

Midway through the afternoon, Magnus was able, to begin with, his questions with Jonas, who now had acquired a lawyer. Magnus knew this particular lawyer, Håkan Karlsson, and from his experiences with him, had a low opinion of him. Magnus regarded him as the prototype for scumbag lawyers. After a nod to Karlsson, Magnus shut the door and went to sit down.

"Let's get to the point," said Magnus and continued.

"I'm not currently pursuing the behaviour of you, Jonas, from the other night. Your name has come up in a murder investigation, among other things, so you better start talking."

"What? Murder? I haven't murdered anyone. This is outrageous."

Karlsson touched Jonas on the arm and gave him a smile to say that he would handle it.

"I'm interested to hear what it is you have on my client," said Karlsson.

"Well, if he would just answer a few questions, then we could exclude him from our list of suspects."

"Please ask the questions, and I will advise my client whether to answer or not."

What a prick, Magnus thought.

"Does your client use the sleeping tablet known as dormicum?"

"He doesn't need to answer that, besides if he did, there are millions of people who use that tablet."

"Fine. We will come back to that. Where was your client on Thursday, July 7th, between the hours of 9 pm and 10 pm?"

Karlsson and his client conferred.

"My client doesn't need to answer that," said Karlsson.

"OK if you want to play it like that, its no problem. Let's look at the facts, shall we? In regard to the murder, a man was found dead. Hung, with dormicum in his system, the same substance your client takes to alleviate his sleeping problems. That in itself may not be too much as many people may use dormicum as you have said. However, when we start looking into Jonas's odd hours he would go out at night, it does beg a few questions. Now if we include a case your ex-girlfriend Malin Lindqvist has filed against Jonas this morning for many separate counts of domestic abuse, well all these things put together doesn't paint a pretty picture."

Jonas decided to speak up.

"Malin is lying! That bitch! I'll wring her neck." Jonas stood up and screamed. Karlsson looked at his client and then back at the table, head down.

"Did you wring Sven Julin's neck too?" Magnus said.

"What! No, no, of course not, it's just a figure of speech."

"Let me tell you where we are. I can guarantee I will get a warrant to search your premises. And believe me, my forensic team will tear your place apart. And if I find dormicum after it wasn't disclosed to me, given the other allegations against you, you become a prime suspect and will have to start with more intensive questioning," Magnus said.

Jonas suddenly sat down and was at a loss for words.

"Can I have a word with my client in private?" asked Karlsson.

"Certainly." Magnus got up and casually left the room.

Once Karlsson and Jonas were left inside the dingy interrogation room alone, Karlsson gave Jonas a grim look.

"Jonas, do you have any idea where you were on that day?"

"Yes, I do."

"Good. Tell them."

41

The woods by the school had to suffice. The two of them had taken the back entrance out of the hotel. They had put a hat over her head as well as a big jacket on her. She was put in between them, one arm over each of their shoulders. Should anyone bump into them, the plan was to act as if she had passed out from a bender of a party. Luckily, with it being so late, they stumbled into no one on route to the back exit and to the rapist's car rental in the parking lot. The parking lot was also unoccupied.

The culprit of this crime had decided to drive to some woods by a school. He had looked up somewhere discreet to get rid of the body which would expunge both of them, even though he wasn't bothered at all about the other man. As long as he was cleared. They arrived at the woods, which were not really woods per se, but more like a wooded area, with some trees and bushes. The second member of this party, the man that through too much drinking had landed up being in the proverbial wrong place at the wrong time, was now extremely pale and trying to control *his fast breathing. He had been prodded into a corner. This hideous incident had taken place in his room, and as the swine next to him had reiterated, they were both in serious trouble. What would the police have said? He had been drunk on the floor in addition to it being his room. It could have come down to word against word, and the process could well paint him in a light that would hardly be flattering. Once the papers got a hold of this, he would go through the mud. Even though he had realised the perpetrator was a repulsive human being, leaving the body in the woods in the way they intended was a way out. What else could he do? He would never forget this dark mistake, even though he couldn't pinpoint exactly what the dark error was. A woman was dead, so somewhere in all this he had made a grave mistake. Was it the lack of action? The drinking that had caused the lack of action? He hardly ever drank either. What a disaster. All he knew was that this was the only way to not land up without extreme consequences. Imagine what a jail sentence would be like. He was a good man, a pleasant man. Someone who always helped his family loved his family. He hadn't raped or killed anyone. However, he hadn't stopped any of it. And now he was covering it up. He looked at the man driving the vehicle and felt nauseated at the sight of this disgusting human being.*

The two men got out of the vehicle, and both accessed if there was anybody in the vicinity. Both had differing emotions inside of them. The rapist felt no remorse; he just wanted to get out of there as quickly as possible and resume life. Occupational hazard, if you will. The other man felt guilty, sad, and a wide range of emotions centred around how this had happened and that he now was in a position to do nothing about it, apart from being a coward. He had a type of hiking rope, on the off chance he would have had time to go and have a quick hike, which was now going to be used for another function — their staged suicide. The agreement had been made that they would hang the woman from a tree, and make it look like she had gone off the deep end. The snapped neck may indicate the women had gotten bad whiplash when hanging herself. Also, with both men being from out of town, and leaving that day, early in the morning, they would hardly be suspected as long as they were careful. The process to get the women in the suicide position was extremely difficult. First, the hiking rope was fitted around the branch of the se-lected tree, with the vehicle they had come in being the apparatus used to get her to that height. The roof was used to stand on to attach the rope. The rope slouched over the roof, to which both men then lifted the woman, so she joined the cord on the roof of the car. The tree that had been selected would leave the women dangling not too far above the ground, which would work well enough. They put the woman's neck through the noose and pushed her off the car slowly. There she now hung. The rapist grabbed a towel and started wiping the dead woman's body all over very carefully. He was trying to remove any traces of them being there. I wonder if he has raped before, thought the man. As he thought that, he felt the strong taste of bile hit his throat. He put his hand in his pockets and looked for his phone. He took it out wondering what the time was while the rapist moved the car onto a grass patch and came back and kicked some dust onto the place they had parked, hoping to destroy signs of their presence. It was a rental anyway, but better to leave no signs. 2.31 am. A piece of paper had stuck to the phone, obviously when the man had taken it out of his pocket. It wasn't important — just a receipt from a meal earlier in the day along with another few bits of papers. The rapist called for him to switch his phone off and signalled to the car. It was time to leave the scene. The other man stuffed the phone and the papers into his pocket. They drove off. All in all, they both felt relief for different reasons.

"We must never speak to each other again. We must move on with our lives and forget about this incident. I don't know you. You don't know me. We have never met," the perpetrator said.

The other man refused to do anything but nod. He was suddenly worried about what an outburst may do. Would he be the next victim? This bastard may be capable of killing him too. He just shut up. He would have to try and live the rest of his life trying to make up for what had happened. The car disappeared out of the woods slowly, and once they got on the main road, the perpetrator sped up a touch. The other man had listened to the rapist in the woods in regard to switching his phone off. The phone was now sitting back in his pocket. What he never realised, was that in his panic, his shaky hands had put the phone back in his pocket, along with the other bits of paper, barring one. The receipt from the earlier meal had missed his pocket and trickled gently to the floor. When ordering earlier that day, there had been a promotion on. Provide your name and number, and you would go into a draw to get your next ten meals free. This was redeemable anywhere. So, he had entered. The receipt he had dropped now had his details on them. The receipt now lay silently with the woman hanging from the tree, able to see what he had ordered for lunch.

42

Alexander was looking at the corpse of the gunshot victim recently found in the woods, very close to where Sven Julin had been located. Kerstin Beckman knew Alexander was not a fan of the general environment down in the morgue even though many times she had explained that with experience and years under the belt, the atmosphere would improve. Alexander still felt as creeped out as he had before. Out in the field, finding a body out in the open was fine. In the morgue, Alexander always felt off-kilter. Kerstin had called Alexander in to discuss her findings, as Magnus had wanted him to take the lead on this body, while the others were preoccupied with the other two victims.

"So how was your little trip, Alexander? All go well?" asked Kerstin.

"It was fine. We didn't get much out of it," Alexander replied.

"Stina seems switched on. How did it go working with her, just the two of you?"

Well, we slept together, Alexander thought to himself.

"No problems. Everything went well."

Kerstin moved onto discussing the body.

"Well, no prizes for guessing the cause of death. Two shots to the chest. One to the left, and one to the right. The left one was the fatal shot. The shooter looks to have been at fairly close range," Kerstin said.

Alexander nodded.

"We had a bit of luck regarding one of the bullets — the shot to the ribcage on the right-hand side. The bullet did not exit like the other one. So, I have sent the bullet off to the ballistics lab for analysis. We couldn't find the other bullet," Kerstin added.

"And ID of the victim?" said Alexander.

"Hopefully we will get a quick answer regarding that. As I'm sure you are aware, the man had no ID on him when he was found in the ground. So, I've sent off a DNA sample to offset against our database to see if we have him on there."

"How did the body, well, come to the surface?" Alexander queried.

"Well, soil erodes naturally. Also, if you add wind and rain, particularly like the downpours we have had recently, the topsoil will move a lot. The body wasn't buried very deeply either. It's no great surprise some fingers were sticking out."

"Well, I'll be off then. Let me know as soon as you have anything on the victim."

Alexander felt much better out in the fresh air. He got in his car and took off down the road shifting the gears quickly. His thoughts quickly turned to his evening plans. Visiting his father. He always dreaded it. Maybe things would go better this time? Who was Alexander kidding? He knew all too well it would be the usual. Alexander would have preferred to not visit his father, but then he would never see him. So, it was a question of losing both ways, losing big or losing huge. His mother had said Alexander should try and make the most when he went to visit, but Alexander was struggling intensely with that. Alexander increased his speed and hoped he would forget about his evening plans, at least for now.

Rolf strode along toward the sight of Friday's discussion with that quirky - to say the least - man Linus. Linus was there right on time. At first, Rolf saw no book until Linus ushered that he had something in a jacket he was wearing. Linus took the book out after giving the area a once over. The book looked like a novel that had been read a good few hundred times. Rolf promptly put out his hand, which had a white envelope in it. The envelope contained their agreed-upon fee. Would Linus accept it? Linus grabbed and opened the top of the white envelope and flipped through the notes, quickly adding in his head. He smiled and took out a greasy hand. He wanted to shake Rolf's hand. Rolf shook. They went into the pizza place, Linus first. Rolf was behind rubbing his hand against his pants.

You see, the police need my book. That's how valuable my book is, thought Linus, who had a proud feeling running through his veins.

Both Rolf and Linus then embarked on pizza. Rolf was happy he had been given 200 kronor for the meal. He *had* to use it, which meant he could get a pizza for himself. This was a case related meal. It wasn't like he was not trying to eat a better selection of foods. This was needed for the task at hand. To top off the negotiation process. Once they had sat down, Linus went into enormous and unnecessary detail about his book with cars, repeating many things he had spoken about in their previous meeting. Please not again, thought Rolf. After what felt like a lecture, Rolf explained he needed to copy the applicable pages, to which there were only 2, for the night in question. Linus could accompany him to his office as Rolf had mentioned during their last meeting.

"I don't know if I want to go to the police station. I've heard there are dirty cops. They might lock me up or even worse, kill me!" Linus exclaimed.

"There are certainly no dirty cops where I work so you can rest assured you are safe with me."

"But if there are dirty cops then you wouldn't know either. These guys lie low."

With some more debate on the apparent corrupt cop contingent, Rolf could see he was getting nowhere.

"Tell you what, how about I get you one more pizza. While you sit here, I'll quickly go and copy these pages. Then I'll come back with your book. Would that be OK?" asked Rolf.

Linus sat for a minute, finger on lip, thinking, and then looked at Rolf.

"Well, OK. That would be fine. A coke zero too please."

Jonas Langberg walked out of the police station with his lawyer Håkan Karlsson looking smug. Eva peered out of her window at the two while they were in the parking lot and couldn't quite make head nor tail of why Jonas would be allowed to leave so quickly. Eva went straight to Magnus's office and wanted an explanation. Magnus was on the phone, to Lena, by the sounds of things.

"Well, if the cut is worrying you it's better

to take her to the vet to get it patched up."

Silence followed with Magnus listening to Lena's response.

"Yes.... I know.... Yes......Yes, I'll pick up some food. Just go and sort out the dog. OK. See you a bit later".

Magnus hung up and looked at Eva.

"The silly dog was playing with the others and evidently managed to cut herself.

"Which one?"

"Which dog? Smilla. You know, the smaller one."

"Yes, I'm aware of your dogs," said Eva, who always received a heroines welcome whenever she went over to the house.

"Anyway, I told Lena to take her to the vet."

There was a slight silence, and Magnus then asked Eva what it was that she wanted.

"Why has Jonas walked out of here just like that?"

"Thankfully, his idiotic lawyer did something bright for once. He got him to start talking."

"And? Tell me."

"Well, he had an alibi for the night of the Sven Julin murder. Simple as that. It does appear that his alibi checks out."

"So, what was the alibi?"

"Do you want to know?"

"Yes, absolutely," said Eva.

"Well, he was with a woman. He gave me her number. I called her, and she confirmed that he was there. Stayed there for most of the night. Left the early hours of the next morning. She was actually annoyed at Jonas as well, telling me that he had promised to leave Malin. Apparently, this has been going on for a while."

Eva said nothing for a few seconds. Magnus could see Eva was fuming.

"You know I told Malin right from the start, that this...bastard was no good."

"A real piece of work."

"Any chance that this woman is lying?"

"Doesn't seem like it when I spoke to her. We have nothing else on him, so unless we find something else out, we can't do anything."

"What about the beatings? He needs to go down for that."

"Eva, you know as well as I do that Malin has not filed a single charge. In the event of her doing so, sure, we could do something, but I think I have come up with a better solution."

"What did you say now?"

"I said that Malin had reported his abuse to us. Also, I said that before I officially made a charge, I suggested that we work out something that would help Jonas in the long run, and something where he would avoid going to court and receiving jail time."

"Which was?"

"I said if he never bothered Malin again, then I would speak to Malin, and get her to withdraw any complaints."

"But Magnus, you can't go around and make up your own rules."

More like a suggestion, thought Magnus.

Eva felt decidedly uncomfortable.

"He agreed. Malin won't see that bastard again, and they aren't my rules. She hasn't laid a charge!" Magnus said.

"How do you know he won't just pitch up at my apartment again?"

"Well technically he could, but deep down he knows he's abused her a lot and it wouldn't be hard to prove. I also mentioned that I would drag him through the mud should he try that. He looked worried. I also threw in some exaggerated stories about how bad the prisons are now. And that women beaters aren't among the popular groups behind bars now."

"But that's such nonsense."

"Of course it is, but he doesn't know anything about the prisons here. I have a feeling he would rather avoid another run-in with our police department."

There was palpable silence.

"It's up to you what you want to tell Malin," Magnus said.

"I'll think about what to say," said Eva and stormed out.

Magnus put his feet up on the desk. He took out his Mons Kallentoft novel.

Time for a break, Magnus thought to himself.

Eva decided to be honest with her sister Malin when Eva arrived home that evening. She had told Malin to stay away from the police station while this matter was being handled, to which Malin had consented. Eva had thought on her way home in the car that by giving Malin all the unsavoury details, that in actual fact, in the long run, it would be better for Malin. Malin could move on and would never go back to Jonas. Malin had said it was over, but Eva still had a sneaky suspicion that it was possible that Malin may be persuaded by Jonas to move back and mend the relationship. She had stayed with Jonas for a good while and endured plenty of abuse before managing to leave, so best to be on the safe side and reveal Jona's activities with the other woman. The emotions in the room had been varied during this conversation between Eva and Malin, which they had during dinner. Eva explained how Jonas had been questioned regarding murder and that it was now virtually clear he had nothing to do with it, which made Malin relieved. Then the tears began flooding out when Eva dropped the news about Jonas's involvement with this particular lady. Eva went around to Malin's side of the table and took her to sit on the couch and let Malin put her head into her chest and cry as much as she liked. Malin's tears had been the realisation that Jonas was indeed a horrible man, and indeed the relationship was done and dusted. Malin many times, had not wanted to admit to herself that Jonas was as bad as the things he had done to her, both physically and mentally. The penny seemed to have at last dropped, and it was as if all of the horrible things he had done to her came together at once and forced Malin to fall apart and ball her eyes out. Eva felt genuine sympathy for Malin. It was not a case of who had been right or wrong regarding Jonas. It was about Malin's life being rekindled. It was about Malin moving on and finding happiness, something that she hadn't had a glimpse of for a long time. She wanted to see Malin's blue eyes sparkle again.

"What's wrong with us? Alternatively, what the hell is wrong with men? We can never meet anyone half decent, can we?" said Eva.

Both Eva and Malin chuckled at this, with Malin sniffling away the tears.

"Things can only get better. Come on, let's finish off our meal and watch some TV," said Eva.

They both returned to their chicken and bacon pasta and were content to continue where they left off, despite the food now being cold.

Round and round thoughts of Alexander went through Stina's head. She was busying doing her dishes, and her magical thinking was back and causing her some of the usual and unwelcome problems, but to a greater degree. In Stina's one-night escapade in Luleå with Alexander, Stina had felt something. She was unsure of what that had been. Maybe she wanted another escapade; maybe she wanted a decent relationship to form. Whatever it was, there had been a feeling of something. A warm feeling that had made her feel better about herself. Now, back at home, her OCD was going through the roof. She had finished the dishes and put them in the cupboard, but she would have irrational thoughts that they were not done correctly. Then Stina did them again. Then Stina would have thoughts as she put them away again that Alexander thought she was an idiot, that he was not interested in her. Also, because Stina would have those thoughts exactly when she put away the now exceedingly clean dishes, she would redo the dishes in question. She said to herself that she would do them once more, and if she had any more of these thoughts, she would just ignore them and put the dishes away. So, in essence, what had started happening was that Stina was redoing the dishes so she could ignore the thoughts if they came again. It made zero sense in what she was doing.

By doing them again, I'm not actually ignoring them, Stina thought.

I have to not do them again to ignore these thoughts, she carried on thinking to herself.

What the fuck is wrong with me?

Eventually, after another half hour, Stina had finished the dishes and immediately crumpled onto her bed and stuck her head under the pillow.

Magnus slouched on the couch after another long day. With Jonas innocent, the case had hit another wall. At least there had been some clouds today, and he had managed to read another thirty pages in his book. Magnus had briefly greeted Lena and the dogs and had been very happy to see Smilla was fine. Smilla had a small bandage over the wound she had been taken to the vet for. Once Magnus hit the couch, he drifted off to the land of nod. Lena came to watch a program about interior design while dinner was cooking. Magnus kept half waking up and drifting off. His dreams, funnily enough, were occupied by Lena and himself discussing colour schemes for some mansion they had just bought. Then there was a knock at the door, and a man from Skatterverket tax office barged in, saying he knew Magnus was only a cop and there's no way he could have bought this place fair and square. Then his son, Sebastian, appeared from the bathroom saying he had flushed all the drugs away. He promptly woke up, very startled and bewildered. Lena asked if he was OK, to which he replied that he was fine. He watched the rest of Lena's television program, but this was hardly relaxing. Back and forth, thoughts of the case and what to do went through his skull.

It's this damned case, he thought to himself.

I can't relax properly.

I have to figure this out.

43

Magnus left first thing in the morning to go to work and wanted to get there earlier than usual to go through a few notes. He was going to get everyone together and have a meeting so they could start from the beginning and pick this case apart. As everyone made their way into work, Magnus quickly informed them of the meeting. Magnus wanted everyone to meet in half an hour. Everybody got to the meeting more or less on time, and the meeting got underway fairly quickly, which at least was a positive start to the day. Magnus explained he wanted to go from top to bottom and began to address everyone while making notes on the whiteboard with a black marker, the customary procedure.

Magnus had summarised the following to everyone. That Sven Julin had been found hanging in a tree just off the camping site, in which it had been ascertained that it was a murder. There had hardly been a cavalcade of evidence. Some red paint found under the nails, as well as a type of sedative in his system, but not a big volume. There was a slight lead in regard to a half-legible tyre track that had been found in a remote entrance to the woods. The problem with this had been the multitudes of possible vehicles in the database that the track could have belonged to. Magnus remained hopeful of narrowing that number down. Alexander interrupted the proceedings saying that he had got some info about the anonymous phone call made to the police alerting them of the victim in the first place.

"I managed to get some information from the phone company, but it was rather limited. The call came from a public phone booth in town, around seven kilometres away from the body. I stopped following up there because there's nothing else I could have found out about the call that would have helped. A public phone could have been anyone," Alexander said. Magnus gave him a nod and continued with his summary. Magnus noted a man named Linus, had become someone of interest as he frequented the camping site a lot and always carried a strange book with him, where he noted down things about cars. Rolf had managed to get copies of Linus's book for the day of the murder. His book may have had some information in it that may help with identifying the vehicle that left the tyre tread. Rolf wanted to say something but decided to wait for the end of the meeting. Eva intervened with an interesting statement. Sven Julin's wife, Viveka Julin had called on her arrival at work and informed her that she had found a bottle of sedatives, which she confirmed as Dormicum, in one of Sven's desks. So, she had told Eva surprisingly that he may have been taking something. However, she had not known about it.

"OK suppose the victim was taking this medication. What does this mean?" asked Magnus to everybody.

Everybody had their five cents worth on this bit of information, to which everyone's comments were somewhat similar. That Sven Julin had taken the medication as he probably usually did, the low amount in his system backing that up. Other than that, there wasn't much to add to the subject.

The place where the killer had grabbed Sven Julin had never been discovered, but it was believed to have been where Sven Julin taught his lessons. However, when Rolf had checked the premises, he had found nothing at all.

"OK, moving on," said Magnus.

Sven Julin had been hung by a generic hiking rope, another proverbial dead end. The client list had offered something interesting. Magnus had received a list of Sven Julin's clients and had phoned every one of them, and one of them had provided useful insight. She had mentioned Sven Julin had helped her with some personal problems, and Julin had mentioned he had struggled with something over the years. What?

"I wonder if whatever Julin had been struggling with started this whole mess," said Magnus. Possibly why he was taking medication, Magnus thought.

Eva quickly jumped in.

"I think there's a link between his murder and the Luleå one. I looked into Julin's old work," Eva said.

"He worked at a restaurant chain - Mat och Prat in Gustavsberg. They have restaurants all over the country, and I noticed that they have one in Luleå," she added.

Both Alexander and Stina had flashbacks to that trip, and both seemed to have images of their sexual escapade dancing around in their heads when Eva mentioned Luleå.

"Well we need to check if our Mr Julin ever went to Luleå on business," said Magnus.

"I contacted an executive, and he was going to call me back," Eva said.

"He better hurry up. Phone him again as soon as we are done here," said Magnus.

The meeting then shifted and focused on the unsolved Luleå case. Around fourteen months prior, Maria Ekberg, thirty-eight, had been found in a tree, hung. Her position was very similar to that of Sven Julin. The cause of death was markedly different, however. A fatal blow to the C1 vertebrae snapped her neck and caused what would have been virtually an instant demise. The rope she had been hung with was similar to the rope used on Sven Julin. Maria Ekberg had also had red paint under her nails. There was no other evidence to speak off other than fragments of skin found under one of Maria Ekberg's nails. She had sex shortly before her death, but there was nothing conclusive suggesting anything forced. The Luleå police had a DNA sample of the skin, but that was not in the database, and there were zero suspects. The consensus in the room after speaking about this was that even though the cause of death was different, there was way too much in common for it to be a coincidence.

Surely there was a link between Julin and Maria Ekberg. But what? Also, why the big gap in between murders? The Maria Ekberg killing was also shrouded in mystery. She had gone to a party with her friends, stayed for a while longer after her friends had left, and then vanished after that. Until she had been found. Her friends had mentioned to the police at the time that she had been seeing someone for a few months. A new guy in her life. She had had many breakups, and finally, she seemed like she had found that special someone. However, she had not told anyone who it was, nor had anyone seen the two of them together. The reason for that was to take things slow and steady. Maria Ekberg had been very nervous about this relationship not working out, so she had kept the relationship very hush-hush. In light of the tragedy, the boyfriend was someone who would be a person worth speaking to. However, no one knew who on earth it was. The bartenders that night also hadn't been of much help, as it had been busy. A couple of them vaguely remembered Maria Ekberg, but there wasn't anything else they could say of any significance. She had been chatting with various people, and certainly, nothing out of the ordinary had occurred. Nothing strange when leaving either. She had walked out the door on her own. The meeting then went onto the most recent person that had been found dead. This was different. A male, unknown name, to which they should have an answer to shortly that had been shot and buried.

Many in the meeting thought that this murder had nothing to do with the other two. Not every murder had to be connected, did they? The timing was odd, however. Magnus suggested after this lengthy discussion, for everyone to get back to work, and reconvene once the identity of the unknown gunshot victim was found. There was also a toxicology report pending, as well as trace and ballistics reports but they were expected to take a while longer.

"Does anyone have anything to add?" asked

Magnus.

"I have," Rolf said and continued by holding up some papers.

"I'd like to discuss our friend Linus's book. I think his book may prove to be very useful."

44

Rolf Jonsson stood up from his chair and proceeded to hand out copies of the page of Linus's book and then elaborate on what he had come across. Rolf mentioned Linus had kept intricate details about cars in his book. Linus never seemed to say no to a slice of pizza either, but Rolf didn't say that. Rolf had only worried about the two pages, namely the pages containing information from the day of the murder. From Rolf's discussion with Linus, he tried to pass on the information and did mention that the reason for the book was "rather out there."

Linus had an evident fondness for cars and spent many many hours looking at cars and writing them down. Linus had explained that depending on where he sat to watch these cars, he would note down details of the vehicles as they drove past him. If it was a busy area, details were a bare minimum. He didn't have time to write everything down as the cars would come and go too quickly for him to keep up with. But if it were a quieter spot or quieter time, then he would put down just about every detail. He had said he preferred detail, so he tried to go for the more tranquil places. This was where it got interesting. Linus liked these quieter places because then he could even include a car's number plate. Linus did like going to the camping site and sitting outside of there or just up the road. There was also a bonus of a meal at least once a week out of them as well. The good news for everyone was that Linus was around on the evening of the murder. He was in the middle of an "event" and to keep things simple and also not to sound completely insane, Rolf merely stated Linus had told him that cars collect points over a specified period based on make and model. The good news was his notes included number plates for the day of the murder.

Definitely has a screw loose, this guy, Magnus thought.

The notes in Linus's book were quite untidy; the proverbial dog's breakfast so to decipher it presented a bit of a challenge. This event had run from 8.24 pm the evening of the murder to 10.39 pm. Two hours and fifteen minutes. When Rolf had chatted with Linus about the evening in question, Linus hadn't remembered anything in particular or seen anything out of the ordinary. He had also told Rolf he had sat at the top of Strandbackavägen, the road leading to

the woods and campsite and recorded his findings from there. Where Linus sat was still quite
far away from both the campsite and the woods,
so it was no surprise Linus hadn't seen anything
strange. In that time, there had been twenty-
eight cars that had come down that road. Alexander wondered even with it being quiet how
on earth Linus was able to note down details so
quickly. It didn't take long for a car to go by. Rolf
had asked Linus this very question. He had some
rough paper to scribble down things and then
transfer that into his book. He also said he had
a "very good memory" and always made sure to
write the number plate first as that was the hard-
est part.

"OK, I've heard enough. Eva - cross-reference all the number plates on that evening of
the murder in Linus's book with the possible tire
matches in the database with Stina. Even though
Linus has written down makes and models, the
number plates will give you the *specific* make and
model and then you can go from there."

The meeting continued, with Magnus asking everyone what they thought had happened
based on everything so far. There was a lot of
talk of some type of revenge, that Maria and
Sven were involved in something together and
that someone had taken them both out. Magnus
sat there thinking while comments went up and

down the meeting table. What about this other body then? Maybe this was the third person involved in whatever Maria and Sven had been up to. Of course, there had been no proof of Sven and Maria even knowing each other. Maybe the murderer was also involved in something with Sven and Maria and was screwed over? Suddenly Magnus interrupted everyone.

"I've got it," Magnus said.

"Got what?" said Alexander.

"We've been looking at this all wrong."

"How so?" asked Rolf pushing his glasses in with his index finger.

"Well, we have been going on Sven and Maria possibly been in cahoots in some type of way. That's not it."

"What do you think then?" Eva asked.

The man with all the answers, she thought. Let's hear it.

"I think Sven did something that got Maria killed. Did he kill her? No, I don't think so myself. But he somehow had something to do with it. And somebody close to Maria knows this and took matters into their own hands. So, they weren't involved in something together. Sven was involved in Maria's death."

The meeting room was quiet for a second. Magnus continued.

"Alexander, I remember you saying that there was a man in Maria's life."

"Yes, but no one knew him. They had been keeping their relationship a secret."

"Sounds like they both were very scared of being hurt again. Then Maria is murdered. How do you think this boyfriend would react?"

"Not too good," Alexander said.

"What that lady said to me also makes a lot more sense now," Magnus said.

"What thing?" asked Rolf.

Rolf, please keep up, Magnus thought.

"That lady. The one who had the piano lessons. She told me that Sven had said he had been struggling with something for a while when this lady mentioned that she had personal problems."

"That answers my question about why Sven packed up and moved so quickly. Maybe it was a way of trying to put things behind him. Even though he didn't live where Maria was killed, it seems like maybe this was his way of a fresh start," Eva said.

"We need to find out if Sven went up to Luleå on business," Magnus said.

"I'll follow up right away," Eva said.

Alexander had been deep in thought.

"There's one thing I don't understand," Alexander said.

"What's that?" asked Magnus.

"Why did this killer lead us to that warehouse? That was risky even though he got away."

Everyone was quiet again, thinking of

what the explanation was to that good question.

Magnus then looked at the whole table ser-iously.

"It was a diversion."

"To lead us away from the evidence?" Rolf asked.

"To buy himself time. Because he's not done."

45

The time is now here. The last part of my journey for revenge is here. Once all is complete, it remains to be seen how I will feel. I don't foresee myself suddenly being happy again, and that all will be right with the world again. I will still be miserable and have a deep void, and that is something I will have to live with. Where do I go after my deeds have been done? What do I do? That is a good question. One I can't answer now as I write this. But at least one thing I do know is these two bastards will have been punished. My destination is not that far away, an easy drive of thirty kilometres to Falkenburg. I won't rush. I'll take it all in. On the way, I will have the comfort of knowing it will all be over, my quest as I call it, completed.

46

About an hour later, Magnus wanted an update about the person from Mat och Prat that was going to call Eva back regarding Sven Julin and any information the man had about him and a possibility that he had been to Luleå before for any business. Eva said he had failed to call her back. Magnus said he wanted the number. It was high time that this person got the message that the police didn't have time to wait for him.

The gentleman from Mat och Prat had been quite helpful once Magnus told him that he was "impeding a homicide investigation" and that if they were to get the local police to come down with a warrant, no work would be done for a few days. With the threat of their business being halted, even though it was just an idle one, the man got into gear regarding the speed at which he could get information on Sven Julin. He explained to Magnus that the head office would have any business-related trips in the accounts with a basic itinerary. Magnus was promised an email regarding Sven Julin's business trips very shortly. With that out of the way, Magnus went to grab some coffee. His pod machine had become quite the popular item, and everyone followed the unwritten rule of bringing your own pods. Magnus kept a box behind his desk on a counter and pulled out an Americano pod. He organised himself his freshly made coffee and went back to his office. He gave himself a few minutes to sit and drink his coffee while thinking more casually about the case. After a few minutes, Magnus decided to open his email to check if he had gotten anything from Mat och Prat. Nothing as yet.

Rolf came into Magnus's office.

Can't I just be left alone for two minutes, Magnus thought.

"I was wondering...."

"Yes, what is it?" Magnus barked.

"Well, I left my packet of coffee pods on the kitchen counter this morning, so I wondered —,"

"Yes, just take a fucking pod and get on with your work," Magnus moaned as he heard his email sound.

Magnus had received three new emails. One was from Svenska Spel, reminding him of the evening's sports events he could bet on.

Keep, Magnus thought.

The second one was an advert from Ikea about savings on outdoor furniture.

Delete.

They can shove their savings up their backside, Magnus thought, still sour after the dealings with the Ikea bigwig Kjell Sandell.

The extremely positive news was that the third email Magnus had received was about Sven Julin's travel information during his time at Mat och Prat. It had been scanned to him and was in .pdf format. He quickly printed all of it out. He went straight for the dates in question, namely the day before the murder of Maria Ekberg in Luleå, the day of, and the day after. It didn't take very long to find what he was looking for. It stuck out like a sore thumb. During his time with this company, Sven Julin went on business up to Luleå only once. The body had been found early in the morning around 6 am, and in the case notes it had stated that death had occurred several hours before it had been found. Sven Julin had been in Luleå then and had left not that long after the body had been found.

Wow, thought Magnus. This is massive. What the hell happened up there?

Magnus went to see Eva right away and told her his findings.

"What? That's huge," she said.

"We need to call the hotel Julin stayed at. See if they remember him. Maybe somebody remembers something strange."

"That's a bit unlikely."

"Yes, but it's worth a shot."

So, what exactly had happened in Luleå? Had Sven murdered Maria Ekberg? If so, why? And to do it while up on a business trip, well that seemed risky. Or did it? If it ever came back to him, that was an alibi - business. The company would verify that he was there for exactly that. Then the next question was who killed him? And who was left to kill? The killer's goose chase had been for time because this wasn't over. So, whoever this next proposed victim was — how did they fit into everything? Or was there more than one potential victim lined up? Magnus called Kerstin Beckman immediately.

"Hello," Kerstin said.

"Kerstin. Listen I need you to pull some strings. I need a DNA analysis done right now."

"Magnus, that's going to be difficult."

"Just try. Make up a story. Lie. Do whatever, but I need this now."

Kerstin heard the urgency in Magnus's voice.

"I'll think of something. What do you need compared?"

"I need DNA compared between Sven Julin and the DNA found on the victim Maria Ekberg, the lady in the Luleå case."

"I'm on it."

"Call me as soon as you have the results."

Within the information that Magnus had been given about Sven Julin's business trips, it contained the hotel name of where Sven Julin had stayed on that trip to Luleå. The Best Western Savoy. He quickly searched and found the number and wasted no time in dialling it. He was put through to the manager, which took a few minutes, in which he had to listen to some utterly dreadful musical tune. Once he spoke to the manager and explained he was a chief detective, and he needed this information, the manager was helpful. He said he would find the relevant details and call him back as quickly as possible. Magnus went out of his office, gulping down his leftover coffee, which was now ice cold. Magnus then went to see what was going on with the tyre treads and found Stina, who was working on them. As usual, her desk was in perfect symmetrical order.

Even though he found Stina a bit strange, he was very fond of Stina. Not that he was going to tell her that. She was really good. And she worked her socks off. Never a complaint.

"Stina, an update on the tyres please," Magnus asked hurriedly.

"Bad news I'm afraid at the moment. The servers to the tread as well as other databases are down. There is network maintenance while they fix the problem."

"When on earth will it be fixed?"

"Shouldn't be long."

What a load of crap, Magnus thought.

It took around two hours for the manager of the hotel to ring Magnus back. The manager confirmed the stay of Sven Julin on those dates. The only other thing he could add was attached to the invoice; there was a slip noting the purchase of two beers and then reversing the charge to create a nil balance. What was the slip for? The manager had a good recollection of having to calm a guest down when he went on a tirade about the shocking service. There were never many scenes, but most of the staff remembered this one, even though it was long ago. There had been some mix-up in the kitchen, and two men had been waiting twenty minutes for their food. The manager couldn't remember the exact details but could recall this incident because the man was so rude. It then went from bad to worse. This man, as well as the other man at the table, had been comped their drinks while waiting. However, this "lunatic" had expected his meal would be for free as well as his acquaintances to which the manager had explained that it would not as they hadn't messed up the food. It was merely late which they were very sorry for. The other man at the table had said not to worry, but the man who was angry didn't let up.

The man proceeded to go berserk and said that both he and the other man at the table didn't want their food, and they had better not receive a bill for anything. The hotel had not made the food so to balance the books and stock, printed up a till slip denoting the nil balance. Who was who then? Was Sven Julin the one going mad, or was it his companion at the table doing that? The manager couldn't say for sure, but what he did say he would do was to find out the name of the second member of this table and then try and recall who was who. Magnus asked him to hurry up. He wanted to know who this other person was. Just as he put the phone down, Alexander came into Magnus's office.

"Doesn't anyone knock anymore?" Magnus shouted.

"Oh, sorry about that. I got the identity back on the buried gunshot victim," asked Alexander.

"And?"

"It's Felix Corvin. The guy who used to hang out with your son."

47

Everyone had heard about Magnus's issues with his son as well as the story of Felix Corvin threatening his wife Lena at home one night. These stories had a way of spreading through the office like forest fires, and by and large, everybody had a good idea of what had happened. Alexander had heard his version from Eva, who had the real facts, as Magnus had spoken to her about it and had also filled her in about the aftermath involving kicking Sebastian out. She had been the only one he had talked to about this scary incident. Magnus, over the years, had been aware that various people knew about it, and at a meeting one day had said to everyone they didn't have to pretend they didn't know about it. He knew they knew. He had then said he hadn't seen his son, Sebastian, since then.

"Oh, I see - that piece of shit," Magnus said. There was a short, stuffy type of silence for a few seconds.

"What?" said Magnus when Alexander

failed to say anything.

"Nothing," Alexander replied.

"Good riddance," Magnus added.

"Anyway, we are waiting on the lab for a few other things, so we don't have much to go on at the moment."

Whoever did this should really get a medal, not jail time, thought Magnus.

"Let me know when you have an update," Magnus said.

"Do you think he was involved in the other murders?"

"Hard to say, but this guy was always involved in something criminal."

Maybe Corvin was the other man in the hotel, thought Magnus.

Corvin and Julin at a table together? That makes no sense.

48

The hotel manager at the Best Western Savoy to his credit had done his level best to help the police and in particular Magnus. He called Magnus back quickly and informed him of the name of the other person who had been sitting with Sven Julin when there had been an eruption about lousy service at the hotel. The man's name was Konrad Dahlen. He had found out that he, in fact, was the one who had gone bananas about the service and not Sven Julin. After speaking to an employee, he had found out that Dahlen had been called "the man in 102" after his antics. By simple logic and seeing Dahlen was the one in room 102, it was clear he was the bad-tempered one. It was clear Julin was the other person at the table, as he was the other person who had received a slip reversing his drinks in and out showing he was due to pay nothing for them. Julin had just sat there, not wanting to get involved either way, which seemed to match what most people had told Magnus about Julin. Magnus moved forward with his questioning and wanted to know if any of the staff recalled anything about either two of them other than this incident. The manager said he would ask again, and if anything came up, he would alert Magnus. Magnus thanked the man very much for his help and ended the call. Magnus pondered the whole scenario again. Sven Julin takes a trip to Luleå on business. When he leaves to return home to his residence in Gustavsberg at the time, Maria Ekberg had been killed. Sven Julin then talks with his wife not long after about starting a new business down in Varberg, and they up and leave. Fast forward about a year and a month from that, and Sven Julin is then found murdered. He is located in the same fashion as Maria Ekberg had been.

We need to find Konrad Dahlen, thought Magnus.

49

Everyone was rounded up for an impromptu late afternoon meeting at 4.48 pm in which the seriousness of the situation was addressed. Magnus gave everyone the heads up about Konrad Dahlen. There was much conjecture about what this meant.

"We need to locate Konrad Dahlen. Rolf, can you get me his details right away?" Magnus asked Rolf.

"Absolutely," Rolf replied and roared off in a type of speed walk which made his stomach bounce a little from side to side.

Where were they on the cross-referencing of the tyre tread in question? Well moving in the right direction, but nothing yet Stina had remarked, although she expected to be finished soon.

"What about the Felix Corvin murder? What should I concentrate on?" asked Alexander.

"This takes priority, for now."

Rolf arrived back shortly thereafter and

had gotten the details on where Konrad Dahlen lived.

"We are in luck - he lives not far away. Pilgatan 32 in Falkenburg," he said.

"Great - Eva and I will go there now. The rest of you keep working. Call if anything comes up."

Magnus took the time to call Lena and tell her that he would be home when he could.

Falkenburg was only thirty kilometres away, in which you would head down the E6 and merge onto the E20. Plain sailing. The drive to Falkenburg was pin-drop quiet. Both Magnus and Eva were having a difficult time knowing exactly what to expect when arriving there at Konrad Dahlen's residence. They reached Pilgatan in just under twenty minutes, and went down it in a slow, steady manner, having a look for the correct address, which they found with no hassle. The house looked a bit old fashioned from the outside, but was in pretty standard order otherwise, except for the entrance which he had refuge bags and old cardboard boxes next to the driveway. Near the front door of the double story house, there were two cars parked outside — a black BMW, as well as a white Volvo pickup. The BMW looked like an old model. They parked, and Magnus and Eva were just about to exit the car when Magnus's phone rang. Magnus answered quickly.

"Magnus, I've finished with the cross-reference on the tyres and got something big," Stina said.

"Yes?"

"Based on that partial tread found at the scene, there is only *one* vehicle that appears in Linus's book that could have a possible tread match to it. Of all the cars on his list, no car could have made that type of tread but for that one."

"What type of vehicle?"

"A Volvo XC90 pickup."

"Can you send me a picture of the model to my phone right away?"

"Doing it now. I'll stay on the line."

Magnus heard a beep, and he had the picture.

"Shit!"

"What?"

"Well, we are outside the house, and there's an XC90 in the driveway."

"Are you certain its that model?"

"Yes. Damn sure. Give me the registration."

"BDV 122."

"What the — The pickup at the house is BDV 122!"

"What? What should I do?"

"Tell Rolf and Alexander to get here now. There may be a situation. Tell them to step on it." Magnus had an image of Alexander and his driving skills and expected them to be there in a flash.

"I checked the registration and got the name of the owner."

"Let me guess. Konrad Dahlen?"

"No."

"Well, who then?"

"The vehicle is registered to a Henrik Gustafsson."

Magnus shuddered. A wave of anxiety mixed with nausea swept through him and for a moment he thought he would throw up everywhere.

"Hello?" Stina shouted after not getting a response.

"Tell them to come now," Magnus said and then hung up and breathed in and out quickly. Magnus felt as if he had no air.

"What's wrong?" asked Eva.

"The tread matches the model and registration of the Volvo pickup in the driveway. We also have an ID on the owner of the vehicle in Linus's book."

"Who?"

"Henrik."

"Henrik who?"

"Henrik. My friend Henrik."

50

Before Magnus and Eva got out of the car at Pilgatan 32, both sat looking forwards saying nothing. Magnus was decidedly stunned. Eva was also stunned to a degree. She knew that Magnus and Henrik were very good friends, and on a few occasions had met Henrik briefly. He had seemed a nice man.

"Are we quite sure this implicates him?" asked Eva cautiously.

"What else could it be?" said Magnus.

"Maybe there's a mistake."

"Well, it's his pickup which I've never seen him driving before. It means he was at the scene and he's here now."

They both looked at each other and realised it was time to get out of the car and go into the house. The answers surely lay within.

The front door was slightly ajar, which automatically garnered a lot of suspicion from both Magnus and Eva. Both decided it was prudent to draw their weapons. It was the first time

Eva had a weapon in her hands since what had happened. Silently, they crept into the house. It was dead quiet. Magnus swept left, while Eva swept right. Living room, dining room, kitchen, bathroom, spare room. Nobody in any of the downstairs rooms. They both met back up in the corridor. Magnus indicated with his index finger, pointing up the staircase that was where the two of them should head next. They very cautiously made their way up the extravagant looking staircase. Once they got to the top of the stairs, both Magnus and Eva were able to make out a brushing sound, not very loud, but audible enough. It sounded as if it was coming from the very end of the corridor. Both Magnus and Eva slowly shuffled side to side towards the door, looking around at other rooms as they made their way there. Once they reached the door, Magnus made a "1-2-3" gesture, and as he reached three, he pushed open the door, and there they found a man painting a wall. Red paint. Presumably Konrad Dahlen. He wasn't painting of his own accord, as quite close to him, was Henrik, Magnus's good buddy. He was pointing a gun at this man. The room was small and very hot. There was a reasonably big glass window towards the end of the room, but that was closed, increasing the temperature.

"Magnus, I'm glad you are here. You can help me put an end to all of this," Henrik smiled.

Konrad Dahlen stopped painting and froze.

"Henrik, whatever is going on I'm telling you this as a friend. I think you should put the gun down."

"Or what? What will you do?"

"Hopefully we won't need to find out, Henrik. Let's sort this out."

Henrik pointed his gun towards Eva.

"Guns down now or I shoot her," he said to Magnus.

Giving up the weapons would leave Magnus and Eva in trouble, but Magnus was very confident that Henrik wouldn't shoot either one of them. Henrik was looking for revenge, and they weren't part of that. It was possible Magnus could reason with Henrik if he and Eva did not have weapons and did not look a threat. What other choice did he have? If they didn't give up the weapons, and Henrik actually did decide to shoot Eva, Magnus would shoot Henrik. Then Eva and Henrik would both be dead. Hardly an ideal outcome.

Magnus told Eva to do what Henrik said.

"What? Are you serious?" Eva said.

"Just do it."

Once Magnus and Eva had put their weapons down, Henrik told them to kick them to him, to which both Magnus and Eva did. Henrik put the guns out of reach, then walked towards Eva and grabbed her. He put his one arm around her and put the end of the gun on Eva's head. Eva could feel the metal prodding into her. Henrik then made his way back to his original position. Magnus hadn't expected that. The position they were in was now markedly worse. Konrad Dahlen was still stuck to his spot.

Henrik Gustafsson started explaining, not taking the gun off Eva's head for a second. It looked as if he wanted to get all of this off his chest. Henrik hadn't lied to Magnus about being in many different places as a child. Henrik had been living in Luleå, as a private computer technician, and had met the women of his dreams, Maria Ekberg. Maria wanted the relationship hush-hush because of her previous heartbreak. She explained to him it wasn't personal, but she didn't want anything to go wrong this time. That suited Henrik because he had also had some bad break-ups. Things had progressed incredibly well, and they had just decided to move in together and had spent an afternoon sprucing up Maria's house as that was where they were going to live. They had painted the whole bedroom red that afternoon. Maria had organised to go out and see her friends that particular evening. Magnus wanted to know more about the paint.

"So, what's with making this guy paint the walls?"

"I want him to get a taste of what we had

been busy doing just before she went out and was raped and murdered. I made the other bastard paint as well."

Both Magnus and Eva looked at each other. It was obvious the other "bastard" being referred to was Sven Julin. Magnus wanted to know more. Henrik took the pause in the conversation as a cue to continue.

Maria Ekberg had gone out with her friends, and the next thing Henrik had heard from Maria was a half-written message that Maria had sent about being raped. His whole world had started to collapse. He had leapt in his car and gone all over the place. Maria hadn't been sure where they were going that evening and had gone to a friend's house first. Henrik had called the friend, and she had mentioned the bar. By the time he had gotten there, the bar was closed. He drove around town, not knowing where to go. He had then thought that if someone was being raped, it was probably away from people, perhaps out in the open somewhere. Henrik had decided, based on that to go and look at parks and wooded areas. After not finding her in the first few places he went to look for her at, he finally found her. Henrik looked as if he was about to collapse when he started talking about this, but he gathered himself. With the gun still pressed against Eva's skull, now shaking, Henrik explained that he had found Maria in the woods hanging from a tree. Magnus felt a lot of sadness for Henrik. He didn't want to say anything, but this whole thing was dreadful. But what the hell had happened? Henrik had broken down in tears at the sight of finding Maria like that. It was incomprehensible to compute. He had been on the verge of dialling the number for the police when it occurred to him there was a possibility that they may never find whoever was responsible for this unspeakable crime.

"A thought came over me while I was in tears, mortified, not knowing what I was going to do. I was just about to call the police; then I thought, what if I didn't call the police? What if I didn't? They would probably muck it up anyway. What if I - excuse the cliché - took matters into my own hands? It was like a eureka moment. Suddenly this made all the sense in the world. I would exact revenge because it was the right thing to do, dammit. Just let me finish off what I started. What would you have done in my situation?"

There was silence.

"Well, what would you have done? Answer me!"

Silence.

Both Magnus, and Eva, even with the gun firmly on her forehead, thought about Henrik's remark.

Henrik continued after the short silence. He had taken Maria's hand and kissed it goodbye. It was heart-breaking that he would have to leave her there, for someone else to find. He couldn't attend the funeral. He wouldn't be able to say goodbye properly. This would be the goodbye. Maria's body was motionless. There was no colour in her face. Henrik started to leave and then stumbled on something he would never have thought of. Evidence. He had not known how he was going to even begin tracking down the person who had done this. Now he had found something—a slip of paper not far from the body. Henrik had picked it up and looked at it. It had been a Subway take away order, with a man's name on the back — Sven Julin, as well as his phone number. He had no idea why a man's name was on the back of the slip, other than that Subway wanted his details when Julin returned for his food. Henrik had thought about the odds of this paper landing up here so near the body, and not being connected with it. A receipt out there. It *must* have something to do with what had happened to Maria. The date was also at around lunchtime the previous day, so that had settled it for him. He had put the receipt in his pocket and had left quietly and sleekly.

Henrik Gustafsson had put his plan into action after constructing a very well thought out one first. His ace in the hole was that nobody was aware that he and Maria were an item. Henrik had always been somewhat of a loner and had one or two friends. Firstly, he had spoken to his friends and said that he had gotten an excellent job in the states and he was to leave in a month. The USA. An IT job for a top computer company. He had then used that month to slowly formulate everything and also not to divert any attention on himself. He had followed the news regarding Maria's death in which the police department had confirmed that it was murder. They had no suspects. Henrik, however, had one. Using his computer skills, which were in the top echelon in his field, he had quickly found out about Sven Julin and where he lived. Gustavsberg. Even though he had great suffering in having to wait, Henrik did nothing for two months. He had left town after a month as he had told his friends and travelled around Sweden not doing much, just waiting. He wasn't going to take any chances and get caught. This was a game of patience. Also, this Sven Julin would be in for a big shock when the day arrived. Off he set on his journey for vengeance. Once in Gustavsberg, he quickly found Julin's old employment and the information that Julin had left and moved to Varberg. This didn't present a problem. Even though Henrik wasn't working, he had sufficient funds to continue for a fair while. He headed down to Varberg, and once he found Julin, who was now working at a piano store of his own, he decided to take his time. Henrik had to cover his tracks. Henrik had gotten a job at an IT firm, a relatively small job, but once they had seen his brilliance, he quickly made strides up the ladder. He hadn't bothered to mention anything to his friends about this and emailed them a few times on a new email, saying his new job in the USA was going very well. Along the way, he had met Magnus, and they had become terrific friends. All Henrik had left to do was to deal with Julin. After having great patience, the day came, and he waited outside Julin's store near closing time and had made sure to be the last "customer" of the day. As Magnus was well aware, Henrik was a big man with bear paws for hands and wouldn't have had an issue subduing Julin. Henrik went in, and quickly by threatening force as well as having a weapon made Julin shut up shop. Magnus, at this point, had chimed in with a question regarding sedatives. Henrik told Magnus to shut up and let him finish. He had given Julin no sedatives so he must have taken them himself.

Henrik had taken Sven Julin to his house, and without having to beat him senseless, had sat him down, and in no uncertain terms explained he wanted to know what had happened to Maria. It hadn't taken long for Julin to work out who Maria was. Julin was quick to clarify that it wasn't his fault, that he had seen what had transpired, but because of being very drunk at the time, he had been unable to do anything. Also, with Maria's death taking place in his room, he couldn't have called the cops. Julin had remembered the perpetrator's name and was happy to tell Henrik if he would just let him go. It would have been hard to forget it after that dreadful experience. Konrad Dahlen. He had raped Maria and had pushed her very hard, which had caused her to hit the marble coffee table and virtually die instantly. Julin admitted he had helped stage the suicide, but it was more because he was in a situation that had gotten far beyond his control. Henrik decided to make Julin paint his bedroom wall, to point out that was what Maria had been busy doing that day. What Henrik and Maria had been doing that day? Once Julin had done the wall, he took Julin at gunpoint to the woods by the campsite, in his pickup. The pickup was specifically for this task. He always kept his pickup in his garage, and never let anyone into the garage. Next was to set the rope up, and Henrik made Julin stand on the back of the truck. Sven Julin had pleaded, but it was to no avail. Henrik put Julin's head through the rope once he had set everything up. Henrik got in the pickup, put his foot gently on the accelerator, took his foot off the clutch and with that Julin was left hanging in the air. Henrik had watched him die and then removed as much evidence as he could from the scene. What Henrik hadn't known was that his little discreet entrance to the woods had left a partial tyre tread. Henrik had been pleased with the sight of rain after he had gone. That would have washed away any evidence, or so he had thought. Magnus had asked why he hadn't tried to change the name of the owner of the vehicle or better yet use another vehicle. Henrik had replied saying that his pickup had a Luleå registration so he had thought that even if the tire tread could be traced, they would surely only look for vehicles from in and around this area.

"So how did you work out it was my car?" Henrik asked.

"Because we are good detectives Henrik," Magnus said.

That and because Linus likes cars, Magnus thought.

Henrik continued his story. Next was for the bigger culprit. Konrad Dahlen. Henrik would follow the same procedure with Dahlen. He would make him admit what he had done. Henrik would address a letter to the police department, explaining a few things, anonymously of course. He would make Dahlen paint the walls, of Dahlen's own house this time, and afterwards, Henrik hadn't been sure if he was going to beat Dahlen to a pulp and hang him or just hang him. That's when Magnus and Eva had arrived. So, these four were now in a room. Magnus, looking Henrik in the eye, trying to think of a way out of this. Eva, who was having thoughts of the gun going off at any second. Henrik, sweating profusely, as well as relieved at telling somebody his story, that he had justification for his actions. And Konrad Dahlen, who was still frozen to the spot, his hand holding a paintbrush dripping drops onto the floor.

51

"You could have come to me," said Magnus.

"I didn't even know you when Maria was killed! Also, even when I did know you, my mind had been made up. I, as well as Maria, will not be denied good old-fashioned revenge," Henrik replied, spit flying out his mouth.

"Henrik, please, this isn't the right way."

"I'll go back to my previous question - what would you have done? I've seen how you are with your wife and your pets; I'll bet if someone so much as put in a foot in the door, you wouldn't hesitate. Hell, I'll bet even if your son were in trouble (Henrik too was acutely aware of what had happened with Sebastian), you would do something drastic."

The motive was killing Sven Julin was well established, as was the going after of Konrad Dahlen.

What the hell do you do when confronted with something like what Henrik had been faced with? After a brief silence, the silence was broken with authority.

"This is what we are going to do," said Magnus and carried on.

"You are going to let Eva go, and then you have to turn yourself in. It's the only way. I'm sure that I can put in a good word for you. Scratch that, I *will* put in a good word for you. Then I'll bring this man in, and he will be put behind bars for a very long time."

"NO. This is what we are going to do. You are either with me or against me. That's your call. If I have to shoot your friend for you to get the message so be it."

No one said anything. Magnus and Henrik just stared at each other. Eva stared at Magnus as well, her eyes asking Magnus to please do something.

The silence was broken when Konrad Dahlen thought he had a chance to make a dash for it. The door wasn't that far away, and with everyone in the room having more pressing concerns to deal with, Konrad decided to make a break for it. He darted from behind Henrik, not looking at him and was headed for the exit. Henrik saw Konrad come past and didn't hesitate. He shoved Eva away from him and fired two shots with both connecting Konrad in the side. Konrad dropped and fell to the floor, groaning as blood started to fill up the floor. While Henrik had aimed and fired at Konrad, Magnus saw an opening and decided to run at Henrik. When Magnus hit Henrik, the impact caused Henrik's gun to fall to the floor. Eva managed to get to her gun, and once she picked it up, she turned and saw Magnus and Henrik tussling with each other. Both were locked together, and both were getting perilously close to the window.

Eva aimed the gun, looking for a shot at Henrik. Suddenly Eva was rooted to the spot.

Not again, she thought.

She had been trying to move on from her shooting that man, and now Eva was faced with another situation that may require her to shoot someone.

What if she killed another person? Worse, what if she shot the wrong person?

Closer to the window Magnus and Henrik went, with Magnus closest to the window. If either went through the window, then they would fall to their certain deaths from that first-floor window.

What the fuck do I do? Eva thought, her palms clammy, her hands shaking.

Eva shrieked.

"Stop right now. NOW. Otherwise, I shoot."

Henrik took no notice, nor Magnus, and he and Magnus continued to fight each other close to the window.

Magnus got in a shot to Henrik's ribs, but

Henrik shrugged the shot off and landed his own shot, and his shot hurt Magnus. Henrik's bear paws pulled Magnus right towards the window frame. As Henrik lifted his fist to try and pound Magnus, Henrik's ribs became exposed and if Eva was going to shoot, the time was now. Eva would have to make a snap decision.

Crack. The bullet left the chamber and in a flash exploded into Henrik's ribs.

Henrik let go of Magnus, feeling for the shattering pain in his side. Henrik was not thinking of anything but the pain and lost balance and smashed through the window. Henrik managed to stop his descent to the ground by grabbing onto the window ledge by one hand. Magnus dropped to his knees and quickly dived to grab Henrik's hand.

"I've got you, Henrik. Don't worry; I've got you. I'm going to pull you up," Magnus said. To pull Henrik up was going to be hard work.

"You have always been my friend Magnus. Don't forget that for one second."

"I know that. But let's not talk about that now. We have to get you up, and you have to help me get you up."

Magnus saw Alexander as well as Rolf running up the driveway.

Magnus started to pull Henrik up, and Henrik started to push himself up too. As Henrik was close to getting up to the frame, he stopped for a second.

"I'm sorry for what I've done. But I had to for Maria's sake."

Henrik pulled himself up an inch more, and as Magnus looked for a better grip on Henrik's hand, Henrik looked at Magnus and let go. Henrik fell silently to the ground.

Crack.

This crack wasn't another bullet. It was the back of Henrik's skull connecting with the driveway pavement.

52

Red was the predominant colour at the Dahlen residence. There was red on the driveway where Henrik had fallen and hit the driveway. The blood was pooling around Henrik rapidly, and Konrad Dahlen was drenched in red. Eva checked Dahlen's pulse. Nothing. He was dead. Magnus was visibly upset by what had happened. He was breathing heavily, and his face was close to breaking into tears, but he held them back. Magnus kept looking out the window at the sight of Henrik lying dead on the ground.

Alexander and Rolf were now at the foot of the body.

"Shit," said Alexander, him and Rolf also having met Henrik.

"Where is Dahlen?" Rolf asked.

"He's in the house. Dead. Henrik shot him when he tried to escape," Magnus replied.

Rolf and Alexander made their way into the house.

Magnus, in spite of what had happened,

pushed on. He proceeded to fill Rolf and Alexander in on what he had found out. Henrik had been the boyfriend of Maria Ekberg, who had been raped by Konrad Dahlen in a hotel room, where Sven Julin had ended up drunk and had seen Dahlen do the act but had been too out of it to even move. Then Maria Ekberg had tried to send a text to Henrik and had been pushed by Dahlen and had fallen and cracked her neck on a marble table and died on the spot. Dahlen and Julin went about staging Maria's death. Julin hadn't wanted to but had thought this was his only way out. When Henrik had gotten a half text from Maria minutes before her death, he had set about trying to track her down and had found her hanging from the tree. He had decided to not call the police. Instead, he had his own plan, and with the help of something he found at the scene, tracked down Julin and killed him. He also had killed Dahlen, even though it wasn't the way he had planned.

"Shit, you don't have cases like this every day," said Alexander.

"Well, I suppose Henrik completed his task then. He got them both," said Rolf.

Once Magnus had gotten back to work to fill in a few details regarding the case, the full force of what had unfolded hit him. Torrents of emotions swept through his head. His so-called friend, no check that - his very good friend had just let go of his hand when Magnus had been trying to save him. He had watched him fall to his death. Of course, Henrik had killed two people, but that didn't mean Magnus could not be upset with what had happened. If only Henrik had thought this whole thing through. Even if Maria's case hadn't been solved when they had met, Magnus would have solved it. There was no maybe about it. Magnus quite simply felt miserable about the whole thing. He had given Lena a quiet call and told her about what had happened. She had taken the news very badly. Alexander entered Magnus's office, looking tired, his eyes with a baggy look under them. Alexander mentioned he was about to knock off and get some sleep, but he wanted to fill Magnus in about what he found out about the Felix Corvin murder. He had checked his email and obtained the findings from Kerstin Beckman regarding the information from the National Forensics lab. The bullets Corvin was shot with were from a Glock. That was all they had.

"I think it's time we all go home," Magnus said and paused for a second.

"This has been a very long day."

"Very long and quite horrid," Alexander said, not sure what to say about Henrik. He decided to say nothing and said to Magnus to rest up well.

Magnus got his things and was about to

leave when he got a call from Kerstin Beckman.

They chatted a bit very briefly about what had happened. Kerstin was shocked to hear Henrik was a friend of Magnus's. After Magnus reassuring Kerstin that he would be OK, Kerstin told him why she had phoned.

"I've got your DNA result back regarding Sven Julin's DNA and the DNA found on Maria Ekberg. No match."

"Thanks, Kerstin, we know who the DNA belonged to now."

53

Magnus woke up the next morning and got ready quickly. He and Lena had talked a lot about Henrik when he had gotten home the night before. There had been many questions they had asked each other back and forth. The biggest emotion in the room between both of them was the sheer shock of Henrik killing two people.

"I would have solved the case for him," Magnus had said possibly ten times in the space of two hours.

Lena was already up when Magnus was getting ready for work and was surprised that he was going in so quickly. Magnus saw the look of surprise in her eyes.

"I'm going into tidy a few things up, and then I'm going on leave. I think we need to get away after all of this," Magnus said before Lena could say anything.

"I think that's wise Magnus."

That morning at work, a final meeting was held to wrap everything up. Magnus liked to end with a meeting to summarise what had happened and allow for any questions anyone had. It had been a short summary. So, the Sven Julin case, the mild-mannered Piano teacher, had been solved.

"What about the other case? The Felix Corvin shooting?" asked Alexander.

Who gives a shit, Magnus thought.

"Well it is pretty clear that the Corvin murder had nothing to do with the Sven Julin case," Magnus said.

"Maybe Henrik didn't mention killing Corvin," said Rolf.

Come on Rolf. Have another cheeseburger, Magnus thought.

"Why on earth would he do that when he confessed everything else? No, I don't think so."

"Well, we will have to carry on and find out who did kill Corvin then," said Eva.

"On that note, I will be going on leave for the next two weeks at the end of today," said Magnus.

54

Magnus, the rest of the day did virtually nothing. He had told everyone he had lots of admin to do, but he sorted out what he needed to be done speedily. Magnus had sat and thought about Henrik a lot. About the good times. Playing tennis, having many laughs at the races, social occasions, and many others. It would take a bit of time to recover from this.

Magnus devoted the rest of the day to reading his Mons Kallentoft novel and was close to completing it by the time he stopped. That had given his mind some respite. Magnus then went to Rosenberg to hand in his leave application. Magnus had a fair amount of leave due, so asking for two weeks was definitely reasonable. Erik Rosenberg had been commended on this case being solved and had taken a lot of the plaudits. He had given a short press conference that morning in which he had been complimentary about the team but had also been quick to make himself out as the driving force behind this case. Rosenberg looked at Magnus's application.

"That's no problem, Magnus. Good job on the case. Very good actually."

"Thank you, Erik."

While I was at gunpoint, you were probably hiding under your desk, Magnus thought.

"You know what, maybe the department can do something about that coffee machine. How about you give me the receipt for the purchase, and it can come out of the budget," Rosenberg said, smiling.

"I think that would be a nice gesture to everyone here. I'll be sure to mention it to everyone."

Magnus said he would see Rosenberg in two weeks and promptly exited Rosenberg's office. He then made sure to convey to everyone that Rosenberg, now out of trouble with his superiors with the case being solved, was going to pay for the coffee machine.

Wait till he sees we used 1000 kronor for a tip-off payment, Magnus thought and disappeared out of the building and to his car.

Magnus wanted to go past the bookshop on the way home. He had planned that he and Lena could go away in a few day's time and more Mons books would be a good idea to take with. Lena had a friend who lived in Spain, so he thought they could visit her and then carry on through the country a bit. Magnus thought the worst thing to do after this horrible case was to crawl up in a little ball somewhere. He needed to carry on with his life.

Magnus would need to find someone to look after the dogs. Someone reliable. Upon driving along and trying to work out who he could ask to mind his animals, he drove past a car he knew—a Sleek dark blue Mercedes.

I'd recognise that pricks car anywhere, Magnus thought referring to Kjell Sandell, the man from Ikea Magnus had had a run-in with.

Magnus noticed something else interesting as he pulled into a spare parking space. Sandell had parked in parking reserved for disabled people.

Magnus couldn't believe his luck and made a type of chuckle and got out of the car. He went past the car just to make sure Sandell did not have a card on his window, allowing to park in disabled parking. On closer inspection, it was clear Sandell did not.

Just as I thought, fucking arrogant arsehole, Magnus thought.

Magnus got out his phone and knew just who to call.

Lennart Gronberg worked at the Swedish transport agency, Transportstyrelsen. He was sixty-four years old, and the biggest stickler for rules Magnus had come across.

An illegally parked car in a disabled zone, well that will get the old boy going, Magnus thought as he was put through to Lennart Gronberg.

"Hello, Lennart Gronberg speaking," said Gronberg in a professional tone.

"Lennart, it's Magnus Markusson, Varberg police department. I had to call you because I noticed something that needs your urgent attention," Magnus replied.

"Yes, hello, Magnus. What seems to be the problem?"

"I just saw an illegally parked car in disabled parking. I thought you would want to know."

"Of course! This is an outrage. Do these people have no respect for basic parking rules?"

"You know, I don't think they do," Magnus said, trying to egg him on.

"Well, I will do something right away."

"What are the rules and fines regarding this Lennart?"

"Incorrectly parked cars may be removed by the local authority. If you park in a parking space reserved for disabled persons, then the local authority has more than enough grounds to remove the vehicle. The vehicle is usually taken to a car pound. The vehicle owner is liable for the costs related to the vehicle's removal."

"You know Lennart; you can't have all these rules breakers going around parking where they like."

"Thanks for calling me Magnus, and don't you worry, I will follow the correct steps concerned regarding this infringement."

The call ended, and Magnus got in his car and made his way home. He needed to call Lennart back in a few hours to find out what he had done. If Kjell Sandell decided to blow a gasket on Lennart Gronberg, he wasn't going to see his car for a good while.

About forty-five minutes later, Kjell Sandell was walking towards where he had parked, and instead of seeing his car parked where he had left it, he saw it being towed away down the road. The look on his was face was priceless, and something Magnus would have enjoyed immensely.

55

Alexander Holström was a bit anxious. Just sitting and thinking. Then he started pacing up and down. Tried to relax on his bed. Eventually, he got up decisively and got his iPhone out. He sent three texts, both saying the same thing.

"I'm sorry, I don't think it's a good idea that we meet up anymore. We both know its been fun, but it's not like it's going anywhere. Keep well and good luck. Alexander."

Alexander then dialled another number. He wasn't quite sure what it was, but he wanted to dial the number. He felt very excited if he was being honest with himself. The person on the other line seemed a little surprised that he was phoning, but that person too was very excited.

"I was just wondering, I'm going to put on some dinner now, nothing fancy, and I thought maybe you might want to join me."

There was no response at first and then "Yes. That would be nice."

"Great. How's forty-five minutes from

now?" Alexander asked.

Precisely forty-five minutes later, Stina was outside Alexander's front door, having managed to lock up her front door on the first try, although she had many uncomfortable thoughts on the way there. For good measure, she touched the front door of Alexander's three times to point out to herself she didn't have to worry about her door being "wrong". She felt a lot better when Alexander opened up and invited her inside.

Rolf was back ordering a pizza. Now that the case was over, he felt like heading back there and having a pizza to celebrate that the vital thread of information was due to meeting and offering Linus a freshly baked pizza. It was fitting. There had been a lot of pizzas recently. Rolf was happy that he had played an integral part in the case. For the first time since Camilla had passed away, he felt as if he could be happy again. Rolf took a window seat, then went to order a new pizza on the menu called meat medley, which, as the name suggested, was packed with various delicious meat toppings. There was also an option of thin base, or thick base, to which Rolf had ordered thick base (why the hell not he had thought). His pizza was ready, and Rolf took a seat and started tucking in. Rolf thought that once and for all, he needed to do something about his weight. This time he had to not joke around and set some kind of a goal. No excuses at all. As soon as this pizza was finished, then he would start. And he meant it this time. He had picked up two kilograms in the last month alone, so now was definitely the time. After about half-way through his pizza, he saw a familiar face outside the window peering in at him. Linus. Linus walked into the establishment and seated himself at Rolf's table and before saying hello, Rolf asked what he was doing here.

"I thought you might be here. People often like their routines," Linus said.

"Well, it's not a routine."

"Did my notes help?"

"Yes. Yes, they did. A great deal."

"I thought they would. They are very accurate, you know."

"How about a pizza? To celebrate?"

"Yes, please."

"I met a guy," said Malin to her sister Eva while they were sitting at dinner and enjoying some home-made meatballs with lingonberry jam.

"Oh Malin, don't go getting into anything silly now."

"I went to a bookstore and turned and bumped into him. He was charming and helped me pick out a book. I said he must have a cup of coffee with me sometime."

"Well, just chill out now. There's nothing wrong with coffee, but just take it easy."

Malin thought for a second.

"Yes, I know, OK. It was just nice for someone to be so genuine for a change."

"Speaking of being nice, I have a favour to ask you. Well, not exactly for me but for Magnus. He's going on leave for two weeks, and in a few days, he and Lena are off to Spain. He needed someone to look after the dogs and stay with them. I thought you would be perfect so I said you would do it. I hope that's alright."

"Sure, I'll do it. That will be fun."

"Great. Magnus will be so happy."

Malin then unexpectedly got up from the table and went and gave Eva a big hug. Eva found it surprising but it gave her much happiness.

"Thank you. For helping me."

"Hey, what are sisters for?" Eva said, a few tears dripping down her face.

Eva was overjoyed at how she and Malin had been bonding of late. While the two of them continued with their meals, Eva thought about what had transpired in the case. She had shot and wounded Henrik. Henrik had then let go of Magnus's hand and had fallen to his demise. Eva had been worried about how she was going to feel about the whole thing and herself having to use a weapon again. However, Eva seemed to have turned a corner. Eva seemed to have realised that sometimes in law enforcement, there are circumstances where you may need to use a weapon. Admittedly she still thought about the day she shot the man who tried to attack his wife with a knife, but she understood now that having to shoot someone in a situation like that, was what she had to do, even though she may have not wanted to do it. As she sat and enjoyed her meal with Malin, Eva felt good. Things are going to be fine, she thought.

After a delightful meal, Alexander and Stina were sitting on the couch. Neither felt the need that they had to climb all over each other. They felt comfortable. As if anything could be said, anything personal be uttered. Alexander put the TV on to see if there was anything good to watch, and that was when he decided to talk about his father.

"I've never told anyone about my father," he said, breathing quite heavily all of a sudden.

Stina could tell that whatever it was, Alexander was nervous about the subject.

"What about your father?" Stina replied.

"Doesn't know who I am."

"What do you mean?"

"He has Alzheimer's. He's in a home now. He's quite happy, but he doesn't have a clue about much. When I go to visit him, it's painful. I hate it. He looks at me as if I'm a complete stranger. He always asks me who I am. I can't take it anymore."

Stina's heart sank, listening to the sadness in Alexander's voice about this.

"That sounds dreadful, but you can't give up. Yes, he may not remember you, but you could go there and spend time with him and doing something fun while you are there. He may not remember, but you will remember you looked after him. I think that's what is important."

"It's not that easy."

"No one said it was."

"It's just so sad to see where my father is now, compared to where he was. I'm not going to end up like that. No way."

Stina understood a lot of what Alexander was saying. With her own problems, namely the OCD, Stina had many thoughts about getting sick, and about dying. She had one thought that she would take a nap and wake up having just had a stroke. One where she would be hit by a drunk driver while she was on the road and die instantly.

"I see where you are coming from, Alexander, I really do."

The conversation fizzled out after more deliberating, and after watching some TV, Alexander turned to Stina.

"This may sound funny, but do you want to stay here tonight?"

"Not it doesn't sound funny. Yes, I would

like to stay here. A lot."

56

The trip to Spain had started well. The weather had been great. Magnus and Lena had got to spend some proper time together and just unwind and put that horrible case behind them. As they were about to begin dinner at a very relaxing restaurant, Lena went to the ladies' room. Then Magnus's phone rang.

"Hello, said Magnus.

"Dad. It's, It's Sebastian."

Magnus couldn't believe it and a wave of emotions coursed through him.

"Hey. How are you?"

"Well, I'm doing much better. After all this time, I have managed to realise how my life spun out of control."

This was the first time Sebastian had ever phoned Magnus since he was told not to come back.

"Well, I'm very glad to hear that. It's good to hear that you are doing better."

"The only thing is something happened,"

Sebastian said worriedly.

"What happened?"

"I killed him."

"Killed who?"

"Felix Corvin."

"What?" Magnus said, stunned.

"He wanted to meet me in Varberg. I hadn't seen him for a while. I had, well, I had been selling some illegal goods for him, and I wanted out. I told them when he called, and he said he wanted to meet in private somewhere. He owed me some money and said he would give it to me and we could parts ways."

"We found him in the woods off the campsite. Did you meet there?"

"Yes. It seemed odd, but he had said he was in Varberg on business for a while. Anyway, I thought that it was a good spot to get a handout of cash. That was until I heard something from another guy who worked for Felix that I was friendly with."

"Well, what did he say?"

"He said there was no way Felix would just let me part ways like that. He said a meeting like that could only mean one thing."

"He was going to kill you?"

"Yes. So, I went prepared. Felix got dropped off and then came to meet me. I was already there. It didn't take long until he pulled a gun on me. He pulled the trigger and nothing."

"The cartridge was empty," Sebastian added.

"What?"

"The guy that gave him the lift. He was the friend of mine who was working for Felix. After he told me about Felix's intentions, we cut a deal. If Felix was out of the way, he would very likely be able to take Felix's place, so it suited him helping me."

"What kind of deal did you make?"

Lena was making her way back to the table.

"I could get out. Leave it all behind me. All I had to do was take Felix out. It was the only way. After I told Felix I wanted out, it was probably only a matter of time, and he would have killed me. Dad, do you think I'll get caught? I read in the paper there was a big investigation going on."

"No, not really, there hasn't been anything to go on other than the bullets, which doesn't really help at the moment. Just let it fizzle out."

Magnus felt very conflicted. Sebastian had killed someone. However, look at the person it was that he killed. Someone that pulled a gun on his wife, and wrecked a proportion of his son's life. Felix was going to kill Sebastian as well, Sebastian just got lucky that someone wanted Felix out of the way.

I'll make it fizzle out, Magnus thought. He could deal with all the conflicting thoughts later. He had to protect his son.

"One more thing, Dad, it was me who called the cops about the man hung in the tree. I saw him as I was getting out of the woods. I went another way, and I saw him. It wasn't a pretty sight. I ran to town and called from a payphone."

"Well, it was good you did," Magnus said, not knowing what else to say.

"I need to go now, Dad, but I want to come and see you soon. I just need some time, you know after, you know, everything."

We need some time to get our heads around all this too, Magnus thought.

"I'll call you soon. Bye, Dad. Tell Mom I say hi."

"Sure Son. Speak soon."

"You look like you have seen a ghost. Who was that?" Lena asked, sitting down after getting back to the table.

"Sebastian. He says hi."

Printed in Great Britain
by Amazon